and the UNCOLLECTED STORIES *of* FRAY ANGÉLICO CHÁVEZ

Edited and Introduced by
Ellen McCracken

Illustrations by Gerald Cassidy and
Fray Angélico Chávez

Museum of New Mexico Press
Santa Fe

 Museum of New Mexico Press is a division of New Mexico Department of Cultural Affairs.

Manufactured in the United States of America
10 9 8 7 6 5 4 3 2 1

Illustration credits:
Pages 3, 6, and illustrations for *Guitars and Adobes*: lithographs by Gerald Cassidy, *St. Anthony Messenger*, 1931-32.
Early Illustrated Stories of the Southwest: illustrations by Manuel E. Chávez, *St. Anthony Messenger*, 1929-30.
Lessons in Love: lithographs by Gerald Cassidy, *St. Anthony Messenger*, 1931–32.
Illustration for 1936 story "Viola Comes of Age" originally published in 1932 in *Guitars and Adobes.*
Courage and Faith: lithograph by Gerald Cassidy, *St. Anthony Messenger*, January 1932.

Library of Congress Cataloging-in-Publication Data

Chávez, Angélico, 1910–1996.
Guitars and adobes, and the uncollected stories of Fray Angélico Chávez / by Fray Angélico Chávez; edited with an introduction by Ellen McCracken.
p. cm.
ISBN 978-0-89013-559-4 (clothbound : alk. paper)
I. McCracken, Ellen (Ellen Marie) II. Title.
PS3505.H625G85 2009
813'.52--dc22
2009015116

Museum of New Mexico Press
Post Office Box 2087
Santa Fe, New Mexico 87504
www.mnmpress.org

Contents

ACKNOWLEDGMENTS

and a NOTE *on the* EDITION

This volume would not have been possible without the invaluable assistance of several people. In Cincinnati, Father Dan Anderson, O.F.M., former archivist of St. John the Baptist Province, made hundreds of documents available to me, allowed me to work long hours in the archives, and sent photocopies of *The Sodalist* stories by mail. Father Jack Wintz, O.F.M., of the *St. Anthony Messenger*, generously allowed me to photocopy *Guitars and Adobes* and other stories in the magazine's offices after hours. Franciscan Fathers Murray Bodo, Jovian Weigel, and Bernard Gerbus provided generous hospitality and information about Chávez and Franciscan life. Current Provincial Archivist, Brother Allan Schmitz, O.F.M., volunteered extra time, despite his busy schedule, to digitize Cassidy's lithographs for this publication. And most importantly, Father Daniel Kroger, O.F.M., publisher of St. Anthony Messenger Press, gave permission to reprint the material in this collection, and took time from his busy schedule to assist me in obtaining copies of the images for this book.

At the University of California, Santa Barbara, a grant from the Chicano Studies Institute supported the digitizing of material for this volume. Graduate research assistant Haley O'Neil spent long hours skillfully doing this work, as well as cross-checking the digital and print versions, under the time constraints of the publication deadline. Maura Jess, digital imaging specialist, professionally produced a number of images for this book. I am extremely appreciative for their assistance.

I am especially grateful to Mary Wachs, Editorial Director, and Anna Gallegos, Director of the Museum of New Mexico Press, for their interest in this project and their sustained work with me in the sometimes complicated process of seeing the book through to publication. I appreciate their recognition of the importance of publishing this volume for the centenary of Fray Angélico Chávez's birth in 2010.

Professor Ilan Stavans of Amherst College graciously advised me on the question of republishing a text with anti-Semitic passages. He astutely led me to alternative sources of information on the history of Jews in Spain and the Spanish-speaking world. I am indebted to his groundbreaking anthology *The Scroll and the Cross*, which provides necessary background for today's readers of Chávez's first novel.

In editing this volume of Fray Angélico Chávez's early fiction, I corrected a few errors in Spanish, added accent marks which were unavailable to Chávez and publishers at the time, and updated occasional spelling anachronisms, such as hyphenated compound words (for example: "to-day"). Nothing was removed from the original texts of the novel or the stories except the pseudonyms. The novel *Guitars and Adobes* was originally serialized in eight installments in *St. Anthony Messenger* magazine. Therefore, the reading experience of the novel in this volume is different from that of the original readers, not only because of our current historical moment, but also because the serialized experience no longer remains. I have not reprinted the "Up to Now" summaries that preceded each installment in the original version, because of the absence of serialization here.

Future literary scholars may wish to investigate these paratexts in studying the original experience of reading the novel.

Rather than republish the original installments as chapters in this new edition of the novel, so that readers could approximate the serialized experience of the early 1930s, I made the decision to follow Chávez's division of the novel into five parts, four of which appeared with their own titles. In one instance in the original publication, material that did not fit in the previous installment was tacked on to the beginning of the next month's story. I therefore returned the first four paragraphs of the April 1932 installment to the end of part three, where they logically belong. Similarly, Gerald Cassidy's circular image of the guitar and Doña Genoveva lying in bed, which appeared at the top of each installment, now appears only at the beginning of the novel. The captions that appear below Cassidy's lithographs and Chávez's drawings in this volume are the same ones that appeared in the original editions.

INTRODUCTION

by ELLEN McCRACKEN

In 1924 a young Hispano from northern New Mexico traveled by train with Archbishop Albert Daeger to enter the Franciscan seminary in Cincinnati. The eldest in his family, the fourteen-year-old boy had been intrigued by the brown-robed Franciscans. When he was a small child living briefly in San Diego, he learned about Fray Junipero Serra and saw the first California Franciscan mission founded in 1769. "From then on I wanted to be a Franciscan," he later told a reporter.[1] This young boy, Manuel Ezequiel Chávez, became the first native New Mexican to be ordained a Franciscan priest in the centuries since the Spanish colonization of the area. He also became one of New Mexico's foremost intellectuals and humanists, writing twenty-four books and hundreds of articles, stories, poems, plays, and translations. A talented artist as well, he did paintings and drawings and restored churches.[2]

Almost immediately after arriving at St. Francis Seminary, Chávez began writing fiction, essays, and poetry, and worked on paintings and drawings. All these works of the 1920s and 1930s were strongly influenced by his separation from the Southwest, where he grew up. The only Hispano in a high school of primarily Midwestern boys, he stressed his ethnicity and his connection to New Mexico. The temporary absence of the geographic and social space that had nurtured and formed him became a strong presence in his creative work.

In particular, the famous writers and artists who had settled in Santa Fe, New Mexico, influenced Chávez's writing and art of this period. While growing up in Mora, Chávez had spent summers with his aunt in Santa Fe, where he saw the construction of the Museum of Fine Arts (now the New Mexico Museum of Art), in 1917, and the development of the Santa Fe style of architecture. In the early 1920s, a number of writers came to the city, some seeking cures for illnesses at Sunmount Sanatorium, others joining friends who had become enchanted with northern New Mexico. Among them were Alice Corbin, co-editor of *Poetry* magazine, who came from Chicago in 1916 with her husband, artist and architect William Penhallow Henderson; poet Witter Bynner, who visited Corbin in 1922 and eventually moved permanently to Santa Fe; and writer Mary Austin, who took up residence in the city in 1924. Other important writers who spent time in Santa Fe during this period were D. H. Lawrence, Willa Cather, Thornton Wilder, Edna St. Vincent Millay, Carl Sandburg, Vachel Lindsay, May Sarton, Robert Frost, John Gould Fletcher, Haniel Long, Walter "Spud" Johnson, and Lynn Riggs. Following their visits to the region, themes of the Southwest appeared frequently in their work.[3]

In Chávez's youth, Santa Fe's cultural life was also shaped by the many artists who came to work in the region in the early twentieth century. Several of them painted ethnic and indigenous subjects, including Carlos Vierra, Kenneth Chapman, Sheldon Parsons, Gerald Cassidy, William Penhallow Henderson, John Sloan, Frank Applegate, Randall Davey, Gustave Baumann, and B. J. O. Nordfeldt.[4] In 1921 five artists banded together to help one another survive and make an aesthetic mark, presenting new visions of the Southwest. Called *Los Cinco Pintores,* they engaged in experimental modernism and therefore encountered difficulties in access to exhibition space and in selling paintings. The group included Fremont F. Ellis, Walter E. Mruk, Jozef G. Bakos, Will Schuster, and Willard Nash. Their first joint exhibition was in November 1921. In the ensuing years they became a mainstay of the Santa Fe social scene, performing creative skits at parties and organizing elaborate costume events. They are especially remembered for their role in reviving the Santa Fe Fiesta, for which they organized new events, such as the Historical-Hysterical Parade and the annual burning of the giant, paper puppet called Zozobra or "Old Man Gloom," designed by Shuster in 1926.[5]

Witter Bynner wrote the following evocative description of the artists' and writers' early get-togethers at Alice Corbin Henderson's house:

> It was a small, pleasant, primitive adobe house, with an outdoor privy and with horses corralled alongside....Visitors would come across distances which now demand motoring; but we came on horseback then by day or at night on foot with lanterns and would kick snow off our overshoes in the welcoming glow of the room with its corner adobe fireplace. Painters from near-by houses on the [Camino del Monte Sol] would be there, Applegate, Bakos, Shuster, Nash, sometimes Sloan and Davey from streets farther away...occasionally a visiting writer, Lindsay with his chants, Sandburg with his guitar, Frost with his wit, Lummis with a red bandanna around his gray temples.[6]

Bynner also noted that Manuel Chávez, not yet called Fray Angélico, came to these social gatherings.

The young Manuel Chávez was profoundly influenced by the diverse elements of Santa Fe's vibrant art scene. The multiple representations of Southwest culture that these writers and artists created imbued Chávez with an aesthetic sense of his own Hispano ethnicity and difference. The writings and paintings Chávez encountered contributed to his developing understanding of personal and communal identity as a Hispano and as part of a distinct region of the United States, in which diverse cultures had been preserved for centuries. When he traveled to the unfamiliar environment of the Franciscan seminary in Cincinnati, with its strong Germanic traditions, Chávez's ethnic and cultural difference stood out.[7] His occasional trips home to Santa Fe for the summer in the 1920s, and his trip home for his parents' twenty-fifth wedding anniversary in July 1934, nourished and developed his Hispano ethnicity further. In the exciting environment fomented by the writers' and artists' groups, Chávez's sense of self as a Hispano writer and artist from New Mexico grew. In his writing, art, and self-presentation in the period from 1924 to his ordination in 1937, a striking sense of ethnicity combines with other cultural elements to publicly display Chávez's unique hybrid identity.

Home from the seminary in the summer of 1928, Manuel dressed as a gaucho for the Fiesta and won first prize for his costume. He presented himself as a Hispano subject through sartorial signs, as well as through his writings that included ethnic themes. His association with the Santa Fe writers' group was overcoded with his ethnic identity as a native New Mexican who included southwestern themes in his work. He met Witter Bynner at the Fiesta and corresponded with him during his remaining years at the seminary. When he returned to New Mexico permanently in 1937, Chávez attended the events and parties held by the writers' group.

Santa Fe and Taos artists also influenced Chávez's understanding of the Southwest and his artistic work of this period. He specifically cites the influence of Taos artists Ernest L. Blumenschein and Joseph Henry Sharp, whose paintings he saw in the Santa Fe Museum of Fine Arts. He remembers watching Cassidy, Shuster, and Nash painting in the city.[8] Early on, in the seminary, Chávez painted and drew in several genres, often emphasizing aspects of his ethnicity and southwestern themes. Like Carlos Vierra, he sketched the old missions of New Mexico; in 1934 ten of his drawings of the old churches were published in an article he wrote in *St. Anthony Messenger* magazine.[9]

The novel and stories published in this volume span the period between 1929 and 1938, when Chávez lived in Cincinnati, Detroit, Oldenberg (Indiana), and Peña Blanca (New Mexico). In August 1929 he entered the novitiate at Mt. Airy, Cincinnati, and formally received his religious name—Fray Angélico Chávez—taken from the Medieval Italian painter Fra Angelico. In September 1930 he began studies at Duns Scotus College in Detroit, where he received a B.A. in 1933. Then, from 1933 to 1937 he studied theology at Oldenberg and was ordained in Santa Fe in May 1937, beginning his first assignment as a priest at Peña Blanca in July of that year.

THE FIRST NOVEL

Guitars and Adobes, published in eight installments in the Franciscan national magazine *St. Anthony Messenger*, from November 1931 to June 1932, presents an alternative picture of the Southwest to Willa Cather's *Death Comes for the Archbishop*. Chávez's story, beginning with the death of Archbishop Jean-Baptiste Lamy in 1888, and ending with the death of an ordinary Hispana in 1929, reconfigures the idea of death in the years before and after Lamy's demise, giving it an alternative ethnic nuance. In the novel a cursed guitar that has come down through the ages, since the reconquest of Spain, causes those who play it to die. The guitar stands in sharp contrast to the motif of the adobe—the traditional means of building houses among Hispanos—that appears throughout the novel as a symbol of life. Overcoming injustice and adversity, the two young lovers in the story escape into the northern New Mexico countryside, marry at Chimayó, and settle in Mora. Despite a smallpox epidemic, one courageous character perseveres.

In addition to several narrative digressions about key figures in Hispano New Mexico history, such as Don Diego de Vargas, María Gertrudis Barceló (known as Doña Tules), and *La Conquistadora*, Chávez integrates motifs relating to the writers and artists who lived on Camino del Monte Sol, and artist Gerald Cassidy's house at 924 Canyon Road. In this intriguing novel Chávez interjects an insider's view of Hispano ethnicity and history into literary and artistic portrayals of the region and period.

Having met Cassidy on one of his summer trips home, Chávez asked the artist to create a series of lithograph illustrations for *Guitars and Adobes*. Cassidy, whose full name is Ira Diamond Gerald Cassidy (1869–1934), studied at the Art Institute in Cincinnati and then worked in New York as a commercial lithographer. In 1890, suffering from pneumonia, he went to a sanitarium in Albuquerque, and began to paint the New Mexico landscape and Pueblo Indians. Later, he moved to Denver and once again worked as a lithographer. After visiting Santa Fe in 1912, he lived and worked in Ventura, California. He received a commission to paint a mural series in the Indian Arts Building at the Panama Pacific Exposition in San Diego, for which he received a gold medal. Coincidentally, the young Manuel Chávez and his family lived in San Diego at the same time, while his father worked on the construction of the Panama Pacific Exposition. The Chávez family returned to New Mexico in 1915, and that same year Cassidy and his wife, Ina Sizer Cassidy, bought a house at the corner of Canyon Road and Acequia Madre in Santa Fe. The artist tragically died in 1934 from inhaling turpentine and carbon monoxide fumes, from a newly installed gas heater in his studio.[10]

Each episode of *Guitars and Adobes*, printed in *St. Anthony Messenger*, begins with the same Cassidy lithograph illustration: a circular image that features a guitar prominent in the foreground and a figure lying in bed in the background. The large size of the guitar points to its centrality in the narrative. Most of the other illustrations have captions directing readers to the scene in the story to which they refer. The depictions of the main characters, landscapes, pueblos, churches, feast days, and religious rituals reflect the style of the Santa Fe and Taos artists of the period. Additionally, Cassidy's images fulfill the conventions of fiction published at the time, which frequently included illustrations. The brown ink used for both the text and images creates a literary work that is a single harmonious whole, and more importantly signifies the color of New Mexico adobe and the brown robes of the Franciscan missionaries who were so closely involved in the history of the Southwest.

Guitars and Adobes was published under the playful pseudonym "F. Chalmers Ayers." Perhaps because other stories, poems, and a translation were appearing in the same magazine under "Fray Angélico Chávez," he employed a pseudonym for the serialized novel. For example, installments one, four, and five of the novel were each printed with a poem by Fray Angélico Chávez in the middle column of the second page. The nom de plume, F. Chalmers Ayers, creatively retains and mixes the order of the initials of Chávez's new religious name, subtly hinting at the real identity of the author, for astute readers who may have been following his writing in the magazine. The pseudonym even retains the diphthong "ch," which is a single letter in the Spanish alphabet. The refusal to mark gender, and the implicit Anglo ethnicity of the pseudonym, point playfully ahead to when Chávez uses female Anglo pseudonyms for other fiction, and hint at his connection to the many eastern Anglo writers in Santa Fe.[11]

At the time Chávez published *Guitars and Adobes,* other novels and short fiction about the Southwest found ready audiences, such as Mary Austin's *Starry Adventure* (1931), Ruth Laughlin Barker's *Caballeros: The Romance of Santa Fe and the Southwest* (1931), and Frank Applegate's *Native Tales of New Mexico* (published posthumously, 1932). In 1929 Oliver La Farge's *Laughing Boy* won the Pulitzer Prize. Plays about Southwest history such as *Pageant of Old Santa Fe* were produced at the annual Fiesta, and other regionally-themed dramas were performed by the Santa Fe Players. The most well-known novel of the period, Willa Cather's *Death Comes for the Archbishop* (1927), is the first explicit intertext in Chávez's serialized novel. He suggests on the first page that in his novel he wishes to present an alternative to Cather's picture of the Southwest.

Chávez continues in *Guitars and Adobes* an emphasis on Hispano ethnicity that he began in his earlier fiction. The novel reveals that he had already been reading about important figures in New Mexico history, whom he would later research and describe in longer historical accounts. As stated earlier, digressive subnarratives within the novel portray Don Diego de Vargas, Archbishop Lamy, Doña Tules, and *La Conquistadora*. Chávez emphasizes the role their legacies played in his fictional characters' lives. He displays his firsthand knowledge of New Mexico places, such as Mora, Las Vegas, Taos, and Santa Fe.

In the last chapter Chávez re-signifies the adobe house that has been the central motif of the novel and subtly suggests that it is the Cassidy home on Canyon Road. He also mentions other members of the writers' group who lived on Camino del Monte Sol in 1929, the year in which the novel ends. By obtaining Cassidy's artistic contribution and by alluding to the writers' group in the plot, Chávez noticeably places this creative work within the burgeoning artistic and literary movements of 1920s Santa Fe.

The novel is framed at the beginning and end by two deaths: the 1888 death of Archbishop Lamy, the famous historical figure, and the 1929 death of the fictional Consuelo Ortega Rael, an ordinary Hispana whose life story the people of Santa Fe have forgotten. Chávez's explicit denial at the outset that the novel is a sequel to Cather's in effect signals the opposite: that he strives to offer a vision of New Mexico in the late nineteenth and early twentieth centuries that more accurately portrays Hispano culture. Chávez presents Hispano culture as an alternative ethnicity to Cather's emphasis on French figures in her novel.[12] As the story opens (at the time of Lamy's death), Consuelo's mother, the widow Doña Genoveva, proudly traces her lineage to a captain who served under Don Diego de Vargas during the reconquest of New Mexico in 1692–93. Doña Genoveva, who hides her fortune under a slab in the fireplace, watches over an ancient guitar from Spain that her husband recovered years earlier from the famous saloon of Doña Tules, and that, according to legend, will bring death to anyone who plays it. Throughout the novel Chávez both affirms and denies the superstition about the guitar. Early on, Archbishop Lamy visits Genoveva's house when she is ill and plays the guitar before she can stop him. She is convinced this is why he dies on February 14, 1888. Meanwhile, her daughter begins to fall in love with Rosendo Rael, an industrious adobe maker who is falsely blamed for a burglary in her mother's home. Doña Genoveva wishes her daughter to marry another young man from a wealthy family, who unbeknownst to her is actually a gambler, troublemaker, and the real burglar.

When Rosendo loses his adobe-construction jobs because of the false accusation, and because Anglo Americans settling in New Mexico were building their houses using other materials, he uses the adobes he has made to construct a house near the Atalaya hills and buys a beautiful piano for it.[13] After Mass on Sundays, he continues to tell Consuelo he loves her and is finally able to spend some time with her at a dance held at a home on Agua Fria Street. At the novel's climax, after seeing Rosendo's beautiful adobe house with the piano, Consuelo elopes with him. They eventually make their home in Mora (where Fray Angélico grew up) and have a daughter whom they name after Doña Genoveva.

At this time an epidemic of *la viruela* (smallpox) breaks out in Mora, and the entire family is infected after Rosendo nurses some of the ill. The narrative then moves to about thirty-five years later (1929) and focuses on the writers' and artists' groups of Santa Fe. Doña Genoveva's house on Acequia Madre has been bought by an artist who has added a second story in keeping with the Santa Fe style of architecture. Up the road, on Camino del Monte Sol, three writers at a gathering hear the music of an untuned piano and a guitar, coming from the nearby Atalaya hills. The old woman with the scarred face who lives in the house calls herself "Margarita" and one night is killed during a violent storm as the house caves in while she is playing the piano. When the writers go to the house the next day, they find no musical instruments there, despite having heard music for many nights. Chávez ends the novel on this note: this mystery is "as intangible and uninterpretable as the one that holds the Old Santa Fe with the New in spite of the years, a tie of race, faith, and traditions, of love and romance, of guitars and adobes." Chávez's historical novel emphasizes realism tinged with the uncertain. He suggests that we cannot know everything about the past, but perhaps Spanish traditions and narratives carried down through the generations provide us with a more accurate account of the past than what appears in Cather's novel.

One key way in which Chávez Hispanicizes Cather's version of events is by linking the motif of death to the ancient Spanish guitar. The Spanish name for the instrument is *la vihuela,* which Chávez creatively connects to its near homonym *la viruela,* the word for smallpox. On the guitar is an inscription that contains words in Spanish spelled with the Hebrew alphabet, which Archbishop Lamy succeeds in deciphering because of his knowledge of Hebrew. The hybrid text gives historical testimony to the period of reconquest in Spain, during which Jews were told to convert to Christianity or leave the country. In a subnarrative, fictively recounted in one of Doña Tules' letters, the legend of the guitar is revealed. Here, Chávez falls into glaring anti-Semitism that he most likely imbibed in the milieu of the Cincinnati seminary. He writes: "Most of [the Jews] had been driven out of the kingdom by the government in order to free the country of a peril more insidious than the open warfare of the formerly victorious Moors; for they had been assuming control of the financial, the political, and even some of the religious affairs, when the Spanish hierarchy sounded the alarm." Seemingly defending the Spanish Inquisition, Chávez creates a character in *Guitars and Adobes* named Salomon García, whom he calls "a notorious leader of the Jews," a "shifty Jew," and a "fanatical rabbi." In the novel, the Inquisition accuses the *converso* (convert) García of being involved in a plot to overthrow the government, and so they burn him at the stake. During the execution, an onlooker improvises a ballad, accompanied by guitar music that criticizes García. The *converso's* youngest son Benjamin then kills the balladeer and inscribes an encoded curse on the guitar: *"La muerte canto—tócame y mueres"* (I sing death—play me and you die!). Eventually, the guitar came to the New World and ultimately to New Mexico with Doña Tules's family.

The overt anti-Semitism Chávez expresses in this first novel, written when he was just twenty and before the Holocaust would wreak its devastation, should be read in conjunction with Ilan Stavans's *The Scroll and the Cross: 1,000 Years of Jewish-Hispanic Literature,* which provides information about the important contributions Jews made to Spanish and Latin American letters.[14] Beginning with the era of cohabitation of Muslims, Christians, and Jews on the Iberian Peninsula, Stavans traces the relations between Jews and Hispanics in the Spanish-speaking world. He presents key texts of the literary and intellectual contributions of Jewish-Hispanic culture, examining the dreams of Jews in Hispanic lands and their reaction to native civilizations.

The Scroll and the Cross also provides information about how non-Jews have reacted to the Jewish presence, including the Edict of 1492 that forced the Jews out of Spain, and the anti-Semitic work of the thirteenth-century poet Gonzalo de Berceo. Representing popular views of his time, Berceo portrays in a poem, for example, a statue of the Blessed Virgin that miraculously claims "the Jews were doing Her injuries severe" (73). Stavans describes how the thirteenth-century King Alfonso X (*El Sabio*) proclaimed a code of law with restrictions for Jews: they should live forever in captivity as a reminder of their role in crucifying Christ, they should wear a distinguishing mark on their heads to allow recognition, and Jews who had sexual relations with Christian women deserved death. Elsewhere in his book, Stavans explains that the poem "To A Nose," by seventeenth-century poet Francisco de Quevedo, "might be one of the most anti-Semitic sonnets ever written in Spain, a peninsula known for its anti-Jewish literature" (134). In contrast, Stavans notes that writer Federico García Lorca wrote a poem in 1930 that highlights Judaism as a reservoir of ancient memory. By also including important writing by Hispano Jews in this volume, Stavans documents and gives voice to a vibrant intellectual culture, often developed under conditions of extreme adversity, and often demeaned or overlooked by cultural arbiters. Stavans's work partially explains the long tradition of Hispano anti-Semitism that Fray Angélico Chávez inherited, along with similar attitudes fomented in the Germanic milieu of the Catholic seminaries he attended. Stavans's book is a necessary companion to any reading of *Guitars and Adobes*.[15]

The guitar in Chávez's narrative is a metaphor for the novel itself on several levels. Linking the themes of the curse, revenge, and foretelling, it provides an enigma that impels the narrative forward. Characters often debate whether playing the cursed guitar does or does not cause death, and although several voices of authority in the novel insist that such deaths are only temporally coincidental, or caused by God, Chávez playfully leaves doubt about the guitar's role at the novel's end. Additionally, Benjamin's encoded curse inscribed on the guitar is like the novel Chávez has written: both involve writing by an oppressed minority that carries a message about the past to future generations. The novel and the curse intend to convey important historical events to succeeding generations, to prevent the forgetting of history. In form, Benjamin's dual-language message is similar to Chávez's bilingual narrative: both encode ethnicity through hybridity.

If, as its title indicates, Cather's novel focuses on the death of Archbishop Lamy, Chávez's novel broadens our overall understanding of death in the period. Lamy's natural death is set in contrast to the tragic deaths of ordinary people. The cursed Spanish guitar symbolizes the anxiety of Hispanos in New Mexico about the pervasiveness of death in their age. Chávez gives the idea of death in the years preceeding and following Lamy's demise an alternative ethnic nuance.

Another signifier of ethnicity that Chávez emphasizes in the title and the plot is the adobe. In contrast to the death symbolized by the guitar, adobes symbolize life—for they are used to construct homes that give people shelter. Rosendo makes thousands of adobes for people's homes, and after two clients reject him because of the false accusation, he builds a beautiful home that he hopes will shelter his future family. In contrast to the guitar's embodiment of *Thanatos* (the death instinct) Rosendo's adobes symbolize *Eros* and life. The piano he places inside the adobe links the home to the aesthetic. Inexorable death triumphs in the end, as nature overpowers culture during a violent storm, in an edifice constructed of adobes in desperate need of repair. The image of adobes also links Chávez to the historic preservation movement in Santa Fe, led by some members of the writers' and artists' groups. Following his ordination, Chávez would extensively engage in preservation work himself.

Hispano ethnicity imbues *Guitars and Adobes*. It is particularly evident in the stories-within-the story that Chávez inserts in the text, as lengthy digressions to explain Hispano historical figures. For instance, citing details written by a chronicler of the period, he tells the story of Doña Tules, who came to Santa Fe in 1820 and established a saloon and gambling house at the corner of Calle del Palacio and what is now Burro Alley. Later, in 1950 Chávez would publish his own revisionist historical account of Doña Tules in the journal *El Palacio*. His scholarly article documented that she died in 1852 when Jean-Baptiste Lamy was a bishop. In *Guitars and Adobes* he augments and re-ethnicizes Cather's version of events by inserting the contemporary narrative about Doña Tules, whom he calls Tules Barcelona, as her name was believed to be at the time.[16] In another narrative digression, Chávez tells the story of *La Conquistadora*, a seventeenth-century statue of the Virgin Mary, officially called at the time *La Señora del Rosario* or *de la Victoria*, according to Chávez in the novel. As Rosendo prays before this figure, which sits on a wood pedestal in the north chapel of the cathedral, to ask for help in winning Consuelo's love, he has a vision of Don Diego de Vargas's reconquest of Santa Fe. In narrating Rosendo's vision, Chávez familiarizes readers with the associated Hispano traditions in Santa Fe relating to the Pueblo Revolt of 1680, when the Spaniards were expelled, and then Vargas's reconquest of the city in 1693, with the same statue of the Virgin that Rosendo prays before now. Revealing that he had engaged in historical research of the period, Chávez suggests that if Rosendo had read the original document that Vargas drew up concerning the reconquest he would have seen the signature of his forbear Antonio Rael de Aguilar, as well as an ancestor of Consuelo's, Francisco Xavier de Ortega. Thus, Chávez selected the names for his protagonists in

Guitars and Adobes to emphasize the authentic connection of Santa Fe Hispanos to the centuries of Spanish presence in New Mexico. And that story, he insists, did not begin with Archbishop Lamy.

Once again, as he undergoes the increasing discipline of the novitiate in Cincinnati, and Duns Scotus College in Detroit, which he entered in 1930, Chávez directs an important part of his creative energy to a compelling narrative that reasserts Hispano ethnicity in the master historical text. His nostalgia for home was shaped by the intellectual, cultural, and artistic preoccupations of the Santa Fe writers and artists, with whom he had become connected during visits home and had stayed in contact with through correspondence. In *Guitars and Adobes* he joins forces with them by obtaining artwork by Cassidy for the novel, and at the same time asserts his own authentic and historically accurate Hispano version of events. Instead of seeking an outlet for publication in the Southwest, or a national venue, he publishes the novel serially in the Franciscan national magazine *St. Anthony Messenger.* Perhaps he did so because of his youthful inexperience, his confinement in the seminary, and pressure from the magazine editor, who wanted to publish more of his compelling fiction.

THE UNCOLLECTED STORIES

In addition to the novel, this anthology gathers together twenty short stories of Fray Angélico Chávez that have not appeared in previous published collections of his writing. Dating from 1929 to 1938, the stories present various themes and are set in locales such as Argentina, Mexico, Spain, New Mexico, and the Midwest. In each story Chávez employs sophisticated wordplay, suspense, surprise endings, and humor to draw readers in. Eight of his drawings are used to illustrate the stories—artwork that portrays aspects of the Southwest, emphasizes ethnicity, and depicts central scenes of the stories.[17] Chávez establishes a visual/verbal hybridity through which readers move back and forth between words and images to experience the particulars of southwestern culture. Text and image enhance one another in partnership.

The Southwest is rendered in images of American Indians in native garb, cowboys, *conquistadores,* Hispana women in long dresses and shawls, brown-robed Franciscans, *cantinas,* elements of local geography, and nature scenes. Many of these sketches resemble the illustrations in the 1928 Santa Fe Fiesta Program, in which the young Manuel Chávez had a poem published.[18] The contemporary style of drawings and sketches being made by artists in Santa Fe influenced Chávez's artistic imagination in this period. The verbal/visual hybridity of these early illustrated texts by Chávez, together with religion, ethnicity, history, and the Southwest, create a complex narrative identity for the author.

From June 1929 to September 1930, during Chávez's year at the Franciscan novitiate in Mt. Airy, he published under his given name a series of ten stories about the Southwest, illustrated with his own signed drawings, in the *St. Anthony Messenger.* Seven of the stories included in this volume, in the section "Early Illustrated Stories of the Southwest," appeared in this series. Precisely as he received the Franciscan habit, took on a new name, and was encouraged to withdraw from the world he had matured in, Chávez reconstructed key cultural elements of that world in his short stories. He continued to assert his Hispano ethnic identity, linking religious themes to Southwest ethnicity, and markedly revealed the influence of the Santa Fe writers' and artists' groups.

One central narrative strategy in Chávez's early stories is that of performance and disguise. "Spanish and Irish" (1929) employs these tropes on several levels. Ethnicities confront one another in the story, as a Hispana and an Irish girl work out their differences through representations of Native American ethnicity. As the girls disguise themselves for their private contest, the competition between them becomes a battle between fake Indian identities. Superior disguise, performance, and acting ability allow one contestant to win. Her performance is superior because it ingeniously engages in doubly-encoded difference, beyond simply ethnicity. Chávez manages to lead readers down a false path by merging the subjective view of the character

Lupe with that of the third-person narrative voice, misguiding readers into trusting the ostensible omniscience of the utterances. Readers, along with the character, mistake the simulacrum for the real.

Easterners displaced to New Mexico, like some members of the Santa Fe writers' and artists' groups of the period, appear in several of these early stories. For instance, in "Old Magdalena's Friend" (1929), the protagonist Clara Bolton is forced into political exile with her father, leaving behind the man she deeply loves, and wanders the globe in search of him, ending up in Santa Fe after failing to find him. She loses her religious faith, but following the example of Magdalena, her Hispana landlady in Santa Fe, she makes a *manda* or *promesa* to St. Anthony, the patron saint of finding lost things (including husbands) and of childbearing. Chávez continues his narrative strategy of performance and disguise by having Clara don the landlady's immensely long "seven-league black shawl" to visit the saint's statue in the cathedral. One might argue that the nineteen-year-old Chávez also "disguises" the landlady through exaggerated ethnicity by transliterating her speech from Spanish into stilted English. Speaking of her relationship to St. Anthony, Magdalena says: "Me and him is fine friends." In this way Chávez overcodes the religious message and the moral of the story with signifiers of ethnicity.

The first-person narrator of "Sierra Moon" (1930) functions as a local expert on New Mexico, and, along with Hispano cowboy Fernando, employs double-coded language as a disguise or costume for the truth. Through linguistic disguise, Fernando humorously leads the city slicker from the East (as well as the readers) down a false interpretive path to achieve a surprise ending. Through carefully crafted language and suspenseful delay, he plays on the fears and imagination of his audience, by taking advantage of the moonlit night on the deserted mountain to enhance the fear of the unknown. Chávez's double-coded language serves as a disguise or costume that temporarily conceals the truth and gives all a good laugh at the end of the story. Another easterner, Tim McCay, in "The Dude of Anchor Ranch" (1929), travels to an Ottowi Canyon ranch to cure his tuberculosis and learns that his body involuntarily takes on the stereotypical characteristics of the cowboys, a result of his new lifestyle on the ranch. Like Clara Bolton who dons her landlady's large Spanish shawl to perform a popular religious ritual, McCay's bodily performance of the New Mexico lifestyle is transformative.

In a number of stories, Chávez validates local Hispano culture while linking it to places outside U.S. borders. He sets the story "Romance of *El Caminito*" on a very narrow path in Santa Fe that locals use as a shortcut to the plaza. As a native insider, he explains to readers the name and tradition of the path, and he recounts a fictional romance that blossomed there because of a young woman's initiative and agency. The narrowness of the path forces two young people to interact with each other. Although the boy seems uninterested in the girl, she attempts to attract his attention by showing him her international stamp collection. The appearance of a Franciscan friar on the path creates a slight impediment and delays their conversation—a scene similar to an event in *Guitars and Adobes*. In the accompanying illustration the Franciscan's back looms large in the foreground, as he faces and surveys the two young people, who appear smaller in size and farther down the pathway. By choosing this event for the illustration, Chávez highlights the chance occurrence that will provide delay in the plot and enhances narrative pleasure. At the same time, he is thematically emphasizing the key role of Franciscans in the Southwest. Moving beyond Southwest culture at the same time that he emphasizes it, Chávez suggests that sharing the exotic stamps from various global cultures will allow the romance to blossom.

While other writers and artists in Santa Fe and Taos were highly interested in, and supportive of, the culture of Mexico in this period, Chávez takes a jab at the Mexican Revolution in "The Blasphemer" (1929). Unlike "Romance of *El Caminito*," in which outside culture plays a positive role, here a visitor from Mexico to the small town of Buena Vista (the name of the Santa Fe street where writer Witter Bynner lived) creates a disruption. Named Zapata, the visitor symbolizes the anti-Church reforms of the Mexican Revolution. Sabino, the owner of the local cantina, tells the men in town that there is no need to go to Sunday Mass or support the padre monetarily. When Zapata takes Sabino's remarks further, arguing that the Church is only out to get people's money, and engages in blasphemy, a physical fight ensues. Hispano and Mexican ethnicities battle with one another here, resulting in religious renewal. Chávez had once insisted to a fellow seminarian that he was Hispano, not Mexican, and when he was in elementary school he had been told by a Christian Brother that the Franciscans did not accept Mexicans as seminarians. However, his criticism of Mexican culture here is related more to a particular aspect of Mexican politics that he and the Catholic Church strongly rejected—the weakening of the power of the Church by the constitutional reforms after the Revolution and the ensuing Cristero War of 1926–29.

In "Notch Twenty-One" (1930), the first story published under Chávez's new religious name, disguise, performance, and storytelling are key once again. He shows his strong interest in New Mexico history by setting the story in 1870s San Miguel County, where Sheriff Miguel Armijo waits to capture "Beely de Keed." Chávez gives clues to the outcome in the first paragraph. Armijo has set his pistols on his desk, waiting for the outlaw to arrive. Behind him and next to an open safe sits "young Jim Slocum," with his guns strapped to his sides. Slocum reminds Armijo that the sheriff of Lincoln County has sent him to help because of his expertise in recognizing Billy the Kid. Chávez then recounts key historical details of heavy outlaw activity in mid-nineteenth-century New Mexico, and refers to a document of the era then on display in Santa Fe.

William H. Bonney, or "The Kid," is twenty-one years old at the time, claiming he needs to kill one more man to match his age. Slocum passes the time waiting with Sheriff Armijo by telling a story about how the outlaw killed his friend in a bar in Lincoln—a scene that Chávez adeptly draws in an illustration for the story. Slocum's tale parallels the story we are reading and prefigures its outcome. Vision is a central motif here, complementing the images of disguise and performance. Chávez's illustration includes several ethnic motifs of the Southwest and focuses on the mirror behind the bar of the *cantina,* in which Slocum and his friend briefly see the image of the outlaw as he enters.

In Slocum's tale, Billy the Kid rapidly kills Slocum's friend while he is drawing his gun. In the larger narrative, the man sent to help the sheriff distracts him with fabrications and storytelling, thereby leading both the character and readers down a false narrative path. The sheriff's vision is impeded with the literal and figurative disguises, and his mistaken reading of signs. Like the sheriff, readers are also fooled into thinking that one character is Billy the Kid, as Chávez leads them down another false narrative path.

Chávez's illustrations for this series portray aspects of the Southwest, in which he emphasizes ethnicity and key scenes from the plots. He establishes a visual/verbal hybridity through which readers move back and forth between words and images to experience the region's culture. Text and image enhance one another in partnership. Chávez renders the Southwest in images of American Indians (and their imitators) in native garb, bow-legged cowboys, Hispana women in long shawls, a brown-robed Franciscan, a rural church, *cantinas,* and depictions of pine-covered mountains, hollyhocks, and the "opaque amber eyebrow" of the moon (in "Sierra Moon"). The contemporary style of representing the Southwest in drawings and sketches in Santa Fe influenced his artistic imagination in this period.

LESSONS IN LOVE, COURAGE, AND FAITH

The stories that appear in the last two sections of this volume—"Lessons in Love" and "Courage and Faith"—were published between 1935 and 1938 in *The Sodalist* and *St. Anthony Messenger.* At the height of the Depression, while he was finishing his studies at St. Leonard's Seminary in Oldenberg, Fray Angélico wrote a series of stories for the young female readers of the Catholic magazine *The Sodalist.* In this period "Sodalities of the Blessed Virgin" were clubs at parishes and schools designed to encourage young women's devotion to Mary and further their moral development.[19] Fray Angélico's stories in this magazine impart advice and morals, with humor, erudition, and witty wordplay. Female protagonists predominate; they are often wiser and cleverer than the men. The stories frequently portray young women who must choose between two suitors. Through the narrative resolution the stories give advice on the most efficacious choices and the qualities of a good husband.

Fray Angélico published four of these stories under female pseudonyms, perhaps because the readers of the magazine might be more receptive to instructional messages if they came from a woman. However, one of his choices for a pen name—"Ann Jellicoe"—used for three of the stories, challenges readers to connect the stories to previous narratives in the magazine that appeared under the byline "Angelico Chavez." By leaving out the religious signifier "Fray," the byline suggests that a lay person is writing the story. This omission also allows readers to make an easier connection to the pseudonym Ann Jellicoe, without an intrusive, non-homonymic extra word. This pen name echoed his real name phonetically, and the stories written under it had similar structures, lessons, humor, and sophisticated wordplay as the stories written by him under "Angelico Chavez." Thus, the pen name subtly invited readers to decipher the singular identity of the two writers. The last of the four stories appeared in 1938, after Chávez's ordination, and perhaps to mark the departure from his studies for the priesthood, he used the one-time pen name "Monica Lloyd."

Fray Angélico may have adopted a pseudonym in 1936 for a more practical reason. In September of that year he published an article featuring his own illustrations in *The Sodalist* called "How to Make Your Own Bookplate," and because one of his fictional tales appeared in the same issue, the editor, or Chávez himself, might have suggested that he invent a pseudonym to avoid the appearance of two contributions by a single author. The same thing happened in the November issue of *The Sodalist* that year: Chávez published a poem with the byline Angelico Chavez, while his story carried a pseudonym.[20] Perhaps Chávez enjoyed experimenting with the female authorial identities, at a time when his real-life identity was about to undergo transformation, through ordination into the Franciscan priesthood.

The gender hybridity of the pseudonym Ann Jellicoe was also marked by a fictional ethnicity—Anglo Irish.[21] Nonetheless, the gender and ethnic hybridity of a name such as Ann Jellicoe allowed observant readers to see the distinct elements of the new mixture clearly: just as a pun moves back and forth between the two or more meanings of the signifier, so do the names Angélico and Ann Jellicoe allow readers to enjoyably waver between male and female, Hispano and Anglo significations. Chávez also engaged in such rhetorical and thematic strategies within the story "Carrie's Notion" (1937), by giving the character Elmer Vogelmeister, whose surname means "Master of the Birds" in German, the pseudonym "E. Byrd Masters."

Besides attempting to socialize Catholic youth, in keeping with the goals of the magazine, Chávez's stories in *The Sodalist* address issues of the day, portray Hispano and other ethnic cultures of the United States and engage in humorous wordplay and cultural references. In "Time and Tide" (1935), for example, New Mexico Hispano culture is only a backdrop in contrast to other stories where it plays a more central role. Twin sisters, humorously named Fructosa and Sinforosa Cana, are unmarried businesswomen who operate a hotel in Mora, New Mexico (where Fray Angélico grew up). The name Fructosa means "the sweetness of fruit," and Sinforosa is from the Latin "full of misfortunes." They share the last name Cana, a play on the biblical story of the wedding at Cana and the Spanish word for "grey hair," thus symbolizing their age. In the story Chávez Anglicizes their names to Time and Tide, diegetically because the educated young people in town found their names too much work to say, and formally to allow the author to play on the aphorism "Time and tide wait for no man." Chávez also references the following relevant lines from "Bill" Shakespeare: "There is a tide in the affairs of men which, taken at the flood, leads on to fortune." In terms of romance, the Cana sisters had only experienced a desert to this point, but, Chávez warns, they were about to experience a flood and disprove "Bill's weather forecast."

While Fructosa (Time) attracts two shady men with her financial "sweetness," Sinforosa (Tide) suffers a temporary misfortune beneath the guise of romance. Chávez foreshadows the outcome with a clever allusion to the real Queen Victoria and her mirrored reflection. With extensive wordplay and clever cultural allusions throughout, Chávez adorns the rather simple plot with references to President Roosevelt and flood relief, Noah's ark, and the wedding at Cana, ultimately giving the women the upper hand by showing that they "wait for no man."

Hispano culture functions more strongly in other stories in the series. "Viola Comes of Age" (1936), written under the byline Ann Jellicoe, is set in Argentina, where Chávez develops identity through ethnicity, religiosity, and family heritage. The protagonist Viola Molinar is a hybrid figure in appearance, personality, and name. She is a blue-eyed blonde—physical traits inherited from the Celts who originally inhabited Spain, according to Chávez—and has pensive moods in which her eyes grow big and dark, which is attributed to her strain of "Moorish fiery blood." Her given name is a linguistic hybrid of her two grandmothers, Victoria and Olivia. The narrative disequilibrium with which the story opens relates to religion and family heritage: Viola has begun to frequent the shrine of the fictional "Our Lady of Roybal" some distance away near the *alcalde's* plantation. Here Chávez has inserted his personal family identity into the narrative—his mother's name Roybal—perhaps to compensate for the absence of his paternal family name in the byline. He has implanted a subtle signifier of identity for careful readers and future scholars to decode.

The principal conflict in this story involves Viola's mother's fear that her daughter's frequent visits to the shrine will lead to her becoming a nun instead of marrying and passing on the family's fortune as the sole heir. The conflict is developed through ethnic images, such as when her mother complains that the trips to the shrine take away time from Viola's practice of the Andalusian gypsy dance that she is to perform at the upcoming fiesta. To depict Viola's Spanish dancing *The Sodalist* included a lithograph that Gerald Cassidy had originally created for the February 1932 installment of *Guitars and Adobes*.

On her visits to the shrine Viola prays to the Virgin that the handsome American miner she has just met will turn out to be single and a Catholic. When the miner sees her at the shrine one day, he tells her that he is indeed both, and an Irishman—"the dark variety of Erin that inherited its brunette strain from shipwrecked survivors of the Spanish Armada." Chávez integrates an inherited strain of Hispano ethnicity into the man who attracts Viola, and casts him as single and Catholic to remind female readers that they should seek the same qualities in the men they fall in love with. They should also imitate Viola's later pilgrimage to the shrine, when she prays for the miner's safe return. The story ends with a tableau of Hispanic ethnicity in which Viola performs her gypsy dance: "Never was her hair more golden, or her lips enticingly poutful, or her eyes more Moorishly big and enchanting. All the youthful *caballeros* applauded and whooped...." Offering readers an emblematic ideal they should follow, the hoped-for match between Viola and the miner conjoins Spanish heritage, devout Catholicism, and maternal approval.

The Hispano culture of New Mexico is also an important element of identity in "Eve of San Isidro" (1937), which was also published under the pseudonym Ann Jellicoe. Although once again the story deals with a young girl's suitors, in this case her choice is a religious vocation rather than marriage. The protagonist is an elderly nun—Sister Consolata—originally from New Mexico and living in Delaware, who tells the story of her youth for the first time. Much of her narrative, identity, and preoccupations coincide with Fray Angélico's own trajectory. It might be argued that Ann Jellicoe has superimposed his/her identity upon that of the character. Like Sister Consolata (nicknamed "Sister Disappointed") Chávez was transplanted from New Mexico to the East and often needed to explain his Hispano culture to other people, and correct misperceptions. In the story, on the eve of the feast of St. Isidore—the patron of the school—Sister Consolata finds she must inform the young graduate, Ellen McIntyre, that this saint was Spanish, not Irish. She explains that there were two saints by that name, the Archbishop of Seville and the Laborer of Madrid, and both the church and school in Sister Consolata's village in New Mexico were dedicated to the Laborer. We can detect Fray Angélico's own nostalgia in the vivid image the nun portrays for the student: "I can still see the little town perched on the mountainside, with the New Mexico sierras looming behind, and the yellow plains spreading below for hundreds of miles. I can see my father's house so plainly, and the little white chapel of *San Isidro Labrador!* I can see the Padre teaching the children their prayers under that old acacia tree by the chapel door." About to be ordained and not having been home for several years, Fray Angélico combines memory of place with a projected future image of himself as a village padre.

Fray Angélico overlays elements of his own story on that of Sister Consolata, who desperately wished that she had been born a man so that she could become a priest. She alludes to her concern about the deteriorating condition of the Southwest missions and the work of the French missionary in her village who had the church restored. In 1937–38, shortly after the story was published, Fray Angélico would begin restoration work himself, at the chapel of Santa Dorotea in Domingo Station, and at Our Lady of Guadalupe Church in Peña Blanca. Here he uses the voice of the nun to outline the religious and community work he expects in his first assignment: rectifying and blessing marriages, restoring the church building, teaching children catechism along with reading and writing, and teaching the people how to better build and plant. When Sister Consolata looks at the crucifix at the end of her narrative and tells Ellen, "I was never disappointed in love," we can imagine that Fray Angélico shared these sentiments about his own vocation.

Several of Chávez's stories in *The Sodalist* center on an aphorism or common saying that is reconfigured both to teach a moral and as part of the author's humorous wordplay. In "A Stitch in Time" (1936), Chávez plays with the motif of sewing to illustrate a young dressmaker's integrity and ingenuity. Protagonist Gertrude Miller's "stitch in time" is needed to save the nine innings of a close baseball championship game. The narrative disequilibrium introduced at the outset involves a rivalry for Gertrude's affection between the pitcher and catcher of the local team. During the game, the pitcher refuses to follow the catcher's signals, resulting in disastrous consequences. Having recently left the pitcher for the catcher because the former was not a gentleman, Gertrude saves the day by an ingenious bit of playacting that she herself chooses and executes. At the same time she figuratively scores a double. Chávez shows the predominantly female readers of the magazine that they can be strong and ingenious despite adversity and men's attempts to stereotype them. The story contains lessons for boys, too, as the author invites them to look negatively on the pitcher, Ashby, who is a bad role model, and instead follow the model of the catcher, who refuses to engage in Ashby's tactics.

Chávez depicts another ethnic culture in his touching love story about an Italian street vendor who competes with a doctor for a nurse's affection. In "Daily Apple" (1936), under the byline Ann Jellicoe, a fruit vendor named Tony Valentino gives the nurse a bright red apple every day, as she passes on her way to the hospital, hoping the gesture will keep the doctor away from her. He promises her an original song, and one day she hears him singing in Italian from the street below—lines that Chávez translates for readers: "O wingless angel, pure and white / You make this hospital a Heaven bright." Almost immediately, the song takes on a more literal significance when the nurse and doctor are called to an emergency.

The stories "Rolling Stones" and "It's an Ill Wind" (1936) play on their respective aphorisms in overcoming characters' dilemmas. The protagonist of the first story, Flora Leech, must decide between two suitors, and between progress and tradition in the face of encroaching Yankee development in her small Tennessee town. The city-bred Algey Ludlow discovers a new species of moss that has gathered on the idle millstones owned by Flora's father, and names the strain "Floralacea" in honor of Flora, whom he wishes to marry. Flora's hometown suitor, Jim Huskin, proposes a clever scheme to revitalize the old mill and sell feed to the government at a lower price than the Yankee company. The decision Flora must make is resolved after she slips into the water, precariously close to the turning water wheel. The adapted aphorism conveys the moral humorously in the last lines of the story, as the new couple converses: "'I ask you for the hundredth time... if you prefer me and the millstones to that cracked moss gatherer.' 'And I answer for the hundredth time,' said she, smiling, 'that a rolling stone gathers no moss.'"

The saying, "It's an ill wind that blows no one good," highlights the thematic and moral elements of the second story. This time, a young man starts to go wrong because he wishes to marry his girlfriend but believes he lacks sufficient money. Like Chávez himself, the man is small in stature and plays a wind instrument—the bass tuba. (Chávez played the saxophone in the seminary.) An exciting, suspenseful narrative draws readers into the ups and downs of the protagonist's initiation into crime, in his misguided attempt to win his girlfriend's hand in marriage. After an ill wind blows into town in the form of two career criminals, who entice him into a burglary, the protagonist utilizes "wind power" to allow a good wind to triumph over the ill wind. The moral lesson for *Sodalist's* readers was to be confident in one's own talents, rather than be defeated by perceived shortcomings, to overcome temptation, and always to be honest.

All of Chávez's pieces in *The Sodalist* teach morals to young women usually through enjoyable plots, wordplay, and linguistic twists, as well as characters that readers can identify with. Chávez inserts himself into many of these stories in unique hybrid constructs that cross ethnicities, genders, and professions, along with history, religion, politics, and linguistic play. He subtly links himself with both male and female characters, including a musician who betrays his family and friends by committing burglary, a nun, and even the Blessed Virgin at a shrine in Argentina. He also presents himself through his given male name and with female pseudonyms. Strikingly, several stories put Hispano culture center stage, pointing to the author as an ethnic subject whose personal expertise corrects the misperceptions about an important, regional culture in the United States.

After his ordination, a few more of Fray Angélico's stories appeared in *St. Anthony Messenger*. In the same vein as his early fiction, "Carrie's Notion," "Beads" (under the pseudonym "Arthur Chapman"), "Mateo Makes Money," and "Honest Art" (June, August, November, 1937, and February 1938) carry over from pre- to post-ordination some of the themes of Chávez's earlier stories. Similar to the story "It's an Ill Wind," in "Carrie's Notion," published just after Chávez is ordained in 1937, a young man wants to marry his girlfriend, Carrie, but as an aspiring writer he doesn't have the income necessary to support her. With advice from the Catholic priest and an idea about a pseudonym from Carrie, he finds a solution. Fragments of Chávez's life are interspersed in the story so that a subtle self-reflexivity overlays the text. This authorial presence overcodes several characters: the priest giving advice, the aspiring writer whose stories are rejected, the designer of the pseudonym, and the winner of the writing contest. As in his stories for *The Sodalist*, Chávez's women in "Carrie's Notion" are strong, play key roles, and often devise ingenious solutions to problems. For instance, Carrie suggests that her boyfriend replace his cumbersome and unromantic German name, Elmer Vogelmeister, with a pen name. Since his name means "Master of the Birds" in German, she suggests he use the more authorial sounding "E. Byrd Masters," reminiscent of Chávez's own pseudonym F. Chalmers Ayers. Chávez also inserts himself into the story as the protagonist, who writes about his own social world using slightly altered names and events, just as Chávez himself does on several occasions. Playfully, he attaches elements of his own identity to the process and plot of "Carrie's Notion."

Part of a group of stories that center on Chávez's notion of role models of courage and faith, "Honest Art" (February 1938) is also Fray Angélico's segue to his first book of fiction, *New Mexico Triptych* (1940).[22] "Honest Art" focuses on Arturo Vásquez, an accomplished *santero* (one who paints or carves images of saints) in Santa Fe. While he is at work carving a *bulto* (three-dimensional religious sculpture) of San José for the chapel at Chimayó, Vásquez tells the narrator about having come to Santa Fe under the Federal Arts Program and wondering how he could raise money to attend art school. Invited to a gathering of the writers' and artists' colony, Vásquez hears a French artist complaining that there is too much dishonesty in modern art. When the rich theatre mogul he is speaking to drops his wallet, Vásquez picks it up, finding hundreds of dollars inside that he decides to keep and use for art school. Later in the evening, the theatre producer praises his carvings and hints that he will help him through school, because he is an honest artist. Vásquez's misinterpretation of this comment saves him; subjective, mistaken semiosis gets him back on the right path. Vásquez learns later that his future sponsor was referring to art that did not cheat, by tracing over a photograph or putting plaster on an imperfection in a sculpture. By ultimately practicing personal and artistic honesty, "Art" Vásquez succeeds both ethically and professionally.

The 1937 story "Beads" might be seen as an extension of Chávez's earlier story "The Blasphemer," in which he criticized the anti-Church activities of the Mexican Revolution. Once again his pseudonym for "Beads"—Arthur Chapman—retains his own initials, "A" and "Ch," as did the nom de plume F. Chalmers Ayers, in his serialized novel of 1931–32. Arthur Chapman is actually the name of a little-known southwestern writer of cowboy poetry who died in 1935. In "Beads," the persona of the author, "Chappy," meets an old friend he knew in Cincinnati, journalist Joe Sterkes, who tells him two related stories that teach the adage "Don't judge a book by its cover." When assigned to travel to Mexico to write an undercover story on the Calles government (Calles was the president of Mexico who implemented strict anti-Church policies and thereby fomented the Cristero War), Sterkes ended up on a military work crew, where one elderly worker passed out. While nursing him back to health, Sterkes learned that he was a Franciscan priest who had been forced to leave his convent in Jalisco during the war hostilities. Sterkes's "beads," on which he faithfully prays the daily rosary, are a sign that assured the priest he was in safe hands. The educated priest quoted Shakespeare,

Cervantes, and Lope de Vega, proving that his bedraggled looks belied his true talent and intelligence. Chávez inserts himself into the story by having it set during a train trip through Denver, like one of his own journeys home from the seminary. After hearing Sterkes's story, Chappy feels inferior and humbly follows his friend into the church to pray the rosary.

Chávez's next two stories, also published in *St. Anthony Messenger* (November 1937 and February 1938), after he began his ministry at Peña Blanca and the nearby Indian pueblos, are firmly rooted in his particular Southwest surroundings. In "Mateo Makes Money," during a thirty-mile walk from Santo Domingo Pueblo to Santa Fe to sell his wares, sixty-year-old Mateo remembers the story of the Virgin of Guadalupe, whose image hangs on his wall at home. Suddenly, he feels he is rising to the sky, seeing stars, smelling a sweet fragrance, and hearing a mild voice that he imagines to be the Virgin's. In fact, wealthy tourists on their way to Santa Fe have hit him with their car. Chávez satirizes their ignorance: "'Guadaloop must be the chief's name,' one man says when Mateo utters the Virgin's name. Another says, 'How about us chipping in for the benefit of Pocahontas' grandpa?'" After the tourists leave him a tidy sum, Mateo believes Guadalupe has performed another miracle. He decides not to tell the Archbishop, who he knew probably wouldn't believe him, as in the case with Juan Diego (who claimed to have had a vision of the Virgin, outside Mexico City in 1531). Nor does he tell the people at the pueblo, who will likely think he stole the money. Having superimposed the modified Guadalupe narrative on his life, Mateo decides it will remain a secret between him and the Virgin. Although he says he feels like one of the clay rain gods he sells to the tourists, who throw money at him, the story does not represent a stereotypic tourist's view of Pueblo Indians. Since 1935, Santo Domingo Pueblo had been placed under Interdict by Archbishop Gerken, which meant that every Catholic religious function was prohibited, except for rites for the dying. On Saturdays, Chávez offered religious instruction at the pueblo and talked with the people. He was instrumental in ultimately negotiating the lifting of the Interdict, in July 1940. In this context, the November 1937 story "Mateo Makes Money," reveals Chávez's view that the people of Santo Domingo retained a deep Catholic faith despite the Interdict.

Courage and faith are again the theme, as Chávez links Hispanic ethnicity to religion and ideals for young women, in an adamantly anti-Communist story published in *The Sodalist* in 1936. Set during the Spanish Civil War, "Spanish Joan" is about a character named María Jaén, a brave Catholic girl who in an instant becomes a militant and faces death trying to save a *convento* of Franciscan friars from a mob of rabid Communists. Here, as in his 1939 essay "*Ni los Sepulcros Respetan*" ("They Don't Even Respect Graves"), published in *El Nuevo Mexicano,* Chávez presents a one-sided, inaccurate picture of the Spanish Civil War, in which those fighting for the Republican democracy were termed "Communists" by the Catholic Church and other supporters of the Fascist General Francisco Franco.

Describing "the night of Red Terror" in Málaga, Chávez portrays the Republicans as less than human: "The Communist mobs surged about like incarnate demons, shrieking blasphemies and applying the knife and torch to everything that was God's." After her father and brother, Manuel, are arrested and burned alive by the "Soviet fiends," María wishes she had been born a man so that she could fight "these foes of her home, her country, and her Faith." Remembering Joan of Arc and the Maid of Saragossa, the seventeen year old takes up her brother's hunting rifle, refuses an escape route offered her, and forces the friars of the *convento* to escape safely, while she holds off the "blood-thirsty throng." As the "human devils" tramp over her body, the spirit of Joan of Arc comes down from the heavens to rescue the soul of the "Maid of Málaga." Chávez invites his female readers to identify with María's militant defense of Catholicism, giving them a strong dose of Catholic anti-Communist indoctrination, cloaked in details of Spanish ethnicity. For example, María wears a rose in her hair as she holds off the enemy—illustrated here by a Cassidy lithograph reprinted from *Guitars and Adobes*. Chávez subtly inserts himself into the story by using his given name, Manuel, for the brother who is killed.

Chávez's last story in *The Sodalist* appeared in 1938, a year after he was ordained, under the pseudonym Monica Lloyd. "Winnie the Breadwinner and Saint Anthony" recounts a young widow's struggle to make ends meet during the Depression, and support her child and older sister. Allusions to the cold windy weather and the *Free Press* newspaper suggest that the story is set in Detroit. Chávez may have written it when he was a student there, at Duns Scotus. This tale contains none of the humorous wordplay, reinterpreted aphorisms, and lightness of his other stories. Winnie and her sister are immigrants from Wales, suffering so much from the Depression in America that their dream is to return to Britain. Meanwhile, the landlord comes to collect the back rent, and thanks to the prayers of Winnie's sister and child, before the statue of St. Anthony in their home, Winnie finds a part-time job that pays one dollar a day. Despite continuing their traditional Tuesday night novena to St. Anthony at a church, Winnie loses the job. Readers experience many melodramatic ups-and-downs until the final resolution. Chávez's erudition is apparent, for he names the specific shrines and holy places of Wales that the family dreams of returning to. The predominant religious message is that a strong devotion to St. Anthony can ameliorate the most desperate circumstances suffered in the Depression. The story also subtly alludes to Fray Angélico's parents' loss of their house during this period, and his mother's devotion to the statue of St. Anthony kept in the living room. After her death, family members found notes with petitions and prayers that Mrs. Chávez had placed beneath the statue.[23]

The culture of Fray Angélico's new surroundings after his 1937 ordination, and his first assignment as a priest at Peña Blanca, imbues these short stories, as well as the poetry he wrote at the time. For example, soon after he publishes "Carrie's Notion," in which he offers strategies and advice for young writers trying to publish their work, he asks his Franciscan superior permission to begin publishing his own work in secular, broader venues, such as *New Mexico Magazine*.[24]

The plight of the Santo Domingo Pueblo Indians, to whom Chávez ministered, is a central theme in "Mateo Makes Money." The deep faith that Mateo demonstrates reflects what Fray Angélico observed in his weekly visits to the people of Santo Domingo—visits he undertook despite the official Church Interdict in force at the time. Also during this period, Chávez continued to socialize with members of the Santa Fe writers' and artists' groups. In 1938 and 1939 he was invited to participate in the annual Poetry Roundups, organized by Witter Bynner, Alice Corbin Henderson, and Haniel Long. In late April 1938, after Bynner sent Long a copy of Chávez's "The Penitente Thief," just published in *St. Anthony Messenger,* Long wrote to Fray Angélico and invited him to submit short pieces to the weekly "New Mexico writers" section of the *New Mexico Sentinel* that Long edited. The writers' group also invited Chávez to publish his first volume of poetry, with their sponsorship, in 1939. The publication of "Honest Art" in February 1938, which depicts the relationship between the Anglo art colony and native artists (such as the character Vásquez), alludes to Fray Angélico's own relationship with these groups. Through the stories published in late 1937 and 1938, Chávez paved the way to his 1940 masterpiece *New Mexico Triptych.*

Chávez continued to publish poetry, fiction, and other creative writing in his prolific career, including *Clothed with the Sun* (1939), *Eleven Lady Lyrics* (1945), *The Single Rose* (1948), *La Conquistadora, the Autobiography of an Ancient Statue* (1954), *From an Altar Screen: El Retablo, Tales from New Mexico* (1957), *The Virgin of Port Lligat* (1959), *The Lady from Toledo* (1960), and *The Song of St. Francis* (1973). After his service as chaplain in the Pacific front in World War II, he focused primarily on historical research. Among his most well-known history books are *Our Lady of the Conquest* (1948), *Origins of New Mexico Families in the Spanish Colonial Period* (1954), *My Penitente Land* (1974), and three books on famous nineteenth-century Hispano priests in New Mexico: Padres Martínez, Gallegos, and Ortiz. For a number of reasons, he left the ministry in 1971 and devoted himself to writing full time. At the time of his death in 1996 his prolific intellectual and cultural production of seven decades had earned him the title of one of New Mexico's foremost twentieth-century humanists.

The stories and first novel republished in this volume reveal the early path of his creativity; his drive to write about New Mexico; and his talents as a storyteller, humorist, and lover of language. Nearly eighty years after its serialized publication, *Guitars and Adobes* now appears in book form for the first time, along with the illustrations Gerald Cassidy created for it. It is fitting that on the eve of the 2010 centenary of Chávez's birth, these stories, first novel, and illustrations can be rescued from the pages of decades-old magazines, now stored in the Franciscan archives in Cincinnati, and made available to a wider public, for future generations to enjoy.

Notes

1. Meg Sandoval, "Fray Angélico Chávez," *Denver Catholic Register*, October 3, 1990.

2. For further information on Chávez's prolific literary, artistic, historical, journalistic, and intellectual work, see the following two books by Ellen McCracken: *Fray Angélico Chávez: Poet, Priest, and Artist* (Albuquerque: University of New Mexico Press, 2000) and *The Life and Writing of Fray Angélico Chávez: A New Mexico Renaissance Man* (Albuquerque: University of New Mexico Press, 2009).

3. James Kraft, *Who Is Witter Bynner?: A Biography* (Albuquerque: University of New Mexico Press, 1995); T. M. Pearce, ed., *Literary America: 1903–1934: The Mary Austin Letters* (Westport, CT: Greenwood Press, 1979); and Alice Corbin Henderson, *The Turquoise Trail: An Anthology of New Mexico Poetry* (Boston: Houghton Mifflin Company, 1928).

4. Edna Robertson and Sarah Nestor, *Artists of the Canyons and Caminos: Santa Fe, The Early Years* (Santa Fe: Ancient City Press, 1976); Marta Weigle and Kyle Fiore, *Santa Fe and Taos: The Writer's Era, 1916–1941* (Santa Fe: Ancient City Press, 1994); Joseph Dispenza and Louise Turner, *Will Shuster: A Santa Fe Legend* (Santa Fe: Museum of New Mexico Press, 1989); and Elmo Baca, *Mabel's Santa Fe and Taos: Bohemian Legends (1900–1950)* (Layton, UT: Gibbs Smith Publisher, 2000).

5. See Dispenza and Turner, and Robertson and Nestor. Some now argue that Eliseo Rodríguez, a local Hispano artist who did chores for several Santa Fe artists and

writers, should also be included in the group as *"el sexto pintor"* (the sixth painter). See Carmella Padilla, *Eliseo Rodríguez: El Sexto Pintor* (Santa Fe: Museum of Fine Arts, 2001).

6. Witter Bynner, "Alice and I," *New Mexico Quarterly Review* 19 (1949): 38.

7. Fellow seminarian Fr. Bernard Gerbus noted that Chávez insisted that he was Spanish and not Mexican and that he was the first one who went to the seminary from New Mexico and had to go through "this damned German culture." Fr. Bernard Gerbus, interview by Ellen McCracken, March 22, 1997, Cincinnati, Ohio.

8. Fray Angélico Chávez, interview by John Penn La Farge, September 14, 1989.

9. "Old Missions in New Mexico," *St. Anthony Messenger* 41 (March 1934): 532–33.

10. Robertson and Nestor.

11. In addition to the pseudonym F. Chalmers Ayers, for *Guitars and Adobes,* Chávez employed the nom de plume Arthur Chapman in the story "Beads," Monica Lloyd in "Winnie the Breadwinner and Saint Anthony," and Ann Jellicoe in the stories "Viola Comes of Age," "The Eve of San Isidro," and "Daily Apple."

12. Mary Austin criticized Cather for having "given her allegiance to the French blood of the Archbishop; [and having] sympathized with his desire to build a French cathedral in a Spanish town. It was a calamity to the local culture. We have never got over it." Quoted in Weigle and Fiore, p. 25.

13. Here Chávez integrates his personal family history into the narrative. His father built the family a home in the late 1920s at 712 Acequia Madre, where his mother played the piano and rehearsed with the church choir she directed. At the time Fray Angélico wrote *Guitars and Adobes,* the Chávez family had not yet lost the house through bank foreclosure, which happened during the Depression, in 1932. With the assistance of a program established by President Roosevelt, they were later able to get the family home back. Chávez Collection, AC 287, Folder 2: Chávez Family, Fray Angélico Chávez History Library and Photographic Archives, Santa Fe.

14. Ilan Stavans, *The Scroll and the Cross: 1,000 Years of Jewish-Hispanic Literature* (New York: Routledge, 2003).

15. As a mature writer, Chávez published better informed work on Jews and Jewish biblical traditions, most notably in *My Penitente Land* (1974)

16. See Ralph E. Twitchell, *The History of the Occupation of the Territory of New Mexico from 1846 to 1851 by the Government of the United States* (Denver: Smith-Brooks, 1909; rpt, New York: Arno Press, 1976), 298.

17. Although the illustration for "Honest Art" (February 1938) is attributed to Chávez, it is unlike any of his other art, and appears to be the work of another artist whose illustrations appeared in *St. Anthony Messenger* at the time. I have judged it a mistaken attribution and have not included the image in this volume.

18. *Official Santa Fé Fiesta Program: 1928*, Vertical File Collection, Santa Fe Public Library.

19. In 1884, when *The Sodalist* was first published, it was sponsored by a 600-member male sodality at St. Francis Seraph Church in Cincinnati and contained articles both in German and English reflecting the immigrant population. By the time it ceased publication in June 1938, it had broadened its readership to include Catholic secondary schools and academies, and all sodalities, and its format was similar to *St. Anthony Messenger*. When Chávez's stories appeared in *The Sodalist* from 1935 to 1937, the editor was Fr. Hyacinth Blocker. See Celestine Baumann, O.F.M., "Notes on *The Sodalist*," *The Provincial Chronicle* 15 (Fall 1942): 20–25.

20. He did have two contributions under his own name in the December 1936 issue: the poem "Christmas Lullaby" appeared on the back cover, and the story "Spanish Joan" was featured inside the journal. In a note to his bibliographer, Phyllis Morales, Chávez wrote that he did not remember why he used a pseudonym for these stories. Having discovered a copy of "Winnie the Breadwinner and St. Anthony" under the name Monica Lloyd in his mother's cellar, Chávez wrote to Morales: "Lo & behold! On seeing [the] printed copy, I recognized it as my own. But why I used 'Monica Lloyd' still stumps me! Maybe [it was the] editor's idea." Fray Angélico Chávez to Phyllis Morales, 5 November 1976, Chávez Collection, Fray Angélico Chávez History Library and Photographic Archives, Santa Fe, NM.

21. An Irish educator named Anne Jellicoe (1823–1880) founded the Queen's Technical Training Institute for Women, on Molesworth Street in Dublin in 1861 and Alexandra College in 1866. It is unknown if Chávez was familiar with this important Irish figure.

22. The story develops a santero figure similar to the two who appear in "The Angel's New Wings" and "Hunchback Madonna" in Chávez's 1940 book *New Mexico Triptych*.

23. Consuelo Chávez (Fray Angélico's niece), interview by Ellen McCracken and Mario García, August 19, 1998, Santa Fe, NM.

24. Fray Angélico Chávez letter to Provincial Ripperger, 15 September 1937, Franciscan Archives of St. John the Baptist Province, Cincinnati, Ohio.

GUITARS *and* ADOBES

Lithographs *by* Gerald Cassidy

Part One
The Archbishop

1

On the fourteenth of February 1888, the first Archbishop of Santa Fe died. In the evening twilight, when the boy Pablito ran into the Cathedral to pull at the rope which set the big bell a-swing slowly, Santa Fe knew that her great priest was dead. The people fell on their knees, and the next morning they came to view the serene features of him who lay before the high altar of his lately-built Cathedral.

This is no sequel to a certain great story of a great prelate. It just happened that death came at a time, and attended by certain circumstances, when Doña Genoveva's mind was in the vein for linking events and interpreting them for herself. She had gone through a nerve-racking night. So unstrung was she, that she had been forced to keep her bed, while Consuelo and Pablito went to see the venerable remains. Besides, the Cathedral was too far for an indisposed lady to walk all the way. Had the gallant Don Vicente Carillo not been out of town, he would have gladly come to drive her down in his swaying, new *carretela.*

Doña Genoveva's mind was all in a whirl. "No; I cannot go down and see his Grace," she sighed. "Consuelo will tell me how he looks in death. *0 mi Dios,* that guitar, that guitar...first my Pablo died...now the Archbishop!" At last she decided to rise and prepare a breakfast for herself and Consuelo. Pablito, who worked at the Cathedral, would not he home until evening.

Doña Genoveva Ortega, prim, reserved, doctrinal, was blood-sister to those widows who parade majestically through the pages of books with Spanish atmosphere. She was proud of her ancestry. Her family sprang from Don Juan de Dios Lucero de Godoy, a dashing captain under the Reconquistador DeVargas, while that of her dead husband came from another conquistador, Don Xavier de Ortega. Not even the Oteros or the Lunas could boast of such a lineage. Prouder still was she of her bygone youth; she was fascinatingly beautiful then; her voice was the envy and despair of every señorita, and her tongue a playing fountain of scintillating Castilian. Of the three, only the last aptitude survived, and all signs pointed to an active longevity. A complete edition of Spanish proverbs resided on her lip's edge, ready for any occasion.

At twenty, her parents gave her in marriage to Pablo Ortega, a wealthy and adventurous young fellow. They lived blissfully from the first, even though their first children died in infancy. Then came the news that Pablo was killed in a campaign against the Navajo. Consuelo, her only living child, was then about three years old, and very shortly after came the boy, Pablito. That was fifteen years ago. Since then, the Widow Ortega lived alone with Consuelo and Pablito, save for the casual visits of an old friend, Don Vicente Carillo. Gallant Don Vicente was rich, a widower with a wild son of twenty-five in proud possession, and there were rumors in Santa Fe.

Consuelo was late in returning. The widow had fixed up her graying hair into a gorgeous stack, baling it with a four-pronged giant *peineta* at the back of her head. She might walk down to see the deceased Archbishop, and she might not. The Señora was worried. She could not trust herself; she might make a scene before the coffin, and what a humiliation that would be. A flood of recollections welled up in her excited brain, vivid memories of last night, which made her glance nervously at the little fireplace in a corner of her room. She shuddered. Among all the lady's countless worries, there were three outstanding ones. Everybody knew her Consuelo, a girl of eighteen who was growing conscious of her bodily charms, while many had suspicions of her hidden treasure, a cache of jewelry of pure Mexican gold and a large bulk of gold and silver coins, both American and Mexican, which lay concealed under a slab in the fireplace. But her chief worry, the greatest by far, stood before the fireplace, covering most of the opening with its curved and bulging sides, as if aware of the treasure it guarded. This was an old and queer-looking guitar, of amber back and sides, a yellow front, and with a tattered red ribbon around its short, hunched neck. To Doña Genoveva it looked like an oversized, tawny tomcat.

The kitchen door opened and closed; hurried footsteps tapped about on the stone floor; dishes began to dance on the kitchen table.

"Consuelo!" called the lady from her room.

"Yes, madre!"

"Daughter, you are late. Did you come straight home from church?"

"I say, madre, this goat-cheese that you bought from the Tesuque man is delicious."

"I asked you a question, Consuelo!" barked the voice from the other room.

"And this black, cane molasses from Embudo,—it's a wonder Pablito did not lick it all away last night."

"I asked you a question—"

"Yes, I came straight home. Not exactly straight, though. You see, I met Pancho Carillo by the Archbishop's garden. He bought a new horse; I mean, Pancho did—"

"And then ?"

"And then I stopped to talk to Rosendo Rael near the *acequia madre.*

And then I stopped to talk to Rosendo Rael.

You know, there is water in the ditch, and this winter has been so mild, that Rosendo decided to save time and make adobes. He's making them for Pancho Carillo's father, and he has two thousand laid out already. Talk about ambition! By the way, I told him that you wished to see him about rebuilding that wall across our patio, and he said he'd be tickled to come over. You know, madre, he winked at me!"

"There you go, Consuelo, there you go!" the Señora began to shout, rather hotly, around the corner. "How often have I not told you to carry yourself like a lady. You started it, you got him going with your eye, I bet you did. *Ay de mi,* what is this generation coming to? We never did that when I was a girl; no, señora—"

"The dear prevaricator," Consuelo thought to herself.

"You musn't encourage Rosendo, even if he is strong, handsome, and good. Every man is good, but not for everything. Rosendo is good for adobes, but, remember, you are class; he's only an adobe-maker!"

"Aw, apricots!"

"What?"

"I said, mother, the old Archbishop looked lovely laid out." Consuelo's lithe tongue was equal to her mother's. She could thrust and parry, and often corner her more experienced fencing mistress. If cornered, Doña Genoveva resorted to her best defensive weapons—Iberian proverbs. One of these, and Consuelo was done for. However, she had the happier gift of changing the topic and distracting her opponent. "He looked beautiful, the Archbishop did," the girl repeated, as the Señora glided into the kitchen.

"*Mi Dios,* that is nothing, daughter. They'll say I look beautiful, and so natural, when I am dead, too. They'll say that of you also, though your face might have shriveled up like a raisin. If only they would tell us such flattering things when we are alive. Alive, call me a rooster; dead, call me the dove of peace, *you know the proverb!* And so it was for the Archbishop, I suppose. The people lived under the shade of the great tree, ate of its fruits, and made nothing of it; but the tree was cut down and planed into a casket; now they say,—'How beautiful and how natural!'" She sat down to breakfast.

"There you go, madre, with your purple preaching. By the way, why didn't you come with us to see him? Were you sick last night? If so, why didn't you call me, or Pablito... my, you look played out, mother..."

Consuelo struck the right chord in her mother's soul. Like her nerves, this string was highly strung, and responsive to the least touch. Doña Genoveva, as what woman does not, loved to talk over her illness. Operations were not in vogue then, not in New Mexico, at least. But the lady was prone to chronic spells which sometimes took a serious turn. Not five months previous, she had one of these attacks. Thinking herself dying, she sent Consuelo to the Cathedral for Pablito and a priest. However, none of the priests were at home. One had gone to Santa Cruz for a fiesta, Pablito explained, and another had accompanied the new Archbishop on a confirmation trip; the one who remained on duty had been called to Galisteo on a sick call. Fortunately, the old, retired Archbishop had come into Santa Fe from his retreat in the hills near Tesuque. The gallant Don Vicente presented himself at the critical moment with his swaying *carretela,* and presently Doña Genoveva had received the last annointing from the hands of the great pioneer prelate himself. An honor and a privilege, indeed; the Señora already counted herself among the blessed. She expected to hear the celestial harps at any moment; and then the fatal thing happened.

Having cleansed his fingers, the old Father began to inspect the room, when his eye caught the quaint guitar in the corner. It sat there, like a big cat on its haunches, waiting for someone to scratch its yellow belly and make it purr. He stooped and casually ran the back of his fingers across the loose strands of ancient catgut. The sick woman was startled at the sound, and it took all the efforts of Consuelo and Pablito, who rushed in from the adjoining room, to calm their mother. Finally she lay still and panting.

"Your Grace," began the patient, her eyes dancing wildly, "you shouldn't have played the thing. Oh, oh !"

"But, my daughter," he replied, perturbed, "what was wrong with that? You acted as though Satan had spoken."

"Ave María Purísima, he did speak. That thing there is accursed. Whoever plays it will die!" She began to weep vehemently.

The Archbishop knelt before the guitar and squinted inquisitively at it. Under the horizontal bar below the round opening, he noticed a number of

He noticed a number of queer rudely-cut characters.

queer and rudely-made characters. The looked very old and seemed to have been branded into the yellow timber, with a hot and sharp metal instrument. The old priest's brows contracted and relaxed alternately, and he smiled. He now thanked the Lord that he had learned while at the Seminary in France, a few things about Hebrew, for these letters were Hebrew, surely. But, as he pronounced them to himself, he found himself uttering a meaningless jargon. He was plainly puzzled, even though his knowledge of that language was better than the average student of his day. After repeating the mysterious phrases over and over again, he arose with a scholar's dignified gleam of triumph. The characters were Hebrew, indeed; but the language was Spanish! *La muerte canto—tócame y mueres.* "I sing death—play me and you die!"

Another man would have borrowed the curious instrument and delved away at its mystery, but his Grace, with no apparent struggle, quickly denied himself the pleasure. That was the foundation of a character which his fellow-men so much admired. And again, he knew that death would come for him soon, and pursuits of this sort bore no more appeal for him. Turning to the sick woman, who lay quietly staring at him, he said:

"Señora Ortega, I am going to die, guitar or no guitar. I shall die of having lived. My time has come for Heaven, God willing. As for that thing there, forget all about it. It's foolish, superstitious. And I want you to put it away from you, or destroy it. Do you promise?"

She promised.

Upon the Archbishop's return to his Tesuque retirement, Doña Genoveva fully recovered, and she put away the guitar. After a few days, however, she grew lonesome for it; at the end of two weeks, she missed it terribly; and the third week found the guitar back in its corner. Almost five months had passed since that occurrence. Last night she had slept hardly at all. Ever since her Pablito had tolled the tell-tale bell from the Cathedral at sundown, when the whole of Santa Fe knelt in prayer, an over-powering fear took possession of her. Sleep came to her late at night, and it must have been shortly after midnight when she awoke in a sweat, in spite of the fact that the room was very cold. In her distress, she had forgotten to close her window the evening before, and a strong, icy breeze from the sierras was blowing in and was being drawn up through the chimney in the corner, producing a terrific draught. She shivered. Then she trembled and hid her head under the covers in a fright, for the guitar in the fireplace was howling, howling like an angry cat! It might have been no louder than the lowest whisper, but whispers, to one in her nerve-racked condition, were screeches in the stillness of the night.

Breakfast over, the Señora went back to her room, leaving Consuelo to do the dishes. She felt so tired and sleepy, she said, "We can't get rid of it," the girl heard her talking to herself. "We can't…it means death. Pablo would not believe it, and he played on it before going to fight the Indians. He never came back… and now the Archbishop…"

There was a legend concerning this guitar, which Doña Genoveva one day related to her two children, but which had never been told again. Not even the old families of Santa Fe had heard of it, and it was by mere accident that the Ortegas came upon it. About the first year after her wedding, her husband bought an old saloon and gambling house at the lower end of the Calle del Palacio, facing a narrow lane, now known as "Burro Alley." Years before, it had been the Monte Carlo of New Mexico under the entrancing management of Tules Barcelona, a renowned beauty and gambler, who had come to Santa Fe from Old Mexico in 1820.

The humble alley was a most picturesque and lively boulevard in those olden days. Within the narrow windows of the old house, so a chronicler relates, could be seen the gamblers sitting at their gaming tables, fondling fierce mustachios, stroking their long beards, smoking cigarettes of Mexican punche; one caught, he goes on, the glint of their pearl-handled daggers, and ivory pistol-butts, amid the bedlam of music, dancing, and clashing of crystal goblets—laughing, singing, loving.... There was no limit in the games. Brilliant women smoked their perfumed cigarettes and wagered their money bags of buffalo-hide full of thousands in gold and silver coin. It was the mode, the vogue, the social rage.

Tules Barcelona herself, the chronicle continues, was a high-spirited woman of vaulting ambition. Rich and beautiful and clothed in costly finery, she visited the country fiestas, arriving in state in her ox-drawn *carreta,* her burros heavy-laden with gold and silver in rawhide sacks, bringing precious jewelry and golden filigree; she bet only in thousands, and wherever she went other gamblers would leave.... In her *sala* in Santa Fe, the elite of society gathered in the evenings, and a list of her patrons included, besides the Governor of the province who fell under her thrall, the names of men written high on history's page in New Mexico.... All this history was, and still is, common property in and around Santa Fe.

When Don Pablo Ortega cleaned up and repaired this famous old house, he found among heaps of barrels and boxes a large, dust-loaded package. Inside was a guitar, and, tied with a red ribbon around its neck was a sealed envelope. Don Pablo and his wife read the letter the envelope contained that night, and thus learned the origin of their mysterious find. The letter was very long and in Barcelona's own dainty handwriting. After a few words of greeting, she began to relate the story of the guitar.

It was in the year 1491, when Ferdinand and Isabella had built the city of Santa Fe near Granada, during the memorable siege of that Moorish fortress, that the spectacular burning of a "heretic" took place in Sevilla. The Spanish Inquisition was then at its height. Moslems and Jews, particularly the latter, were continually being condemned to the stake. Segovia, Córdova, and other cities of fair names, reeked with the stench of human holocausts. Now, this event at Sevilla was an extraordinary one; the victim was a notorious leader of the Jews; and Torquemada himself presided, or at least lent solemnity to the occasion with his presence.

Alarming though their numbers were, comparatively few Jews remained in Spain at the time. Most of them had been driven out of the kingdom by the government, in order to free the country of a peril more insidious than the open warfare of the formerly victorious Moors; for they had been assuming control of the financial, the political, and even some of the religious affairs, when the Spanish hierarchy sounded the alarm. The monarchy and the Church immediately set up a court of inquiry; the Pope appointed the Dominican Torquemada as General Inquisitor; and the Jews were given their choice, either to submit to exile, or to Christian baptism. The greater number left Spain, while the rest, a vast number at that, stayed and were baptized. The Spaniards, perhaps because they joined the good Christian in his repast of pork, called these Hebrew converts *Marranos,* hogs; but the events that followed on the heels of this wholesale conversion threw more light on the name. While openly professing to be Christians, even partaking of the sacraments with the faithful, in secret they came together and devised means and made plans for the overthrow of the Spanish government and the Catholic religion. Several dangerous plots were laid bare. Spain had to act, and act quickly. The Inquisition developed, almost overnight, in the hands of the civil power from a tribunal to a funeral pyre.

To these Marranos belonged old Salomon García. For a long while, this shifty Jew had matched his wits with the Inquisition, and effectively, to Torquemada's chagrin. However, he was finally seized and brought before the court, then functioning in Sevilla. Political charges, charges of having vilely desecrated the Sacred Host, and a litany of other incriminating accusations, all these the fanatical rabbi acknowledged with a curse on his enemies. They led him to a stake in the shadow of the Giralda, and the executioners applied the torches to the woodpile under him. The orange flames reached up and began to lick his flowing garment and his long patriarchal beard, while the multitude looked on in a grave silence, a silence broken only by the contented hum of the hungry fire and the satisfied chuckling of the logs. Suddenly, from a high balcony somewhere, like the call of a muezzin from his minaret, and as merry as the song of the soaring lark, came the voice of a young Spaniard, accompanied by the sonorous strum of a guitar. It was a merry ballad tune, with verses improvised in mockery of the former defiance and curses of the burning victim. Among the crowd, some took it light-heartedly, while others listened in surprise and awe. Even the hardened officials frowned. Torquemada scowled. Unseen by anyone, a young spectator stole away from the throng and noiselessly sped up the stone steps that led to the high-flung balcony. A few strains after, the singer stopped with a stifled shriek, and his body came hurtling down into the throng of amazed bystanders on the square.

The next day, the guitar, bearing the branded characters, was found on the front steps of the cathedral. The family of the murdered troubadour took it as a remembrance, ignorant or regardless of the curse laid upon it, and as an incentive for revenge. People afterwards said that the slayer was none other than Benjamin, the executed Jew's youngest son, who from that day was seen in Spain no more.

How the guitar came to the New World, the letter continued, nobody knew for sure. Certain it was that it had been in the Barcelona family in Mexico for several generations. According to some, it had been brought along by an adventurous don on one of Columbus' later voyages, and many attributed the various misfortunes that fell, not only upon the great discoverer's head, but also on the different colonies in the Indies, to the cursed instrument. Others even ventured to explain, with as much certainty, that it had come to Mexico in the great expedition of Cortez, and they fully believed that, had Montezuma not fingered its strings before mounting the walls of his palace, he would not have been killed by the arrows of his own subjects. They even laid the blame for the famed and much-lamented *Noche Triste* on its baneful presence! Here it is evident that the probable legend had passed into the province of mere fable.

When Tules came to New Mexico, the guitar came with her. But she had kept it so well concealed, that no one had laid eyes upon it, not even those who had been on exceedingly intimate terms with its beautiful mistress. Not once had she mentioned a word about it.

The last clause of the letter read: *I, Tules Barcelona, bequeath this guitar to whosoever chances to find it. I cannot vouch for the truth of its history, which I just finished telling. The "vihuela" must be very old, since it differs in many respects from the guitars we have been accustomed to see and use, and, as I know nothing of ancient alphabets and cryptic writings, I cannot swear that the letters upon it are Jewish. They might be Moorish, for all I know; or they might be a fashion of gypsy signs. And, too, the guitar perhaps never saw Spain; it might have been made down in Mexico, and marked with Mayan or Aztec symbols; quién sabe? I said before that I can't read anything else besides Castilian. At any rate, here it is. Take it. May it bring you good luck. As for me, I have played the guitar—and in more ways than one! May the good Lord spare me.*

Thus ended the legend of the guitar which played such an influence in the life of the Señora Ortega. It is true that some people knew of a guitar, queer and old, in her possession; but then, there was a guitar in every other home in Santa Fe. The rumor of her hidden fortune was more widespread and well-founded. As for her other treasure, Consuelo, there was no doubt that such a treasure existed, for it was too much in evidence to remain a secret.

2

The Archbishop was buried a few days later. It was the largest and most impressive funeral ever witnessed in Santa Fe. At least, so said the few bystanders who had seen the solemn procession, as it poured out of the Cathedral down the Calle de San Francisco, circling the Plaza, and disappearing again through the arched entrance of the great church, under whose altar the Archbishop was finally at rest.

Pancho Carillo, a cigarette dangling under his sprouting mustache, leaned against one of the white wooden columns in front of Seligman's store. Save for himself and a few Yankee cattlemen down from the Pecos Valley, the street and the Plaza front, with its endless colonnades of white, were wholly deserted. From out the open and crowded doorway of the Cathedral now and then came the voice of some officiating priest. Pancho paid no heed.

"Say, Carillo," came a voice over his shoulder.

"Oh, hello, Mr. Seligman. That you?"

The Archbishop was buried a few days later.

The merchant tugged tightly at the corners of Pancho's vest, and spoke with a serious tone into his face. "Listen, young man, you better foot up that bill of yours in the store by tomorrow, no later. It's one hundred dollars already, and I must have the money."

"One hundred *pesos?* And by *mañana?* Why, man, I can't—"

"You must, or I'll have to ask your father, Don Vicente, to pay for you."

"But I can't; I can't, see! Last night I lost about two hundred at monte!"

"So I heard. Don Felipe Delgado, down the street there, says you owe some fifty dollars in his store, and he saw you lose last night. You're too reckless at playing monte."

"Delgado won't tell—"

"No, but he might kick the fifty out of you!"

"Well, let me see. By tomorrow, you say. Fine. Now, leave me alone." Left alone, Pancho pulled out a five-dollar note, all the money he had left. He returned it to his pocket. On lifting his head, his eye rested on his lately bought horse across the street, where he had tied it to the white picket fence encircling the park. While the semi-bronco impatiently stamped its hoof, Pancho surveyed with pride the sleek and well-proportioned lines of the animal. "Thank God," he consoled himself, "at least the horse is paid for."

The people were beginning to come out of the Cathedral, and Pancho, confident of meeting Consuelo Ortega, sauntered up to the terrace in front of the church. Among the first to appear was Rosendo Rael, who, on spying Pancho, slapped on his tattered and bandless hat and approached him. "Carillo," he said, "I want to ask you something."

Pancho regarded him with a sardonic curl of the lip.

"Sir," began Rosendo, "were you up by the *acequia madre* last night?"

"What if I was? Jealous because I went to see Consuelo?"

Rosendo bit his lip. "I just wanted to make sure that it was you who spoiled some of my fresh adobes last night, you see."

"Were those your adobes by the ditch Rosendo? *Por Dios,* I'm sorry, really. You know, I couldn't control that new half-bronco of mine, and he danced all over the place. I'm sorry—"

"You should be, because those adobes were for your father."

"No!"

"Sí, Señor; these were the last batch I made, so as to complete the two thousand which Don Vicente ordered for his orchard wall. Now, you either pay me eight dollars, or I must explain to the Señor Carillo."

The young Carillo produced his five dollars. "Look at this, Rael. That's all I have. But watch me raise three hundred with it tonight at monte. Last night *la fortuna* was against me, but watch my game tonight, my friend. Then I'll pay you eight pesos tomorrow. All right?"

"All right," replied Rosendo, his rugged, handsome features beaming, not on account of the offer, but because of a figure vanishing around the curve of the street. Consuelo, unnoticed by Pancho, had left the church and departed in the direction of her home or, perhaps, the Sisters' convent. This last was Rosendo's unspoken guess, and he prepared to take leave of his companion.

"Hold on," Pancho said, on further thought. "Are you working now?"

"Sure; I have to rebuild a wall for the Señora Ortega, and must also mend a leak in the ceiling of her room."

"Good pay?"

"The Señora didn't say how much, but it will be good. She always pays well."

"I can't yet understand," Pancho began to scratch his head, "how that family lives the way they do. Why, the only one who works is Pablito, and here with the Padres. I'm sure he doesn't get much, the simpleton. The three dress well, while Consuelo goes to school with the Sisters, and even takes lessons on the piano. Do you think that it's true, —I mean, what the people say?"

"That the mother has money hidden somewhere? Well, that could be, since Doña Genoveva won't trust the bank; she's afraid of bandits, you see,—bandits like Billy the Kid, who got killed some ten years ago. I don't know, though. Well, I'll see you tomorrow about that money, and then that makes us quits, eh?"

"Sí, sí, Rosendo. Kindly commend me to the Señora Ortega."

As Rosendo hastened away in the direction of his adobes (or the convent), Pancho went up the front steps of the Cathedral and paused under the big arch. His brain was ticking. A plan was unfolding itself slowly but definitely, and with exceeding care. With every new development in his head, the prospects for sweeping off the gambling table with a mere five dollars began to dwindle to a very slender probability. And Pancho needed money, lots of it, by tomorrow!

Pablito came out just then. "Hello, Don Pancho!"

"Why, hello, Pablito. Going home so soon in the morning?"

"Yes, the Padre Vicario let me off today, on account of the funeral. I might come back, though. Things don't go right when I'm away."

"I see. I see. Do you get much pay from the *curas?*"

"Not much, Don Pancho. I don't care either; I'd work here for nothing. Besides, my mother has plenty of money—"

"Not in the bank—"

"No, in her own bedroom!"

"And how is your dear mother?"

Consuelo

"Sick. She's sick, more so since the Archbishop died. It must be the night-cold that gives her chills, —but she won't let me or that lazy and vain sister of mine build a fire in her little fireplace...well, I must be going. Good-bye, Don Pancho! Let me ride your new horse some time...."

Pablito wheeled an imaginary steed around and galloped away.

Meanwhile, Rosendo had been conversing with Consuelo outside the high, rear wall of the convent garden. He had overtaken her, just as she laid her fingers on the knob of the gate, or wooden door, that opened into the garden.

"Consuelo," he asked, "is it true that you are learning to play the piano?"

"Didn't you know that? Why, it's two years almost since I began studying. The Sisters say I learned very fast. You know, Rosendo, I can play 'La Estrellita' already, and it's a difficult piece. Oh, how I wish we had a piano at home. I'd play for you while you built that wall—"

"Your mother ought to buy you one."

"She will. She promised to present me with one on my wedding day. Since the railroad came, she says, pianos are not so costly as they used to be, and she intends to order a new one from St. Louis!" Consuelo showed her pretty teeth and looked into the young man's eyes. But he looked perturbed.

"Whom are you going to marry?"

"Mother wants me to be the bride of some man of class, she says,—an *americano;* she thinks they are the last word, but—"

With a speedy glance, Rosendo surveyed himself. His mud-encrusted shoes, his faded blue shirt, his pants bulging fearfully at the knees,—his own self, an adobe-maker! Surely, this was not class. "Consuelo," he urged, importunately, "whom are you going to marry?" As she stood there, holding the door knob, he felt like grasping both her hands and making her answer what he wished her to answer.

"Mother is always proposing Pancho Carillo."

"And do you love him?"

"Don Vicente and mother have been talking of that for long. I hear them sometimes." She turned her face aside, while her Spanish comb, coquettishly tilted behind her ear, grazed her slender shoulder. A moment after, when he repeated his question, she thrust her tongue in her cheek. "He's not bad-looking at all, and he's very popular with the girls. They laugh at his jokes. Also, his father is rich."

"But do you love him?" His big, rough hands closed around hers, and the gate she had been holding flew open. A Sister, flushing crimson, and clapping her hands in utter disapproval, came hurrying down the path under the bare trees. Slipping her slender wrists out of his now loose grasp, Consuelo sighed "Rosendo" sweetly, and slapping him naively on the cheek, disappeared into the convent garden as the door slammed behind her.

The touch of Consuelo's fingertips rested tenderly and long on his cheek. The convent, the Archbishop's house and garden across the street, the ground at his feet, Santa Fe itself, all—all seemed to vanish in a haze. Only Rosendo was; nothing else mattered. All he felt, besides the thunder in his breast, was that lingering, tingling sensation on the side of his face. Oh, for another such slap, a hundred, a million more! Such punishment he could stand until he was black and blue in the face.

Just then, Pablito drew up on his prancing pony and, on beholding the enchanted adobe-maker, he stabled the steed for the present in the stall of his imagination. "Don Rosendo," he shouted, shaking him, "are you coming over to the house? Mother is anxious about the leak in the ceiling. She's afraid of a sudden storm."

As the two walked up the winding Alameda, the boy began to wonder if the Archbishop's funeral had so affected his companion, that he had lost his sense of speech—and his sense of sight, maybe; for at this moment Rosendo bumped into a giant cottonwood that grew in the middle of the street.

That night, Doña Genoveva lay in bed waiting for sleep to come, but the longed-for visitor was late. Nine o'clock, ten, eleven. Still no sleep. Not a sound was there, save for an occasional snore from Pablito's quarters, the kind of snore made by those who sleep with their mouths open. From Consuelo's room now and then arose some quick, unintelligible phrase, as though she were dreaming of many things. The whole city rested comfortably in slumber, it seemed to the Señora, which made her feel all the more awake. It reminded her of those hours, a few nights before, when the Archbishop had passed away. She began to feel cold, for once again she had forgotten to close her window.

"I wept when I was born, and every day explains why," she quoted to herself, pityingly, and arose to shut the window. The night outside was lit by the moon, somewhere behind the house, and the widow could plainly make out the heights of Fort Marcy and the Garrita across the valley. Clearer still were the flat-roofed houses and gaunt naked trees that made up the upper part of Santa Fe, while, close to the slope where her house stood, the fields and fences and the willow-lined course of the *acequia madre* were flooded in a mellow light. Doña Genoveva fancied she could even count Rosendo's rows of orderly piled adobes by the *acequia,* when her gaze was arrested by a figure moving among the rows. Her alarm subsided as soon as she recognized Rosendo, who was covering his adobes with sheets of canvas and pieces of tin, weighing them down with planks and stones. Immediately, she saw the cause for the young man's hurry when she lifted her gaze to the northern sky beyond Fort Marcy. Though the sky overhead was now clear, she knew that in the morning Santa Fe would wake up under a thick blanket of snow. Making the window tight, and thankful that Rosendo had repaired her ceiling that afternoon she went back to her pillow.

Another person was closely watching Rosendo at his work. So close was he to the night-toiler, that he could hear his heavy breathing as he tugged at the sheets of canvas. When the task was completed, Rosendo heaved a sigh of relief and for a while stood admiring the moon that rested on the dark summit of the Monte Sol. The scene, somehow or other, reminded him of a holy picture that the old Archbishop had once given him—a white disk, surrounded by rays, and suspended above a chalice. No sooner had Rosendo vanished up the road toward the Atalaya, when the watcher emerged from a leafless thicket of willows by the ditch, and began to inspect the Ortega home. It stood sharply outlined upon a gentle slope, quite alone, except for some nude apricot trees near the kitchen door. Close to these was a deep arroyo. A few miles behind arose the kingly Monte Sol, and upon it the bright, round moon. To the spy, the moon looked like a white poker chip, about to roll off the table.

Pancho Carillo was now ready to act. His horse he had tied within a grove of old cottonwoods farther down the *acequia madre* road. Keeping himself in the shadow of the log fence that skirted the sunken road leading to the house, Pancho soon found himself under the apricot trees. Sure of his route, he opened the kitchen door softly, and silently felt his way to the door of the Señora's bedroom. Here he paused and listened, before crawling in on hands and feet.

Doña Genoveva had not yet gone to sleep. She was almost certain she had heard footsteps outside a few moments before; she could hear someone breathing in the kitchen, by her door; she looked at the faintly visible guitar in the fireplace and waited for it to howl, but it wouldn't. At last she upbraided herself for being so foolish, hiding her head under the covers, nevertheless.

Pancho

Pancho began to crawl in over the noiseless homewoven rugs. His eyes were unaccustomed to the dark interior, but he had made sure where the fireplace stood. His hand touched the clay ledge in front of the fireplace, and his fingers, reaching forward by inches a little farther into space, touched something at last. A bass, discordant growl, when the guitar fell over on its side, brought Pancho to his feet and Doña Genoveva to her seat. She screamed. With a mad rush, the thief was out of the room, out of the house, out under the apricot trees, until he found himself sliding headlong into the arroyo. Picking himself up, he found his way swiftly along the shadows of the fence, despite the pain on his face and the sand in his eyes.

By the time he reached his impatient horse and mounted it, Pancho saw that the house was all lit up, with shadows hurrying to and fro across the windows, and, as he trotted towards the Carillo hacienda downtown, he congratulated himself on not being as yet seen. The thick, fine dust of the road felt and sounded like velvet under the horse's hoofs, so that no one was aroused. On approaching his home, Pancho jumped off, chased the beast away with a volley of pebbles, and staggered into the house, into his room.

Rosendo Rael arose early next morning and, as was his custom, entered his old mother's room to fire the small logs which he had placed in her little fireplace the evening before. The old woman was still asleep. Having lit the stove in the kitchen, he opened the door and stepped into the snow-covered yard. A marvelous sight greeted his eyes. Behind the house, the Atalaya was a dome of glistening whiteness, while the mountains farther back loomed up in a series of undulating purity, as though God had shaped them overnight out of snow and stuck the pines on them afterwards one by one. The city below, too, was a quilt of white, with dun patches of adobe walls and trees, while the tiny river and the *acequia* threaded their way through the length of the blanket, hiding and reappearing among the patches. Most wonderful of all, however, was the sky, a rich blue sky, like an April heaven.

When he went back into the house, the mother was up and getting breakfast ready. "Madre mía," he said, kissing her wrinkled, brown cheeks, "it snowed last night!"

"Thanks be to God, son. It will help the farmers. If it snows this month and the next, the *acequia* will have plenty of water for the alfalfa and wheat fields, and for the *adoberos*...did it snow on your adobes?"

"No, mother. I got up about eleven last night, because I felt the storm coming, and I ran down and covered them all up. They're safe."

"Gracias a Dios," she said.

It was late in the morning that Rosendo first decided to walk down to the Plaza. On the way down, he wondered how the Señora Ortega's roof had fared during the night. He was astonished on noticing that the sunken road, leading over to the Ortega house, was much trampled upon. There were wheel tracks, footprints, and hoof marks, going back and forth on the wet and now melting snow.

He knocked at the door, which was on the instant opened by Consuelo. Before Rosendo could speak, she stepped hack, wide-eyed. He could tell that she had been crying, but the pained expression in her stare paralyzed his tongue. She was about to say something, when Doña Genoveva appeared.

"Sir," she shouted sharply. "Do us the honor of staying away from this house from now on!"

"But, Señora Ortega, I do not understand—."

"Ah, thieves and liars are first cousins, young man!" she screamed. "Out—out! Never talk to me again, nor to my daughter!"

"But, Señora, what does all this mean? Besides, that wall—"

"Never mind, I'll get somebody else to build that wall, thief! You have played the guitar, and in two ways! Away, then!"

The door was shut in Rosendo's face, and he walked down the road, well aware that he had been accused of something he had not done. Ah, the widow's fabled treasure arose in his mind. Had it been stolen? Most likely not; otherwise the sheriff would have come to arrest him last night or early in the morning. And what did she mean by playing a guitar? He could not understand. In painful flashes that look in the eyes of Consuelo returned to his bewildered memory, and his heart grew heavy within his breast. His anthem in the morning had tuned down to a dirge in the day.

On his way to the Plaza, Rosendo met several persons but they greeted him with the usual, *"Buenos días le de Dios."* If they had heard of the matter, they did not choose to show it, Rosendo surmised. As he passed the Cathedral, he caught a glimpse of Pablito shaking his fist at him before disappearing into the sacristy. Finally, he walked into Pancho Carillo under the long, wooden porch of La Fonda.

"My friend, Rael, I have been waiting for you."

Rosendo stared at him sorrowfully.

"It's eight dollars that I owe you, is it not? Here, take this ten-dollar bill."

Rosendo drew away, his eyes riveted on Pancho's sand-scratched forehead, nose, and chin.

"I realize how you must feel," Pancho continued. "Nor do I believe what they say about you. Come, take this anyway."

Hesitatingly, Rosendo took the proffered money and looked inquiringly at the giver.

"Pancho, where did you get this? Did you win last night?"

"I didn't play last night. You see, I started to go to Española instead, because I had heard there was a big dance over there. But my bronco went loco by that arroyo outside of town. He began to buck, and I found myself pulling my head out of the sand. The blamed horse ran off, and I had to walk home. Really, I looked as though I had fought a gang of bandits with tooth and knife, for my face and hands were smeared with blood, and my clothes were torn to rags. When my father saw me this morning, I told him what had happened, and he grew very soft-hearted. He was glad his only son wasn't killed, you see. So I told the old boy about my debts, and he's paid them all!"

"Is Don Vicente at home?" Rosendo spoke at last. "I want to see him about the adobes. They're ready, most of them."

"I'm afraid you won't do much with him, Rosendo. He really believes that you broke into the Ortega home last night. This morning he and I were over there, because Pablito had come to tell us very early this morning. When the old lady Ortega explained to the old man how it all happened, and that she had seen you outside before it happened, and that you had fixed her ceiling that same afternoon,—well, my old man was convinced. He also said that he wouldn't take your adobes."

Rosendo gasped. After a long pause, he asked if anything was stolen.

"No; nothing. Let me tell you. It's funny. There was a guitar in front of the fireplace, where the lady had her bank. The thief knocked the old thing over. This woke up the widow, and the fellow ran out like a coyote. Now Doña Genoveva says she has hidden most of her treasure where nobody will find it, not even Pablito or Consuelo."

"And—Consuelo?"

"She was with me in believing you were not guilty. But later on I heard her say that she hated you. I didn't like that. But it's true."

The young adobe-maker's wine of happiness was now soured to the sourest vinegar. It was apparent that all took him for a thief, if Consuelo did. His love lost, his trade ruined, his character besmeared with clay, not adobe-clay, but with real mud, all this bore down on his spirit with the weight of many sierras. Without another word, Rosendo turned around and made his way back to his humble and solitary hut on the hill, to the only person in the world who would uphold his innocence and share in his suffering,—his little old mother on the slope of the Atalaya.

Part Two

3

May in Santa Fe! Like the enthusiastic artist who, on finding a time-worn masterpiece, uses his utmost skill to restore it to its original beauty and freshness, May took the faded winter picture and, with a few magic washes of the Spring rains, brought back the vanished green to the trees and fields, gave a turquoise sheen to the sky, and brightened the dull drab of bare hills and adobe walls with orange and carnelian, shaded with light and varied purples.

It was evening. Doña Genoveva Ortega stood at her open window viewing the scene. She was as happy as her nature would allow. She was glad to know that her ancient and naked apricots by the kitchen had made themselves coverings of leaves. To her this was a symbol of rejuvenation. The newborn alfalfa on the field below and the olive-hued willows by the *acequia madre* brought a tinge of joyful green to her large, aging eyes. One thing she missed, though—the piles of adobes near the ditch.

"Consuelo," she said, without as much as turning her head.

"Yes, madre," replied Consuelo, who sat half-dressed before her mother's large mirror. The clouds of powder thinned out as she searched her neck for unpowdered spots.

"Consuelo!"

"Yes?"

"My daughter, I wonder what Rosendo Rael did with those adobes, after Don Vicente and I refused to take them. He took them away last February, soon after his mother died, I remember—"

"You should have seen her laid out at the Cathedral; she looked so natural in her plain coffin."

"They'll say that of us, too—but I asked you a question, Consuelo."

"Mother, do you know what I found Pablito doing with my white mantilla?"

"I asked you a question!"

"Why, didn't you know?" the girl replied.

"When his poor old mother died, Rosendo had no one left in the world. He hated to stay in the old house. So he built himself a new house across the river from the Atalaya with those adobes. He couldn't sell them, you see; and he had to do something."

"It serves the thief right that he can't sell them," returned the Señora. "Anyway, people are beginning to use brick and lumber for building. That's the American fashion...and, Consuelo, is it true that Rosendo bought Mrs. Taylor's old piano, when she moved to California?"

"Yes, madre; he did. I don't know why he bought it; but the lady was glad to sell it to him—"

"But, to Rosendo?" Doña Genoveva turned around.

"To Rosendo. The people have forgotten about that night last February."

Consuelo was almost finished with her toilette, save for the white mantilla which she held in her hands. "Yes, mother, the poor and the simple easily forgive and forget; only 'class' nurses a grudge till it grows too big to handle."

Taken by surprise, the old woman began to look gigantically down upon her daughter. "What?" she exclaimed. "Do you even talk to that robber?"

"There is nothing certain to prove that he is guilty, mother. I always talk to him after Mass on Sundays. Rather, he stops me and begins to plead his innocence, and he tells me that he loves me!"

The Señora began to pound her temples with her bony knuckles. *"Ay de mí*, even my own flesh and blood betrays me—"

"But calm yourself, mother dear. I wouldn't marry him, were he as stainless as that bit of snow on those Sierras. No, not I. Since I have been going out with Pancho Carillo...well, I begin to realize what I would miss by marrying a poor man. So rest your excited nerves on that, madre!"

Immediately Doña Genoveva felt much better. "Pancho and his father ought to be here soon," she said, softly. "Hurry on, my daughter. You are so slow."

Consuelo was getting ready for a dance somewhere on the Agua Fria down town. It was to be a big affair, a *gran baile*. Ordinarily, the Señora Ortega deemed it unseemly for a young lady to be going to dances, especially if unattended by her mother. But she and Consuelo had received a formal invitation from the gallant Don Vicente Carillo and his son. That made a difference. To refuse such a sign of courtesy and courtship, the widow judged, would be like surrendering her daughter to an adobe-maker. And, since she herself could not go, it had been agreed upon that Pancho should take Consuelo to the ball, while Don Vicente stayed at home with Doña Genoveva.

As Consuelo bent forward, so that her mother could see if her Spanish shawl was in place, Pablito came in and slapped his sister with enough fraternal force to impart a sting.

"Pablito, you half-wit!" Consuelo screamed standing up in a rage.

The Señora intervened. "My son, that's not nice to slap your own sister on the back. And, Consuelo, you shouldn't yell so. The neighbors over on the hill will think we are scalping you. For shame—"

"Precious little you care, mother," the young lady retorted, "when I'm the one who gets slapped. What is more, look what that son of yours was doing to my white mantilla."

The May devotions were carried out with simple grandeur.

"That is enough, daughter. Get ready for the Carillos now. Do you want Pancho to find you looking like an Indian dancer?" The Señora turned to the boy, who stood grinning behind her. "*Pablito mío,* it is almost time for the May devotions. Run ahead, or you'll be late, and the Padre will be pulling your ears."

When Pablito's make-believe galloping had died away down the road, Consuelo called her mother and held the mantilla before her eyes. "See here, madre. I wanted to tell you this since we started talking. Do you know what I found that brother of mine doing with this? He had it covering a weed with big leaves out on the patio. It's true. He said that the sun would shine through the veil, and the leaves of the plant would in a few days be marked with the flower-design of the mantilla!"

"Ah, those are the ear-marks of a budding genius!" said the proud mother.

"Ear-marks, you say?" Consuelo mumbled. "Plenty of room on the donkey's head for that."

"What?"

"I said, mother, that he almost spoiled the mantilla. And it's the one that Pancho Carillo gave me!"

"Listen, girl. That thing isn't worth your tears. Even though Pancho paid a good price for it at the store, no one can tell me that it's not from the States. It's not a genuine mantilla. I'll give you one that will make all the women at the dance feel as though they have infants' wrappers on their heads. Just wait." With a swift gesture, the Señora pulled out a low hand-carved wooden chest from under her bed. Consuelo had not seen it opened before. Quickly, the old lady drew forth a small, flat box, and shoved the chest back to its place. With curious interest, the girl watched her open the box and take out a bit of folded black cloth, no larger than her palm. Doña Genoveva, pinching the corners of it daintily, gave it a sudden shake, and the piece of black cloth spread out before Consuelo's staring eyes into a large black silk mantilla, as airy as a magnificent cobweb.

"Observe, daughter, the flowers and the *caracoles*; and yet you can see through it. If spiders spun black thread, and if they would weave designs instead of straight lines on their webs, they would be merely imitating this. Now, let me put it on for you. This is a genuine mantilla that my father imported from Spain, when I was a girl. And, daughter, the real Spanish mantilla is black."

Consuelo inspected herself in the mirror and stood admiring the charming and romantic portrait she made, while her mother, arranging the fairy folds from the peak of the Spanish comb to the graceful shoulders, whispered: "Only class can give you all these things, my dear. You won't find them in an adobe-maker's home."

The two women did not have to wait long before the Carillo four-wheeler drew up outside. As soon as they came to the door, Don Vicente handed the reins to Pancho, stepped off, and bowed like a French courtier. To humor the old man, Consuelo offered him her hand, ladylike, and he helped her unto the seat beside his son, as adoringly as though she were the King of Spain's daughter. With a kiss, blown over the length of her fingers, to the old couple, Consuelo turned her attentions to the driver, and the *carretela* went swaying down the sunken road.

"A fine pair they make," said Don Vicente, with the grunt that follows a draught of raw spirits. "And you, Señora Ortega—you look charming this evening. Feeling well, I'm sure!"

"Would you care to sit out in the patio, Señor?"

"It is immaterial—if I can do anything for you, command me."

Without another word, Doña Genoveva led her guest into the house and out on the porch of the courtyard. They sat down on a Navajo blanket that covered a rough bench.

"It is a beautiful evening," he spoke at last.

"Sí, Señor; a beautiful evening in May."

During the brief silence that ensued the old Don's eyes wandered across the patio. "I notice," he spoke at last, "that you have not repaired that wall."

"Not as yet," she replied. "I haven't had the ambition to call a man to do it. As you know, I had hired Rosendo last February. By the by, Don Vicente, did you note on your way here that Rosendo removed his adobes?"

"Yes, yes. I noticed that a long time ago. He built a new house with them on the slope opposite the Atalaya. Adobes are going out of favor, you understand. Only the poor will use them in the future, and the poor make their own themselves. So Rosendo made good use of his before they spoiled. He's a very practical youth, that Rosendo Rael."

"I think we should have brought the thief to court when it happened, Don Vicente. I am sorry that I took your advice. It was a concession to your wish."

"Oh, Señora, it was better to let the matter drop, better for us all. The court proceedings would have raised unpleasant scandals. My son Pancho and I weighed the circumstances and thought it more advisable to let Rosendo go. As you well know, the court would have sent him to jail, and what would we get out of it all? Besides, it was his first attempt at theft, unsuccessful at that, and he learned a lesson. It was a gesture of charity on our part and yours, understand?"

"Yes, we let the thief go; but there is the guitar! He played the guitar, and the robber must die!"

"Now, my good woman, that is not true."

"It is true. I've told you about the guitar...about my husband...and about the Archbishop!"

A shadow flitted across the old man's eyes, and he grew restless for a moment. "Very well, let us speak no more of the guitar. But did you know that Rosendo has sold me this strip of land near your house? I bought it with a purpose."

"No wonder, then," the lady exclaimed, "that he bought Mrs. Taylor's old piano!"

"Oh, well, Rosendo has some money saved. He's a hard worker and no spendthrift. He has no one but himself to maintain since his mother died. And, Doña Genoveva, Rosendo has turned out to be an excellent brick-layer."

"Ah," she remarked, "the rattler always finds a hole to crawl in—"

"Now, now, Señora. We must admit he's clever. Now, listen to this. Rosendo was hired some weeks ago to repair an old adobe hacienda on the Calle del Colegio. And what did he do? He got some red brick and fringed the edge of the flat roof all around with a crimson cornice. Then he plastered the walls white, painted the shutters green, and there you are! To my thinking, it surpasses the Spanish tile-roof. *Por Dios!* it fits Santa Fe! Many are beginning to imitate the style on their old homes, and I am so charmed by it myself, that I got Rosendo to fix my hacienda in the same manner."

"Ave María Purísima!" was all she said.

"And my house will be a palace by the time my Pancho and your Consuelo move in. I told Pancho the house is for them!"

"You old schemer, Don Vicente. I knew you were coming to this all the while!"

"Doña Genoveva, so you at last decide to be my Pancho's mother-in-law?"

The Señora Ortega assented and, although a sickly lady turned fifty, she gave herself an air of vivid romance, like her apricot trees.

"And, my d-dear woman," the old gallant stammered. "You would make for my Pancho...er...a good step-mother, too!"

"Your wife?" she laughed. "They say that he who marries a widow will have a dead man's head often thrown in his dish."

"But if you only understood—I am such an old and lonely man. And, Genoveva, your beautiful, big eyes, they—"

"A woman should be chosen by the ears, sir, and not by the eyes."

"But your ears—"

"And I hope you don't think my ears are also beautiful and big. Now, don't be silly, Señor Carillo. It is all right for our children; but we are old and gnarled, like those twisted old apricots—only a few leaves..."

The sun had already, like a golden spider, crawled behind the Jemez range of mountains in the West, pulling its fan-web of golden rays along with it. From among the homes on a neighboring elevation came the strum of a guitar, as some poor laborer soothed his tired bones with a song after supper.

"Harken," said Don Vicente, "it seems as if that scamp must have heard us. He is singing: *'Cuando Uno Quiere a Una'* (When a Youth Loves a Lady)."

"It seems that way," agreed Doña Genoveva. "Now listen to the next verse."

Over the stillness that follows after darkness, they heard the singer clear his harsh throat, and the song flowed on beneath the light of giggling western stars:

All the maiden girls are golden,
Silver the married ones have been;
But the widows are of copper,
And the old ones merely tin.

The May devotions for the day were carried out with the usual simple grandeur. After the outdoor twilight procession had filed back into the Cathedral, little "maids" in white frocks and veils walked up to our Lady's altar, following their little "queen," and all bearing a tribute of lighted tapers and wild flowers. This was followed by the rosary and litany, and then Benediction. When the sacristan sent Pablito out to extinguish the candles on the altars, the people surged noisily out of the edifice, leaving Rosendo and a few black-shawled old women crouched in their pews, as though overcome by the heavenly perfume that comes only from the mingling of incense aroma and the attar of wild bloom. Rosendo then arose and quietly made his way along the dim side nave to the north transept, where stood his favorite shrine.

The shrine presented no imposing spectacle. It was a mere wooden pedestal, bearing a small and curiously wrought image of the Virgin. Her head was carved of wood, primitively painted, with a stiff, yet appealing, expression. Over a white lace veil was perched a coronet of roughly cut silver sheet, or perhaps tin, while the rest of her was but an inverted cone of silken dresses, of uncertain number, gradually spreading out from her neck and reaching the pedestal, not unlike the cope on the Infant of Prague. In another part of the Cathedral, stood an American-made statue of the Virgin, which had a beautiful face, and which was clad in flowing robes of blue and white. But Rosendo liked the old one better.

"Oh, María, Madre mía," Rosendo whispered kneeling down. "I love you, I love you, I love you." His lips ceased to pronounce the words, but his mind, his heart, went on saying: "I love you, I love you..." He couldn't pray, he thought. He felt so tired, after working hard all day on Don Vicente's house. That is why he kept on repeating the same words. As he raised his

"O María, Madre mía!" Rosendo whispered.

gaze to the painted eyes that seemed to look nowhere, yet everywhere, his thoughts began to adjust themselves. All the people of Santa Fe knew this New Mexico Madonna. Some called her the Señora del Rosario, or de los Remedios, or de la Victoria; but mostly all knew her as La Conquistadora.

"Queen of Heaven, Lady of Victory" he said, "I love you. I love you because I love you. That is all." Rosendo was not looking at the image any more; on the retina of his soul's eye there stood the live picture of a beautiful Queen, a woman with the moon under her feet and chasubled with the sun. Near the Queen he seemed to see his own mother. "Ah, Mother of God" his heart went on. "I know that my mother is with you. I know, I know. She must be—because she taught me to love you! And now I come—you know why, as I always do...I...Consuelo."

Then followed one of those wary distractions that with amazing stealthiness feel their way into a fervent prayer. The vision of Mary was slowly drawn away to a pinpoint, and, unconsciously, Rosendo began to watch with interest the shining cavalcade of helmeted halberdiers before the ancient Governors' Palace by the Plaza. Now Indians, in paint and feathers, arrayed themselves facing the soldiery, while a singing band of Franciscan friars, some of them bearing a large wooden cross, filled the center of the scene and erected the holy symbol in their midst....

There is a tradition about the statue of La Conquistadora which is near and dear to every heart in Santa Fe. On December 29, 1693, the Spanish Royal forces of the Governor General Don Diego DeVargas stood in readiness on the present site of Rosario Chapel outside the city: DeVargas, by order of the Spanish Viceroy, had come up from El Paso del Norte with a company of 100 soldiers and 70 families, in order to re-take the city of Santa Fe, which years before had been captured and inhabited by the Tanos Indians, after a terrible massacre of the missionaries and the Spaniards. A re-enforcement of 200 men, sent by the Viceroy, had overtaken the expedition during its approach to the city. With these added resources, DeVargas prepared an attack on the settlement, since the Tanos, after having received the new colonists kindly a fortnight before, had of a sudden taken a hostile attitude, stationing a multitude of warriors behind the walls and entrenchments that surrounded the city. Furthermore, a blind Indian and his companion had come to DeVargas the previous evening, to inform him that the Tegua and Picuris Indians from the north were already on their way to aid their besieged kinsmen, the Tanos.

DeVargas himself arranged the order of assault that morning. First, each division, led by its captain, knelt before an altar, and every man with a loud voice made an act of contrition. Father Salvador, the Superior of the friars, gave the absolution and encouraged them with a forceful sermon. Then the General publicly made a vow to the Virgin Mary, whose statue he had brought from Spain, that if to him were granted the victory, he would have a chapel built on the site, promising also to have the said image brought yearly in procession from the main church to this chapel, where a novena of Masses was to be said. On the ninth day, the statue was to be returned in procession to the church, there to remain until the following year.

The army arose as one man and followed the Royal Standard, upon which the Virgin had been conspicuously placed. They made the attack, but without effect. The battle was on, however, with neither side giving quarter. The whoops of the besieged almost drowned the Spanish war cry of "Santiago" amid the smoke and roar of musketry and the showers of

The Franciscans sang hymns and Te Deums at the foot of the cross.

stones and arrows. At noon the plumes of the Picuris and the Teguas appeared above the northern hills; these the cavalry readily put to flight. But the besieged Tanos held on without a show of weakness until evening, when darkness called off activities on both camps.

After a night of watchfulness, the Spaniards surprised the fortified city at daybreak when the infantry clambered over the unguarded walls. Their presence within the city turned the astonishment of the Indians to a panic. The gates were thrown open, and the Conquistadora, with the rest of the army and the colonists, entered in triumph. In front of the Old Governors' Palace, which for the past years had served as the Indian chief's abode, DeVargas, having assembled his men and the vanquished natives, formally received the submission of the Tanos and "the Villa of Santa Fe, Capital of the Kingdom and Provinces of New Mexico," for his Catholic Majesty, Charles II of Spain. The Franciscans sang hymns and the Te Deum at the foot of the large cross which had been erected on the Plaza, and addresses were made by DeVargas and Friar Salvador, into whose hands the Governor General delivered the custody of the Kingdom of St. Francis. The Lady of Victory had won; she was the real Conqueror—La Conquistadora.

Later on, DeVargas built the chapel, now called Rosario, on the spot where he had made his vow. Ever since that time, his heroic promise had been fulfilled every year with great ceremony (and is so done to this day), by the descendants of that army of soldiers and settlers who came with DeVargas. Rosendo always looked forward to this yearly occurrence with overwhelming joy. Still, how much happier would he not have been, had he ever chanced to read the original document of the reconquest, drawn up by DeVargas himself, and signed by his military staff, one of whom, beneath the signature of Francisco Xavier de *Ortega,* had written his own name—Antonio *Rael* de Aguilar!

Rosendo Rael awoke as from a dream. He could see the image no more. The whole Cathedral was pitch dark, save for the reddish glow of the sanctuary lamp, the little ruby flame of which was ceaselessly genuflecting before the Tabernacle. For a few moments, Rosendo knelt at the communion rail, saying a prayer for the old Archbishop, who lay under the high altar. What a privilege for his Grace, the young man thought, to have the Tabernacle for a monument, and for a neighbor and guardian—the Conquistadora. Outside, Rosendo made sure that the dark Sunday suit he had on was in respectable shape and, with mingled thoughts of Victory and Consuelo, he walked down the steps of the terrace and made for the dance, which by now was at its height, down on the Agua Fria.

4

The dance hall on the Agua Fria fairly overflowed with the silvery rhythm of *"Sobre Las Olas."* Over the waves, smoothly heaving and sinking, Consuelo and Pancho Carillo glided among the dancers, now carried along with the stream, now pausing on the crest of a billow, now twirling in a corner of the dance floor, as when a merry brook circles two or three times around a stone and is gone.

Consuelo peered over Pancho's arm, as over a galley's side, taking a complete panoramic view of the dance hall at every dreamy turn. All around she met eyes and eyes following her course. Even the two fiddlers and the guitar-player tried to do two things at the same time. Along the walls sat the women, whose gazes moved with the rise and fall of Consuelo's precious mantilla. The youths and older men who crowded the entrance, she knew, anxiously waited her approach, while no less expectant were those others on the musicians' platform at the opposite end of the hall. The men-folk were not attracted by her mantilla, she complacently admitted to herself. But where was Rosendo Rael? She had looked for him in vain. Ah, he was in mourning for his mother,—and then, there were the May devotions.

The waltz over, the portly *mayordomo,* or gentleman in charge, clapped his hands and announced *"Las Cuadrillas"* for the next dance. Straightway there was a rush for positions. The lines formed as for a reel, and it was then that Consuelo discovered Rosendo in the ranks opposite. He was breathing heavily, as though he had been running, while his eyes kept on searching for Consuelo's. She grew conscious that he was looking for an opportunity to speak to her; in fact, he must have come solely because of her, since, in either disinterestedness or haste, he had chosen a bashful partner with eyes that betrayed a strong leaning for each other. Good, honest Rosendo, she thought; but Pancho Carillo was so jealous.

During a phase of the old dance, when partners are exchanged for a few brief spins, Rosendo saw to it that he captured the wearer of the rich mantilla. The hearts of both leaped when their hands touched, although Consuelo tried to conceal her confusion by turning her face aside, as if looking for Pancho. She felt like a hypocrite. Had she not been looking for Rosendo? And now she wished he hadn't come.

"Consuelo," he breathed, "I have long wished for a chance like this."

"Would you please call me Señorita Ortega," she answered, trying to appear nonchalant, perhaps bored. "Our time is short, Señor Rael. Is there anything I could do for you?"

"Yes; please—please sing 'La Estrellita' for me, the way you used to do!"

She wondered that Pancho had not interrupted them, for the music had died down, and the dancers were beginning to leave the floor. Just then, the round *mayordomo* came up to the two, his palms clapping lightly. "Ah, so here you are, Señorita Consuelito!" he said, courteously. "Don Pancho has kindly asked me to take care of you, as he was suddenly called to the Plaza on business—some old friend of his, understand? Yes. But, ah! Rosendo is with you—go ahead, then, my boy. I delegate you as her guardian." With another bow he was gone.

Consuelo breathed deeply and met Rosendo's gaze squarely for the first time. "Yes, Rosendo, I will sing for you. It may be for the last—"

But Rosendo did not hear the end of her sentence. He ran up to the musicians and asked the guitar-man for his instrument, which was surrendered readily. As Rosendo took the guitar, the young men on the platform began to cheer. The jolly master of ceremonies came up, exchanged a few words with him, made a space for himself on the platform, and clapped his hands.

"Señoras y Caballeros!" he announced. "We have the honor tonight of hearing the Señorita Ortega sing 'La Estrellita' for our pleasure, accompanied by the Señor Rael on the guitar!" He assisted Consuelo to the little stage he had made, and the crowd surged forth *en masse,* like a thick forest bending forward, neither swaying nor still, under a heavy gale.

The silence became more pronounced as Rosendo deftly plucked a few chords. Consuelo looked at him for her cue; he winked, she smiled, and the song began. Slowly and dreamily, reminiscent of Andalusian groves, her words and voice cast an oriental spell over the throng, only to transport them in sudden cadences of fast and tripping Spanish to the proud and severe plateaus of Castille, like a warbler that suddenly leaves the low, shady luxury of a tree and climbs with each ascending note unto the very top, and then drops back with a breath-taking strain of love to the abode of shadows from where she started. Back to Castille, and back to Andalusia, up and down "La Estrellita" went, until it died away with an upheld tremolo—back in Santa Fe. The men and women gathered their wits and began to applaud.

"Rosendo," Consuelo said, musically, "how well you play the guitar."

"Is this what your mother meant last February—about playing the guitar?"

She blushed. "No, Rosendo, I'll tell you about it some day." And she pressed his hand against the guitar-strings.

In quick response his fingers began to play with the passion that his blood dictated. One of the violinists took the fever and began fiddling something akin to a tango. *"Las castanuelas, las castanuelas!"* someone shouted, and the

The dance was on.

cry was reechoed through the crowd, like the amplified noise of many leaves. The guitar-man, who happened to carry a pair of castanets, handed the little black shells to Consuelo. The *mayordomo,* assisted by some of the men, pushed the eager people back against the walls. Consuelo stepped down to the floor, arms akimbo; then she raised them above her mantilla, drummed the floor with the heel of her slipper, and the castanets in her grasp began to chuckle saucily in time with the music. The dance was on.

"That surpasses Tules Barcelona," said a wrinkled chaperon to her young charges. "I was smaller than you when I saw her dance in her gambling salon, years and years ago."

"Yes," chimed in another old woman. "But do you remember Peregrina Martínez and her golden slippers? Ah, she was more beautiful and a better dancer than Tules Barcelona. Tules was a trifle heavy—but beautiful, nevertheless. They say that both women were... But look at Consuelo now!"

At the point of exhaustion, and drunk with the night's triumph, Consuelo Ortega gave the final touch to her performance. Spinning like a brightly colored top, she slowly began to sink to the floor, her face suffused with smiles, until she knelt there motionless, her wide, spangled skirts spread out like the silken wings of a large monarch butterfly upon a leaf.

The applause broke out again along the walls, and with fresh vigor, when Rosendo abandoned his guitar and gracefully assisted Consuelo to her feet. Still holding her hand, he was about to bow with her to the acclaiming audience, when he saw Pancho Carillo coming across the empty floor, his eyes burning red, and an ugly twist of the lip under his small mustache.

"Rael," he exclaimed, "what a friend you are, stealing my sweetheart!" Pushing the girl aside, he began to curse into Rosendo's face—Rosendo smelt whiskey. "Stealing!—Ah! a thief once, a thief always. You broke into the Ortega home, and you shall be brought to court for it after all. You played the guitar that night... Ah, I saw you through the window just now when she was dancing for you. Yes, you play the guitar very well for a bandit!"

Consuelo stepped in front of Pancho, flushed with indignation. "Pancho, I am ashamed of you. We are going home right away!" Swiftly she sped out the side door nearby. Pancho followed, with Rosendo at his heels. The *mayordomo* clapped his hands at the musicians, and, as the music started, the floor filled up with the dancers, laughing, as if something of common occurrence had taken place.

Outside in the alley, Consuelo had already taken her seat on the Carillo carriage. Pancho turned to Rosendo and began to curse him again. He was swaying drunkenly, and all the more excited for it. "We better settle this right now, Rosendo," he said. By the light from a window, Rosendo caught

Pancho was drunk.

the gleam of a pistol butt as Pancho dizzily fumbled for it. His arm shot out, and Pancho fell senseless to the ground.

"You have put yourself in a lot of trouble, Rael," said one of several youths who had come out of the hall. "They'll send you to jail sure—"

"But that is not so bad," spoke another. "Pancho is a desperate fellow when he drinks—you saw him just now. So better watch yourself!" They helped him lift the unconscious man to the rear seat of the *carretela,* while Consuelo looked on, speechless. Rosendo jumped up on the seat beside her, took the reins, and spoke to the horses.

On the way neither said a word. As they turned from the *acequia madre* road to the one leading to the Ortegas, he handed the reins to her. "Here, you yourself can drive from here. Pancho is groaning and will soon come to."

"What are you going to do?" she cried, as he jumped off.

"I'm going home," he answered. "Then I'm leaving this town tonight."

"But where can you go?" She could hardly speak for grief. The horses began to pull away.

"South. To Albuquerque, maybe—" she heard his voice, as he disappeared in the night shadows up the road.

When the horses came to a standstill before the Ortega house, Don Vicente came out, with Doña Genoveva leaning on his arm. "Back already?" the old don said. "Why, it's only ten o'clock!"

"Ave María Purísima!" Dona Genoveva exclaimed, as Consuelo stepped into the light. Behind her staggered Pancho, his face dark with blood. "See, Don Vicente," the Señora continued. "Leave the kittens out without their mother, and a dog worries them, or they scratch each other!"

"Here's your son, Señor Carillo," Consuelo shouted, waxing brave. "Never again will I go out with such a drunkard—no, I will not marry the coward!" Flinging off her mantilla, she went into her room and locked the door. But she had hardly changed into an everyday dress, when the boisterous conversation of the three in the next room made her press her ear to the door. Pancho was explaining his plight, to his own honor and the utter disgrace of Rosendo. The frequent interjections of the old people told Consuelo that their indignation toward the unfortunate young man was growing stronger. They at last decided to carry on court proceedings for the February incident. Don Vicente had money, and Doña Genoveva had money—it was easy. Pancho, however, did not seem to be satisfied, for his pride had been injured more severely than his nose. "Rael told Consuelo that he was running off to Albuquerque," she heard him say. "But I'm going to settle it with him this night, as soon as I wash off this blood!" He was still under the influence of whiskey, and she knew what he meant.

Consuelo stole away from her room through a window, leaving it open for her return. Past the apricot trees, she followed the shadow of the sunken road as far as the *acequia* whence she cut across a field toward the canyon road. She knew where Rosendo's new house was; it was rather far. But she must warn Rosendo in time. Twice she caught her skirts on a fence, and, on crossing the stony bed of the river, she fell and bruised her knee. But she must beat Pancho to it. At last she saw a feebly lit window on the solitary slope of the hill. To a giant, the sight of her, as she ran up the road, would have seemed like that of a weary, broken-winged moth, fluttering over the ground towards a fire. Out of breath and dizzy, she came up to the door and began to pound madly with her fists, but with no response from within. She opened it.

"Who is it?" came a voice from the darkness behind her. She stepped aside, and the light of the open doorway fell on Rosendo, who was cinching a saddle on his horse. "Consuelo, is it you?" he asked, astounded. "What has happened?"

"Oh, Rosendo. I came to warn you—Pancho is coming to kill you!"

"I thought so; I'll be gone when he comes. But why are *you* here?" He took her hands in his, saying: "You are crying—come, what's wrong?"

"Please. Rosendo, I wanted to—I want to—"

"You want to say good-bye?"

"No. Yes—no! Rosendo, I don't want you to go, you can't go! I need your help; mother will marry me to Pancho Carillo, and I hate him, I hate him!" She hung to him, sobbing. "Why don't you stay—please!"

"Don't, Consuelo, don't! If I stay, I'll either go to jail for theft, or I'll be shot down by Carillo. The only way to stop such a man is to kill him; but I choose to flee like a coward rather than do that. So I must be going. You—don't let him find you here!"

"Rosendo" she cried. If you go, I'll stand here, just like this, and let him shoot at me in the dark...or I'll...I—I am going with you!"

Rosendo's heart leaped. This was unforeseen. Kindly, he put his arm around her and, as they walked into the house, he felt the helplessness of her. Many years before, he had found a lost baby deer in the canyon forest, and it had felt the same way, when he took it in his arms. On seeing the interior of the house, especially on noticing the piano in a corner, Consuelo forgot her tears.

"I bought it from Mrs. Taylor," he gave answer to her inquiring look, "when you told me that you could play—"

"When?"

"On the day the Archbishop was buried, the same day of the attempted theft!" He, too, lost thought of the danger they were in. "Don't you recall,

Consuelo, when the Sister saw us by the garden gate and you slapped me?"

"I remember, Rosendo. And I am sorry I slapped you. Here, take this now..."

At this moment, he awoke to the realization that they were alone. What a fine target for Pancho Carillo! "Consuelo, if you are going with me, we must hurry. Some day, after all this trouble is over, we can come here. We'll make good; and every evening you can play the 'Estrellita' for me..." Seeing that she had no covering for the cold night air, he brought her the large black shawl that had been his mother's, and she put it over her head.

"Consuelo, that fits you much better than a mantilla. You look like—like Our Lady of Sorrows!"

"But I am so happy, Rosendo."

"And so am I." He blew out the lamp, locked the door, and helped Consuelo to the saddle. They had delayed too long already. As there was no saddle for the old mare which he led out of the shed by a halter, he leaped on her bare back and gave the word. Instead of turning south to Albuquerque, and possibly meeting Pancho, they made for the hills to the north. Beyond stretched the huge *cordilleras* of the Rockies, and Rosendo explained that the hidden mountain country north of Santa Fe was safer, as nobody would think of following them there. He had some three hundred dollars, all his savings which would help them for a long while. And so they went forth, silently, each with his own thoughts. For the events of the night, of the last hour, had been many and varied and unexpected. Consuelo thought of home and the Carillos; but Rosendo was thinking of Consuelo, and of the "Conquistadora" in a dark corner of the Cathedral.

The riding, even by the light of a friendly moon, was slow, on account of the many hills and dark arroyos. After an hour's travel, the horses began to pick their way into a deep and black ravine. As they reached the bottom, Consuelo sighted a little spire to the right, close by on the mountain slope, and brushed with a stroke of moonlight.

"The country home of the old Archbishop," Rosendo said. "God rest his kind and holy soul. Were he living, he might straighten out matters for us—and marry us, too!"

"Yes, Rosendo, it's too bad. And poor old mother—she thinks that her old guitar brought death to the Archbishop!"

He turned to her inquiringly, and she began to recount the story of the guitar.

The middle of the morning flooded the Chimayó valley with grandeur, as the two night-long travelers paused on the brow of a hill and surveyed the scene. The lazy green river, green with the many motionless cottonwoods coloring its course, meandered through fields that were young with the sprouting maize, chile, and alfalfa. The orchards gayly blushed with blossoms, and even the sandy hills, usually drab, shone with what the artists and writers now describe as cinnamon, crimson, mauve, and lavender. There was the silence of a picture.

At last Consuelo directed Rosendo's eye to groups of people in the distance, some on foot and others on wagons and horses, departing from an isolated grove, out of which arose two graceful adobe towers.

"That's the Santuario of Chimayó," Rosendo told her. "The priest must have come and said Mass there. See! How fresh the church looks!"

"Rosendo, everything seems bright and new, as though it rained during the night. Do you remember that distant thunder last night?"

"I do. The edge of that storm must have touched Chimayó, just enough to refresh the crops and wash those twin-towers."

"Yes," Consuelo replied, looking at him. "Washed for company, for us. Let us go over and see."

When they approached the overhanging grove of thick cottonwoods before the chapel, they noticed three horses beneath them. Two of the animals had an Indian blanket on their backs, while the third was tied aside a large western saddle that lay on the ground. Rosendo opened the wooden-grilled gates of the adobe wall, and Consuelo followed him into the patio of the San-

"That's the Santuario of Chimayó," Rosendo told her.

tuario. By the white cross in the middle of the sunny court stood an old priest, talking to a young Indian couple.

The Padre spied them immediately over his low-perched spectacles. *"Mon ciel,* but Our Lady does grant my prayer at once!" he exclaimed. "Come, my friends, I was just going to send for witnesses at the village. I am Padre Roque. These children here came to get married, when everybody had left after Mass. Surely you will not refuse to be their *padrinos!"*

Rosendo's eyes met Consuelo's own for a silent parley. The old missionary watched them as he excitedly tugged at his faded cassock, once a black cassock, but now showing greenish in the morning light. "With pleasure, Padre," said Rosendo. And then they can be our *padrinos* in turn."

The priest rubbed his bald pate. "*Ma vie!* But did you elope, too? My, such excitement! Here I was about to saddle my horse and go home, when these two came and asked me to marry them. The boy is a San Juan Indian, the girl a San Ildefonso. The parents and chiefs objected because of clan traditions, and so they put on the wings of love last night! And where are you from? What clan?" The priest, smiled benignly.

"From the Villa, from Santa Fe," Consuelo answered, returning the smile. "We belong to the adobe and money clans; the chiefs objected and we flew!"

Father Roque laughed aloud. "I see, I see—from Santa Fe—well. You knew the Archbishop who died, not? Yes, yes." The priest began to squint at them seriously. "Children, I cannot marry you without sufficient reasons. I must know this and that and, oh! so many, many things; sabe? If things are in order, I will gladly help you. *Bien,* let us go inside and look matters over."

An hour later, the wedding procession made its appearance under the front porch of the church. First came the Indian couple, the young woman radiant in her red striped blanket and white buckskin leggings, and her husband grinning under his long hair and scarlet headband. Behind them marched the other pair. Consuelo's fair features stood beautifully framed in her black shawl, the joy of her smiles reflected in the eyes of Rosendo. Flocks of little goldfinches were piping sweetly from the willowy crests of the cottonwoods, with the effect of the *vox humana* of an organ. Countless gossiping sparrows poured down tiny showers of sand-grains from the beams above the portico. From the cedars on the hills, a pair of turtledoves cooed in bell-like tones, like chimes at Consecration.

Father Roque joined the couples by the cross on the patio, where they were waiting to say good-bye. "Consuelo," he said, kindly, "next week I'm going to Santa Fe, and I'll see your mother about this. A little talking might help."

"Many thanks, Father," she replied. "Do try and make her see."

"But now," said the priest, looking up at the sun, "you are not going away so soon. No, no, no! Rest yourselves—awhile. We had a double marriage, a nuptial Mass, and a wedding march, all to ourselves. Now we must have a wedding feast, a fiesta!"

The others stared around in wonder. Fiesta? But with what? Neither party of runaways had brought provisions along. Chuckling to himself, the Padre led them through the grilled gate and out under the giant trees. From his saddle he untied a sack, filled with boxes and packages. "Since I said my second Mass for you, I cannot go to my next Mission. It was too late, anyway; they can wait till next week. Here is my dinner that I brought. It will do for us all, because the newly married don't feel like eating much!"

Rosendo and the Indian youth spread the blankets on the bare ground, while the women silently arranged the rustic banquet upon them under the supervision of the priest.

"This is like the Wedding Feast of Cana," said the Father after the blessing. "That's when our Lord turned water into wine, after His Mother told Him there was no wine. But we have wine; this old steward did not forget!" Out of the sack came a long, thin bottle. "This is not one of the dear French brands, but it's an excellent substitute—*vino de Bernalillo.*" As only two tin cups were available, the Padre put one between Rosendo and Consuelo and the other between the Indians. He filled them to the brim and stood the bottle by his own place.

During the feast, Father Roque did all the talking. Now and then, a remark from Consuelo brought a chuckle from the laconic Indians and a hearty laugh from the old Frenchman. "You know, my little children," he spoke after some thought, "you remind me of the far, the far past. I eloped, too!"

"That's true," he continued, enjoying the intense surprise of his hearers. "Long, long ago, I was a newly ordained priest in France, when the first Archbishop of Santa Fe went over to look for missionaries for New Mexico. I offered myself gladly; and so were my father and mother and sister glad that I would be a missionary. But we could not part when the time came.

My people cried, and I cried. Oh, it was hard…" The gray eyes behind the spectacles became misty. "At last I prayed to my Patron Saint for strength, to Our Lady of Victories. I had a picture of her. 'My son,' she said to my soul, 'be true to your Love. Forgive yourself the pain of parting, and leave home secretly. I will aid you.' And so I ran away with my Lady of Victories to New Mexico, and ever since I have been here, and happy, because she is with me. Children, if you choose her for your companion, you will always be happy of heart!"

Rosendo thought of La Conquistadora in the Cathedral at Santa Fe. She was the same Lady of Victory whom the Padre loved. She would help him also. The priest then asked the Indians where they intended to go. The youth spoke: "We go Taos pueblo, maybe Picuris pueblo. They no take us, we go mountains. Plenty game there." He grinned triumphantly.

"Ah," said the Padre, his eyes sparkling after the mist, "this reminds me of another story about folks like you. This happened in California. Many years ago, when Kit Carson—you knew Cristóbal, not?—well, when Carson returned from a trip to San Diego, he told me a tale that was being passed around over there. That was before the railroad came. The girl of the tale was called Ramona, and she lived with her rich aunt, who was somewhat as you described your mother to me, Consuelo. Now, Ramona fell in love with an Indian sheep-shearer, called Alessandro. To her old Spanish aunt this was a crime; she locked Ramona up and tried, oh! she tried in every way to change her mind. But Ramona loved her Indian so much. She prayed before the statue of the Virgin in her aunt's room. I suppose it was an image of our Lady of Victories, because Ramona succeeded in running away with Alessandro. They went to Alessandro's pueblo, but, to their sorrow, they found it burned down and deserted. However, they did not lose heart. They went to live on the top of a high, high mountain near the sky, and Alessandro made a little cottage there. That's a beautiful story, isn't it!"

"Padre," said the Indian boy, "did they have one, two, three papoose?"

All laughed. "I do not know," the Padre interrupted the laughter. "Kit

Carson has been dead all these years, and I have met no one else who has been to California. Perhaps, matters turned out all right, and they went back to the old aunt. Or they might still he dwelling happily up on the mountain, alone. The mountains are a wonderful place when you are all alone, alone near God."

From their position, Rosendo and Consuelo gazed longingly northward, where they knew the high Sierras were waiting for them and welcoming them, just as the mountain had welcomed Alessandro and Ramona, and they seemed to see a small adobe cottage on the blue crests far away, away—up near the sky, up near the sky.

Part Three

The Vengeance

5

"Three years! Three years is much too much," sighed Doña Genoveva Ortega, her big eyes staring blankly into the fireplace. "Ay, Don Vicente, three long years of separation.... And where can she be, my dove, my Consuelo. She might be dead. Oh, Don Vicente, how very true is the old saying: 'The dead child is the dearest!'"

Don Vicente Carillo had been waiting for the proverb, as it foretold a welcome span of silence. He, too, began to stare at the fireplace, at the guitar. He had learned to enjoy these quiet moments with Doña Genoveva, the same Genoveva whom he had loved secretly when she was a sparkling señorita, years before she had been given to the now long-dead Pablo Ortega. Silent reflection was their mutual balm. Day after day, for three years, snowfall or sunshine, he had come to her in order to console and be consoled. For, with the escape of Consuelo with Rosendo Rael (only God knew where they had gone), his wild son Pancho had become altogether incorrigible. Pancho was always drunk; if he came home at all, it was for money, more money. Don Vicente's heart was already broken by all this! It bled within him whenever Pancho answered his fatherly pleadings with jeers and curses. What had caused all these misfortunes? Who?

The Señor Carillo instinctively fixed his gaze on the old, dust-furred, cat-like guitar. The Señora Ortega, aware of the old man's glance, thought to herself pityingly: "If he only knew what that guitar has cost me."

And he, staring woefully at the thing, uttered, inaudibly, "If she but knew."

They would have mutely challenged each other's thoughts for the rest of the afternoon, had not Pablito suddenly broken into their meditations. "Mother!" said the youth, with both hands on the door-frame, "why do you two sit there, staring, like wooden *santos? Manitos!* you would think that ugly guitar was giving you a sermon—and you sleeping with your eyes open!"

Don Vicente regarded the intrusion tolerantly and propped his palms under his chin. "My son," spoke the woman, "did the Archbishop let you off?"

"No madre," came the reply. "I came to tell you that I saw Padre Roque at the Cathedral—you remember Padre Roque! Well, he came from Mora this morning and is on his way back to San Juan and Chimayó, and he said he would come to see you this evening. He has good news, he said."

"Good news!" she echoed. "*Dios de los cielos!* Good news! The Padre has at last found my daughter.... I wonder, I wonder...." She broke into sobs and sat down beside Don Vicente.

Pablito could not see why his mother should make so much over Consuelo. These three years of absence had not made Consuelo different in her young brother's mind. Had she not always scolded him, pinched his arm, called him a *tontito,* a nitwit? Had she not always angered her mother, talking back at her? Why, then, cry for her? Thus Pablito argued with himself. In three years he had grown taller and more serious-faced, although he still indulged in riding an imaginary horse when nobody was looking. A genius in his mother's eyes, he had failed to make an impression on his teachers, the Christian Brothers at San Miguel, or they on him. The alphabet remained a sealed mystery to him, and school was supplanted by the Cathedral sacristy and the Archbishop's garden. He still experimented with plants; since his advent into the Archbishop's garden, he had graduated himself from sun-printing cabbage leaves with altar-veils and mantillas, and had succeeded, the Lord knows how, in growing a double-petaled variety of hollyhocks, or *varas de San José*. His Grace was amazed, Doña Genoveva proudly pleased, and Pablito knew it. Why, then, howl for Consuelo? With a wry look at the guitar, Pablito started back prancing to his work, thinking it quite a lark if he could but steal the instrument from his mother and send it to Consuelo, did he know where she lived.

With Pablito's exit, the two old people began to converse about Father Roque. "I could never forgive that priest for marrying my daughter to Rosendo Rael," the Señora said. "He came to me shortly after the marriage and tried to make me see—imagine! tried to make me see that Consuelo was justified in marrying Rosendo. Ah, Señor, that first day when he talked to me, I was mad—mad! He came again and again, you remember that. And then, when I asked him where Consuelo was, he didn't know, he didn't know. They went up north into the mountains, he said; and by that time your Pancho had scoured the whole country south towards Albuquerque, even as far as Belén! What a foolish old man, that Padre Roque; I had him trembling once, Don Vicente—yes, really trembling! And still he comes... with good news?"

"But what will you do," the old man asked, "if he has found Consuelo? She has a husband, you know—."

"Yes, Rosendo! But Rosendo must be gone by now—dead. Dead! Remember, my friend, Rosendo played the guitar!"

The Señor Carillo winced, as though his heart had spilled boiling drops of blood on his entrails. He sat in pain for a while and, his features lighting up, added: "And if Rosendo is really dead, Genoveva, would Consuelo marry my Pancho?"

"She will."

"And then, dear Genoveva, you and I also?"

"Por Dios, Don Vicente! Are you bringing that up again week after week? How often have I told you that we are too old, like those hardened apricot trees outside? When you begin to talk like that, it is better that we remain silent—"

"But you often say, my dear woman, that 'silence is lovers' rhetoric.'"

"Well, then, let's talk about something!"

"Our marriage," continued the old man, "would not be one of passionate love—leave that to the young! Ours would be one of necessity; it would be together fortunate—"

"Only he is fortunate with women," she quoted back, "of whom they take no notice!"

"But we are left alone," he pleaded on, "whatever happens to our children, good or ill. We need one another, as an old adobe buttress upholds an old adobe wall, and the wall holds up the buttress...."

The Señora Ortega had stolen out of the room into the kitchen. "There is nothing in the world worse than an old man with a fancy," she called to him after a while. But Don Vicente Carillo was well on his way home down the willow-lined *acequia madre,* wondering what could be the good news of Padre Roque.

Long after the evening Angelus had chimed from the Cathedral, Doña Genoveva spied Pablito and Father Roque in his fusty cassock climbing up the arroyo bank behind the apricot trees. She set the hot coffee-pot on the kitchen table, as if about to begin her meal. As Pablito opened the door, she began to pour coffee in her cup; she spun around, expressing her surprise at the Padre's early visit.

"Padre Roque," she exclaimed, "you come at the right time. Will you please sit down with us? It is our custom to dine late."

The Padre had already dined at the Rectory, but he sat down readily. As a rule, weathered old missionaries never hurt people's feelings. The Señora had counted on this, as she wanted very much to keep this man away from her room, which served as a parlor generally. If the old Archbishop, she reasoned, with his quiet and reserved manner, had been tempted to pluck at the guitar, how much more this nervous old man, who always moved about like a mouse in a granary! She remembered well the first time Padre Roque had come, three years previous, with the news of Consuelo's wedding. She had caught him looking across the room at her fireplace, much like the boy who discovers the first red cherry on the tree, when it occurred to her that his Reverence must see the window in the next room from which Consuelo had made her escape. Never again had she received him into her room; in fact, she wanted no priests there, for fear that they might ask questions and, like the old Archbishop, advise, or even command her, to destroy the guitar.

"Your son doubtless told you I had good news for you," the Padre spoke, peering officiously over his spectacles.

"Sí, sí, Padre," she replied. "Have you really—"

"Thanks to God and our Blessed Lady of Victories, I have located her."

Pablito stood behind the priest's chair and watched his mother's lips quiver, pucker up; then he saw her bury her face in her hands. Such strange folk these women, he thought; such a strange woman his mother. She cried when Consuelo was lost, and she cries when Consuelo is found. At last Father Roque, rising, lifted the old lady's crouched form gently.

"Ah, Doña Genoveva," he said, "how beautiful are such tears. Your daughter wept the same way when I met her."

The woman turned to him, half-dazed. "But where, where is she, Padre?"

"In Mora."

"In Mora?" she gasped. In Mora these three years, and Mora not more than fifty miles across the sierra! Incredible. She began to recall how Pancho Carillo, on the girl's disappearance, had ridden in hot haste to Albuquerque, because he had heard Rosendo Rael mention Albuquerque to Consuelo that same night. He had inquired in Bernalillo and even at Belén further south, but no sign of the fugitives. The Indians at Santo Domingo had seen no one pass by who answered to the descriptions given by Pancho. Then, when Father Roque had told the Señora Ortega of the marriage at Chimayó, Pancho had futilely searched the whole Santa Clara Valley northward, there to hear of a strange young couple who had settled down near Los Ranchos de Taos. To distant Taos he rode, only to find a young Indian couple instead of Rosendo and Consuelo. "They marry when we marry at Chimayó!" they told Pancho. "They were our *padrinos,* and we theirs. But we stay here; they go up the mountains...." and the Indians swept their arms toward the north, where the Rockies waved and waved themselves up into Colorado.

That had been the final judgment of Doña Genoveva and the Carillos, that the runaway lovers had fled into Colorado, and God and the bears knew the place.

The Padre began his news by explaining how he happened to go to Mora. It was his first trip there. The Pastor of Santa Gertrudis de Mora had been his classmate in France, and he had invited Father Roque to celebrate the feasts of Santiago and Santa Ana, which occurred on two consecutive days. But Doña Genoveva was not interested; she wanted to hear about Consuelo.

"I met her the second day of the fiestas, the feast of St. Anne. She and Rosendo came up to me at the sacristy door. 'How is *mamá*?' was the first thing Consuelo asked me. *'Muy bien'* I said, 'and she thinks of you often.' And that poor girl began to cry beautifully, just as you did now, Señora! And Rosendo also asked about you—"

"Rosendo!" she started back. "I thought Rosendo was dead!"

"What made you think he was dead, my good woman?"

"Nothing," she said, catching herself in time. "I must have dreamt it."

"Well, they invited poor old Roque for dinner, and so I told the Padre of Mora, my host, that he could save my share of his banquet till later. Rosendo had built his house of adobes at the upper end of the valley, and I rode in their wagon. Oh, the Mora Valley is a beautiful, beautiful valley—a Paradise, Señora! Mountains and mountains, covered with pines, crawling all around in a circle, and white and blue sierras rising behind them at the upper part, like these Sangre de Cristo peaks. But wait, Señora, and the green grasses in the valley, the big orchards, the river passing through the middle—"

"Yes, yes, Padre," she interrupted. "More about Consuelo, *si gusta.*"

"They had a fine adobe house, nice and clean. Also, a barn and fields, right on the mountain slopes, where wild daisies—yes, wait, Doña Genoveva! Besides the horses, fine animals, they have a cow, a calf, and—guess! a baby!"

"A baby? Why, Padre, why didn't you tell me that before? A baby!" The Señora Ortega was distraught for the moment. It had never occurred to her that Consuelo, by this time, might have a child. So much had she centered her attentions on her own grieved self, so much had she dwelt on the pangs, the wrongs, the sorrows brought down on her own motherhood, that she had never thought of picturing herself a grandmother!

"And the baby," the Padre explained proudly, "she is such a little angel! You can almost see the wings—"

"A girl!"

"Yes, *una mujercita*—about two years old, and toddling. When I saw her mother lead her out to me, I saw right away how our Lady St. Anne must have looked when she led our little Lady Mary by the hand. You see, it was Santa Ana's day!"

"O Dios mío, Dios mío," cried the Señora. "Oh, for a sight of the little one! What is her name, Padre?"

"Guess!" the Padre smiled. "Consuelo thinks she looks like you, and so she called her *Genoveva,* like her grandmama—"

"Oh, Father Roque, you must be making all this up, you must—"

"No, Señora; it is all true. And, dear lady, Consuelo did say the child looks like you; you must have been beautiful in your day!"

The Señora Ortega made no reply. The Padre removed his glasses and began to wipe them vehemently. After a while they began to talk again. The bright moon had soared far above the Monte Sol when Father Roque left. Standing and waving at the door, mother and son could barely distinguish the Padre's small dark form as he waved back and shouted: "Call them back to live with you, and you'll be the happiest grandmother in the world!"

Tenderly, as when a silent blanket of snow settles on the mountains, Consuelo drew a white spread over her slumbering baby. Little Genoveva did look like a tiny sierra, apparently motionless, even when her mother bent down to kiss the tanned little brow. But, under the miniature canyons and ridges of the coverlet, she could feel, as though it were in her own body, the healthy pulsation of the lovely little life beneath. The child was tired, and Consuelo knew that she would sleep through the rest of the afternoon until the supper-time. They had been out on the mountain slope since noon hunting daisies, as Genoveva put it. Ever since May, when the small white flowers hung upon the slope like patches of mist, Genoveva had insisted on going every day after *margaritas,* the daisies of the Mora valley. Even though they were quite sparse now in late July, the little one still grew impatient until her mother led her out to hunt *margaritas.*

Consuelo kissed the sleeping form again, looking up lovingly at the guarding angel above the little bed. This was a picture which good Doña Isabel, the baby's godmother, had given her. It was a brightly tinted, rather stiff-winged angel, passing a bow over a little violin on its left shoulder—a printed reproduction of one of the several musical angels that surround a Madonna of Fra Angelico, the *Madonna dei Linajuoli.* At all events, Doña Isabel said the picture had come from the States: years ago Kit Carson had brought it to Taos as a present for his devout Spanish wife, Josefa Jaramillo. Carson's wife had given it to Doña Isabel's mother, and Doña Isabel to her godchild. All agreed that the angel was very angelic.

"What is my guardian angel doing with his arms so?" the child had once asked.

"He's playing a violin, *vida mía,*" Consuelo had replied. "Do you hear it?"

From that time on, Genoveva always said that she heard the violin; whenever Rosendo and Consuelo kissed her good-night, she would put her

Genoveva had insisted on going every day after margaritas.

elfin finger to her lips and whisper: "Sssh! Listen to the violin!" And they listened.

Consuelo had gone outside to pick a few pieces of firewood, as a preparation for supper, when she caught sight of Rosendo running up to the house. He was waving something white in his hand. Consuelo dropped her wood. What was Rosendo bringing? He never came back from work so early. He was excited beyond words.

"My girl," he shouted, as he approached, "a letter! The first we ever got in three years!"

"From whom?" she asked in a whisper, hardly able to speak.

"I can only guess, Consuelo. See! It's addressed to you."

The letter was addressed to "Señora Consuelo Ortega"; it came from Santa Fe, and the nervous flourishes of the script looked familiar. A letter from Doña Genoveva at last! Padre Roque had delivered his message! The envelope fluttered down among the chips, as the two sat down on the woodpile. Consuelo began to read aloud:

"My daughter, my daughter, my dove, my love. I have found you, and my heart sings like a meadowlark because I sometimes thought you might be dead. Three long years of sorrow and anxiety, my beloved. How could you leave me, without a word, a kiss? Often, often, I told you that haste is a fool's passion, my 'chiquita'..." And so on for two pages.

Pages three and four were a chronicle of Santa Fe. *"Last Sunday, daughter, the Padre came out to say Mass with his chasuble on backward. That would not have happened had my Pablito been in the sacristy."* After a generous eulogy on Pablito's prowess as a sexton and a naturalist, the Señora Ortega described the coming Fiesta in the bright colors of a Spanish conquistador's escutcheon. The colorful weekly dances were reviewed, the latest songs from Mexico quoted. The Señora did not omit the petty scandals of the town; she vehemently deplored the ravages of style, for some wealthy American ladies had dared to abandon their high lace necks for low fronts. *"The Governor's wife had one of these dresses on the other day, Consuelo; and they say that a greenish lizard fell from a 'viga' and dropped right in her bosom."*

The pages about Consuelo's baby were weighted with caresses and motherly counsels. Consuelo shouldn't pin the little one too tightly around the knees, because it stopped the blood. Consuelo should watch like a vigilante that nobody give her the "evil eye." Doña Genoveva deplored the frequent visits of that Isabel woman, whom Padre Roque had lauded to the clouds, but who must be watched. Most of all, Consuelo must have some "ocha" around the household. "Ocha" was a medicinal root, a sort of panacea, which grows in high altitudes and which Doña Genoveva surmised ought to grow in Mora. She charged Consuelo to procure some without delay. *"My dear, its leaves resemble those of a carrot, and it grows in damp, shady nooks of forested sierra canyons. It cures anything. Make the baby chew some once in a while, even though she will not like it. Now, listen to this absurdity, daughter! A rich lady from the East was lecturing to some society women of Santa Fe on our customs. She said that 'ocha' had been used for centuries by the Indians and Mexicans to flavor their soup! 'Ah, ah, malaya!' I seem to be made of fire within me when I hear these strangers call us Mexicans. As if the old Spanish Conquistadores were Mexicans, daughter. Whatever they might say, we are the children of the army of colonists who came with the great DeVargas; some of our people may even call themselves Coronado's Children!*

"The brightest day of my life came when Padre Roque described to me the graces of little Genoveva, the very picture of her grandmother. May all the angels keep her. Give her an embrace from her grandmother. Also remember me to Rosendo. By the way, since Padre Roque told me how well he has taken care of you, I have begun to forgive him. Gratitude without forgiveness is ingratitude, they say. However, I cannot allow you all to return to me. No! Rosendo played the guitar! The guitar must have its blood sooner or later. The time must be near. Until then we must all bide our distance. After that, my dearest daughter, you may come back to me with your baby, back to patch the broken heart of your poor, affectionate mother."

For several minutes, Rosendo and Consuelo sat in silence. A shadow of longing flitted across Consuelo's face as she sighed for the great Fiesta, for the dances, for all the color that was colonial Santa Fe, and of which isolated Mora knew almost nothing. It was little Genoveva who brought her mind back to reality, back to the mountains. Rising, she went into the kitchen.

"Papá! Papacito!" Genoveva greeted her father, running into Rosendo's ready arms.

"You lazy little woman," he said, with a kiss. "You have been sleeping all day, eh?"

"No *papá. Mamá* and Genoveva were out hunting *margaritas,* and then Genoveva lay in bed and listened to the violin!"

As she huddled close to his breast, Rosendo smiled up at the twilight sky. What had he to fear? With Consuelo and the baby, with a good home among a hospitable people, what reason did there remain for complaint? Had not his Lady of Victory taken care of him? True, he had been persecuted in Santa Fe; but in Mora he found peace. On one side of the mountains there was sorrow for him; but on the other side, happiness. Rosendo turned musing, toward the setting sun, thinking how much less sorrow there would be in this world if all men realized that, when the dying sun darkens one side of the sierras, he also tints the other with gold and with the colors of the rainbow.

Several weeks after Father Roque had brought his good news to Doña Genoveva, and two days before the feast of San Gerónimo, Don Vicente Carillo and his son Pancho paid a visit to the old widow. Don Vicente had important things to tell her. Doña Genoveva saw them arrive, the old man and his *carretela,* and Pancho on his bronco. As she led them into her room, she voiced her surprise that both did not ride in the carriage together.

"My Pancho leaves for Taos in a short while," the don explained. "The day after tomorrow is the feast of San Gerónimo, you know; and Pancho wants to be there for the games. But, Señora, I have something to tell you."

Apparently Doña Genoveva was not listening. She had run to her pillow and brought out a letter. "I received another letter from Consuelo, the third one already. My daughter tells me she's getting more homesick every day."

"Why homesick?" Pancho asked. The old woman, ignoring the question, or not hearing it, began to read aloud part of Consuelo's letter. *"Dear madre,"* she read, *"it is not that I am dissatisfied. I have the best home, the best husband, the sweetest baby. But I miss Santa Fe so much, the 'bailes,' the fiestas. Here in Mora everybody is kind to us, especially Doña Isabel; yet, Mora knows nothing of Castilian glamour. I have to act like the people, and they, even Doña Isabel, think we're from the sierras near Taos, for that is whence they saw us come. We never told them we came from Santa Fe, for fear that we might be*

The envelope fluttered down among the chips, as the two sat on the woodpile.

found by Pancho Carillo.... Isolated Mora has forgotten the Spanish traditions: the people never heard a castanet; there are only two guitars in the whole settlement; and, most of all, they think nothing of it when the Americans call them 'Mexicans'...."

Doña Genoveva folded the letter and addressed her visitors. "My poor Consuelo is only a girl, you see. She was used to a different life. In all her letters she says the same things, protesting, nevertheless, her devotion and love for Rosendo."

While she spoke, the Señora had been watching Pancho. At the mention of Rosendo's name, she had caught the cruel curl of his lips and the savage glint in his eyes, eyes and lips which were degenerated by the evil habits of the past three years. No more was he the handsome Pancho of those days. Doña Genoveva realized this, like the pining father of the parable on beholding the returning prodigal. Would that Pancho were half as repentant, she sighed; in his present condition, he was no fit companion for her daughter, surely.

Conscious, perhaps, of the old lady's scrutiny, Pancho Carillo grew furious of a sudden, not at the Señora, but at Rosendo, like the raging bull which overlooks the toreador and centers his attention on the red mantle with which he is tantalized. He began to curse and talk wildly. Even Consuelo began to share in his threats, when Don Vicente, rising, tried to calm him.

"Listen, you two" Pancho shouted, with a determined slap on his holster, "I'm going to the San Gerónimo carnival at Taos. But from there, from there I'm crossing the mountains to Mora. Do you hear me? Rosendo Rael will surely get his due then—"

"My boy," Doña Genoveva said calmly, "that revenge is not for you. Remember, the guitar will take care of that!"

"The devil take the guitar, and you also!" he spat back and left the house. As the hoof-thunder of the bronco died away down the sunken road, leaving the two old people in the awful silence that follows a storm, Don Vicente began to talk, more to himself than to the Señora.

"He's drunk, drunk again. Drunk as ever," he said. "He's beyond cure...."

Doña Genoveva removed his trembling hand from his heart. "Come, Señor, let us forget it for the present. Now, what is the important something you wanted to tell me? You may propose to me, if it does you good."

"Ah, but you guess rashly this time," he answered, regaining his composure. "Genoveva, a friend of yours is dead."

"Dead? Who? Tell me!"

"Old Padre Roque."

"Padre Roque!" she gasped, shaking her head. Padre Roque dead? She could not believe it immediately. Finally, without any wish or effort, she began to picture the old priest in Heaven, running hither and thither, examining every nook and corner of his Father's Mansions. The Padre dead! Why did he die? She instinctively turned to the guitar in the corner. As far as she could recall, he had not touched it.

"Not that, not that," said Don Vicente, understanding her gesture. "The good Padre didn't die from playing the guitar. If death had to depend on that, why—"

"Yes, yes, I comprehend, Señor. We talk, but God does what he pleases!" she quoted, disarming him. "But go on talking, please. Tell me, how did you find all this out?"

"This morning I was coming over to see you. As I passed the Cathedral, the Padre Vicario stopped my carriage and asked me if I had the time to do him a favor to take him and the Archbishop to Santa Cruz. Word had been received that one of the missionaries had been found dead in bed. We went to Santa Cruz and entered the room where a few old women were telling their beads beside the corpse. Imagine my astonishment when I recognized the pallid face. Father Roque lay there as they had first discovered him; he had been dead for more than a day before they found him, they said. His eyes were half-opened, seemingly fixed on a little picture that he still held upright over his breast. There was a happy smile about his lips. The Archbishop closed the eyes, took the picture from the ashen hands, and showed it to all of us present. 'My friends,' his Grace said, 'this was Padre Roque's passport to Heaven!'"

"Don Vicente, what kind of a picture was it?"

"A *santito,* a holy picture of the Virgin. There were letters printed at the bottom, like *Notre*—yes, I think it was *'Notre Dame des Victoires.'* His Grace told me it meant 'Our Lady of Victory.'"

"La Conquistadora! the Señora repeated, slowly and with unction. "Padre Roque, the good Padre! Who would believe that such a beautiful soul dwelt within that rough, uncomely exterior—"

"But, Señora," the old man corrected her, "in death the Padre looked so young and so beautiful!"

"Ay, they said that of the old Archbishop three years ago. They'll say that of us, too. We never tell people such flattering things when they are alive and could appreciate them. Take yourself and me for examples. We are old—"

"Yes, old, old!" Don Vicente broke in, waxing brave. "Old and at an age when we should be thinking of many things. Oh, the emotions that the sight of Padre Roque stirred up in my soul! For that moment my heart felt as if it were whole. A holy death was his, because he lived a holy life. Señora, the sight of him made a lasting impression on me."

6

The pueblo of Taos shone a bright cinnamon in the mid-afternoon sun, its square outline of five terraces rising, tier on tier, against the dark blue of the mountain behind it, like a staircase for giants or an unfinished Babel. Again, it seemed unreal and devoid of life, as though it were a canvas, a cubistic conception; for there was that selective arrangement in which one cannot tell whether the ochre pile of cubes had been painted for the mountain, or the cobalt mountain for the cubes. Yet, there was reality, there was motion at the foot of the pueblo, for it was the feast-day of San Gerónimo, the patron of Taos.

A close view of the pueblo, when the dark mountain sank away from the scene, changed the first impression. The Indian games and dances which had been in progress since early morning were now at their height. One thought of the Circus Maximus, with all those spectators, the white-sheeted Taos Indians, lining the ascending terraces and looking down with the avid interest of Roman citizens in white togas. One expected to see a door on the ground storey fly open and a black Numidian lion crawl with swaying mane toward the naked, painted dancers. But this was Taos, not Rome.

Pancho Carillo had watched the Indians race and dance all day. He was tired of them. His head was throbbing vehemently, more on account of his frequent visits to the saloon in the old Spanish town of Don Fernando de Taos, than on account of the hot sun or the dancers. Whatever the cause was, Pancho's ennui grew stronger. Mounting his horse he rode back to Don Fernando de Taos. On the way he came upon a small party of men who were shooting *blanco,* the target being a whiskey flask a difficult distance away. They were using six-shooters.

Pancho prided himself on the use of the pistol. From the days when he was obliged to climb on an adobe *tapia* in order to mount the saddle, he had begun to practice the art with a little revolver his proud father had given him. The prickly pear of the nopal cactus, the round cone of the piñon, the inquisitive head of the prairie dog, these were his targets. His one ambition had been to rival the fame of Kit Carson, whom his father had known intimately, and whose grave lay not far away from where the men were shooting.

With the bravado of a knight-errant, Pancho joined the lists. The men drew aside prudently when Pancho's turn came to shoot. He could hardly make out the flask, so bleared was his vision. He shot once but no sound of broken glass followed. Again he shot; the bottle stood intact. Angrily, he emptied his revolver without results. He could hear the stifled laughs of those about him. Now he began to realize that his hand was unsteady, his vision defective. In fact, during the past three years he had noted that his shooting was becoming less accurate. Now it wasn't accurate at all! How, then, did he expect to make Rosendo Rael pay for his insults, for stealing Consuelo?

At the thought of Rosendo, Pancho asked the men if anybody from Mora had come to Taos for the fiesta. Nobody knew, they said. A man from Chimayó had been to Mora the week before, selling melons and chile in his covered wagon, they told Pancho; but he had promptly returned because in

It was the feast-day of San Gerónimo, the patron of Taos.

Mora there was an epidemic of the terrible *"viruela,"* the small-pox. Maybe that is why no Mora people had come. *Quién sabe?*

Pancho laughed and rode on to the town. "Small-pox!" he mused. "Small-pox! Rosendo would get his small-pox with a vengeance in a couple of days!" Pancho began to reload his pistol.

His horse, as if by habit, started on a trot for the hitching posts in front of the saloon, when both steed and rider were attracted by the alarmed cry of a rooster. A horseman rode past with the struggling and screaming bird under his arm.

"They're going to play the *gallo,"* a boy told Pancho. "There's a big prize, and they're getting ready for the game right now."

He followed the boy until he came upon a large concourse of eager spectators crowded on both sides of the road. Farther down the thoroughfare, the man who had passed him a moment before was busily burying the rooster. In front of Pancho a dozen young horsemen were waiting for the signal to start.

Making known his intention to an important-looking gentleman hard by, the young Carillo gave his name and took his place in the file of riders.

By this time the *gallo* was ready; the fowl's neck was left exposed so that it would breathe, while its tied legs cropped out of the ground, like an old yucca root, ready to be seized by the best rider. Ordinarily, the cock's legs stuck out some six inches above the surface, but now there was a handsome prize for the winner, and the rooster-man had left room for but two fingers and a thumb. This was a difficult task, all knew. The first horseman to pull up the cock was supposed to run away with it. The other contestants would follow him and try to wrest the fowl from him. If he outran them, he won the game. If they overtook him, he had to fight them off with the *rooster!* Most games ended in flying feathers, and with bits of entrails and gory down clinging to shirts and saddles.

The signal was given. The riders charged down upon the rooster at a thundering speed, one contestant a few feet behind the other, to prevent any chance of slowing up as the rider reached for the cock. Pancho was fourth in line. The first horseman bent down, lost heart, and swerved off the line of action. Pancho saw the second man touch the bird's legs and nothing more. Already he himself was beginning to stoop down off his bronco's side; he was determined to show these Taos men that Santa Fe produced real *caballeros.* He saw the third rider, a cowboy, stoop low, too low, as he missed the object and flayed his fingers on the sharp sand. Now was Pancho's turn. All he could hear was the beating of hoofs and hoofs; all he saw was the thing sticking out of the ground, as it appeared to come toward him. Down he swooped, like an osprey after a fish. He was now under the horse's belly as the bronco bore down on the rooster. He reached for it—ten feet too soon! Desperately he made a second attempt by jerking himself back and reaching for it. His head swung in the path of his steed's hind hoof. There was a dull, sickly thud. His hand lost its grip on the saddle, and he hung down, his boot caught in a stirrup. With a spontaneous cry of horror, the crowds beheld the spectacle. Another cry of consternation arose, as Pancho's bronco, the same bronco he had ridden on the night he tried to steal Doña Genoveva's treasure, became frightened by the cries and by the dangling body under it. The horse began to buck and kick and stamp. At every motion, its master's head struck either the hard ground or a harder hoof. Finally, all of the horsemen succeeded in surrounding the animal, until it stood still and trembling.

Silently they removed the dust-covered body of Pancho Carillo. His one leg was twisted and mangled from the stirrup; his head was a limp tassel of blood and sand.

One afternoon, some days after the feast of San Gerónimo, Doña Genoveva sat at her window, writing a letter to Consuelo. She was recounting, step by step, the tragic end of Pancho Carillo. His death was a most severe blow to poor old Don Vicente, who loved his only boy despite his shortcomings. *"Yes, daughter,"* she wrote, *"the Señor Carillo looks ten years older since it happened. He spends most of the day here with me. You know the saying: Guests and fish stink on the third day. Yet, I cannot help but pity him... even now I see him coming up to the house..."*

Don Vicente entered and sat down. "Genoveva, I've wanted to tell you something since it happened, and I cannot keep it to myself any longer. I must tell you, even if you chase me out of your house forever."

"Calm yourself, Señor. Are you mad? *Ave María Purísima!* Why should I run you out of my house?"

"Señora, you remember that night, three years ago, when a thief entered your room here—"

"Rosendo Rael, you mean?" she asked.

"No; it was not Rosendo. That thief was my own son—Pancho!"

At first she thought the old man had gone mad. But when she peered into his eyes, she began to understand why Don Vicente looked so much older than he actually was. "Now, now. Who told you this?" she asked, still suspicious of his right senses.

"I knew it all the while, all this time, Señora. For three years I have known it!" Don Vicente began to speak in earnest. "That night, that *Noche Triste* when someone broke into your room, I was waiting for Pancho at home. I saw him pull up his horse out on the street; I saw him jump off and deliberately chase the animal away with handfuls of pebbles. I followed him to his room and saw, to my surprise, that his face was scratched and his clothes torn. I asked him what happened. Then he began to tell me a story about his bronco going wild in an arroyo outside of town and almost killing him. When I told Pancho that I had seen him purposely chase the horse away, he humbly confessed everything to me. *Mi Dios!* What a disgrace! Such a disgrace brought down upon my name!

"I didn't know what to do that night, for I was certain that you had recognized my Pancho as he rushed out of your room. Then you can picture my joyful relief when Pablito came in the morning and told us that Rosendo Rael had broken into your house. 'So they think it was Rosendo!' I said to Pancho. We decided to let it go at that. To cover up my suspicions, I paid all of Pancho's debts and, like a Pharisee, came to your house to pronounce judgment on poor innocent Rosendo. Now you know why I was so anxious that Rosendo shouldn't be brought to court. Investigations would have raised scandals, indeed.

"I tell you, my conscience began to hurt me after I refused the adobes that Rosendo had made for me. That is why I later hired him to repair my hacienda. That is why I bought his fields near your home for a good price, to get him away from my guilty sight, to bring my family closer to yours!"

Doña Genoveva was listening, without raising an eyelash, without a word.

"And all this trouble is of my own making," Don Vicente continued. "Look at your own sorrows; look at those of Consuelo; look at those, particularly, of Rosendo. Now, do you wonder why my heart bleeds within me? Do you guess why I fear you will run me out of your sight like a stray cur?"

"Don Vicente," the Señora murmured gently, "I will not chase a lonely old friend away. You have suffered enough. On the contrary, I invite you to come and live with us here, for your own home must be a sad place to you now. Do you see this letter I was writing? I will tell Consuelo all that you have just related to me, and she and Rosendo and the baby will come back to us. Rosendo will make his adobes once more in those same fields by the *acequia madre;* he will build up the wall that was never rebuilt; he will enlarge this house for us all to live happily in it."

Don Vicente Carillo was sobbing gently like a child.

"Don't you think this plan is better, Señor, than if we married?" Doña Genoveva put her arms around him, something she had never done before. She stroked his grey hair, she spoke kindly in his ear. "Consider, Señor, that in this way you will be relieved of all worries. You will not have a first husband's head thrown in your dish; and yet we can talk to each other all day!"

The old man was tremendously pleased. He was glad now that he had but yesterday willed, in a formal document, his residence down town, the fields he had bought from Rosendo, all his money, to Doña Genoveva Ortega. He arose to tell her this, when he backed into the fireplace, and the guitar toppled over with a groan. Carelessly he grasped it by the neck and put it back in its place.

"Ave María Purísima!" the Señora exclaimed in horror. "You played the guitar!"

Don Vicente smiled back complacently. "That's nothing to me. That's a foolish notion of yours, Señora!"

"But, Señor! You recall what I told you about my husband and the old Archbishop! Remember, sir, your son Pancho!"

"Yes, I do recall. My Pancho died from playing the guitar, but not your old guitar. Yours is but a symbol of the real guitar—sin! And sin is death! That is why man has to die anyway, because of sin. The real guitar sings death, all right! Oh, since holy Father Roque died (and he didn't play your guitar), I have thought much, Genoveva. If the history of this guitar be true, then that young Spaniard of Sevilla was a sinner; so was the Jew; so was Tules Barcelona!"

Angrily, he emptied his revolver without results.

"Yet, Don Vicente, you would not say the good old Archbishop was a bad man!" the old woman managed to break in. "He played the guitar and died. Padre Roque did not play it, and he died, too! Why?"

"Why?" the old man said. "Why? Just because! This shows that your guitar is nothing else than an old relic of decayed wood and cat-gut. Now, listen to me. You have not actually played the guitar; but you have played it, nevertheless. For you have acted wrongfully in keeping it and believing in it. I have played the guitar, and in more ways than one. I have been too indulgent a parent. I spoiled my boy, my lost son, by not bringing him to task many a time when I should have done it!"

The Señora tried to interrupt him as Don Vicente waxed eloquent. She failed. The timely proverbs would not come. She merely listened now.

"As for the deaths of the Archbishop and Father Roque, it was their time to die, God's time. God alone knows why many good people die suddenly, why good persons, like Rosendo, have to suffer untold mental anguish. God alone knows the answer now; the Last Judgment will show us all the answer. Now, do not for a moment think, Señora, that you are listening to the dreams of an old man's fancy. Yesterday, I had a long talk with the Padre Vicario at the Rectory, and he agreed with most of what I told him. The Padre comes to my house tonight, he promised me, to talk of other matters. And he also said that he would come to see you later about that guitar."

Doña Genoveva listened on, speechless. Don Vicente continued to show her how foolish was her belief that the guitar caused people to die until Pablito came home from work. As the sun began to hide behind the distant Jemez range, he bade the old widow good-night and walked away homeward. Enchanted by his words and by her own speechlessness, the Señora followed with unswerving gaze his slowly vanishing form, like one of those stone statues near the pyramids, watching the solitary flight of a flamingo as it fades into the far, crimson sky.

That same night Don Vicente Carillo passed peacefully away. The Padre Vicario was by his bedside. On the next day, Doña Genoveva went to view the corpse at the Cathedral. She said that he looked so young and natural in the coffin, in spite of herself. After the funeral, she slowly made her way home on foot, as there was no gallant Don Vicente to drive her over. She reached her room with a heavy heart, a heart which almost stopped beating altogether, when she discovered that her guitar was gone from the fireplace!

Part Four
La Viruela

7

Two days after the mysterious disappearance of the guitar and the burial of Don Vicente Carillo at Santa Fe, Consuelo was bidding a good afternoon to the Sisters at Mora. Since the coming of Rosendo and Consuelo to the Mora Valley, they had been fast friends of the Sisters, and Consuelo, whenever she came down to the village, she always paid a visit to the little convent. How surprised she had been this afternoon when she learned that the good religious had received a piano lately! It was the first piano she had seen in the valley. For a whole hour she played "La Estrellita" over and over again, while the Sisters listened, amazed. Now, as she said "good afternoon," she wore a radiant smile, for the nuns had asked her to come and play often.

Consuelo had many a time thought of getting a piano, but had given up her dream, after summing up the difficulties entailed in transporting one up to the isolated mountains. The nearest railroad was at Las Vegas, more than thirty miles away; the road there was little else than a pair of thin parallel wagon ruts twisting over steep hills and through rocky canyons. Rosendo, moreover, could not well afford a piano now; besides, he had one in waiting for their return to his adobe house across the Atalaya in Santa Fe. Consuelo had yearned all during the past three years, to play "La Estrellita" once more, and now her wish had been fulfilled conveniently. The kind Sisters of Mora had a piano.

These Sisters were no richer than Rosendo Rael. They had their convent and school near the parish church. The structure was of adobe and flat-roofed, somewhat as long and oblong as five or six drab box-cars on a side-track. The nuns belonged to that heroic band of Loretto Sisters whom the first Archbishop of Santa Fe had brought from Kentucky across the fever- and Comanche-ridden plains, where one of them had died. It was said that the old Archbishop had given up in his search for some community to work in his frontier diocese (The Sisters of Charity came later) when he came upon these "Friends of Mary at the Foot of the Cross." They readily volunteered, urged undoubtedly by their love for the two little red Hearts which they wore on the front corners of their black veils. As it was, they had come to the poor as poor, living poorly. It was a wealthy donor from Missouri who had thought of their loneliness and sent them a piano.

Still thinking of her last hour in the convent, Consuelo unhitched the waiting horses in front of the merchandise store and climbed on the wagon seat. As she reined the horses homeward, the postmaster hurried out of the store.

"Señora Rael, Señora Rael!" he shouted. "Here's a letter for you. Just came!"

Consuelo took the letter and thanked the man, asking politely: "How is your wife today...and the baby?"

"The child is well," he replied, with a note of anxiety, "but my wife has developed a rash all over her body. She thinks it isn't serious. But, as you know, several people are down with *la viruela!*"

"La viruela!" Consuelo repeated. "Let's hope it's not that—not the terrible small-pox!"

On her way up the valley road, Consuelo lost all thoughts of the small-pox as she devoured her mother's letter. Its contents held her spell-bound. A dread took hold of her as Doña Genoveva's description of Pancho Carillo's violent death took shape before her mind's eye. Tears welled up, reverently joyful tears, when she learned of the death, the holy death of Padre Roque. Then a kind of wild exultation seized her on reading that her Rosendo had been vindicated of the attempted theft of Doña Genoveva's treasure. Reading further, she became more serious and sympathetic at the sudden demise of Don Vicente. This was at the end of the letter, like a codicil added to a last testament. It modified the spirit of the entire letter, as the postscript in large generous characters showed. It ended with: *"And now you can all come back home! You, my dearest daughter, and my Rosendo and my little Genoveva!—All, the three of you, come back to me. I laugh for joy, I weep for joy, I await you with joy!"*

With a loud happy cry, heard only by the crickets at the road and the jays in the pines, Consuelo urged her horses onward. She could hardly wait until she could tell Rosendo. The few tears for Pancho, the well of tears for Padre Roque, the less generous but earnest tears for Don Vicente, all poured down her cheeks at once, undisturbed, like virgin dew on the grass, like the strings of pearls on the image of La Conquistadora. She turned her face to heaven in thanksgiving, and the sunlight turned the pearls to diamonds. She was looking through a screen of rainbows. How glad would Rosendo be! To go back home, to Santa Fe, to their little adobe home near the Atalaya, to the piano on which she had long dreamt to play "La Estrellita" when Rosendo came home in the quiet evenings, in the joyous evenings!

The trees sped by, the boulders sped by, the fence-posts sped by; Consuelo drove on as in a dream. At last her big dream was being realized. Her exile was over. Long were the days, since her mother's first letter came, when she began to brood over her lonesomeness, and longer far the nights, when she used to lie awake, dreaming day dreams in the night. Then she could hear the peaceful breathing of her baby, listening to the angel's serenade on the violin; then she could almost feel the contented and healthy slumber of Rosendo

At last the wagon stopped in front of the adobe house.

beside her; but, in her own sleep-bereft mind, there throbbed a melody which haunted her—"La Estrellita." She would repeat and rehearse it note-by-note, measure-by-measure, moving her fingers over the imaginary keyboard on her blanket. With it would arise pictures of Santa Fe. Consuelo would imagine the music-teacher at Santa Fe teaching her the movements. A vision, that of Rosendo grasping her hands by the garden gate and a Sister clapping her hands in disapproval, would flare up and fade. She would find herself singing the song in the brightly-lit dance hall on the Agua Fria, while Rosendo fingered the guitar deftly. Lastly, she would linger on the scene of that night when they ran away, she, looking in astonishment at the piano Rosendo had bought, as he gently placed a black shawl over her head and shoulders, saying that she looked like "Our Lady of Sorrows!" "But I am so happy," she replied. ... And thus she would fall asleep.

At last the wagon stopped in front of the adobe house on the mountain slope, and Consuelo, waking up, climbed down. Doña Isabel met her at the door.

"Forgive me, Señora," Consuelo said, "for staying so long. I hope the baby didn't bother you much."

"How could she, Consuelo! the other woman replied, kindly. "She's a good girl, my godchild is, even if I must say it. She's been sleeping for over an hour, the darling!"

Doña Isabel was a queenly woman, some twenty years older than Consuelo. She was tall and straight, almost masculine. An incipient goiter added to the proud poise of the head, as if her neck were accustomed to a big Elizabethan ruff. On the other hand, she was also queenly on account of her soft round eyes and her pious soul, reminiscent of that royal namesake, Isabel of the Spaniards. She and her American husband were the closest neighbors of the Raels, and, as they were childless, they lavished all their affections on little Genoveva. Even Rosendo and Consuelo they had become accustomed to regard as their own children.

"But, my Consuelo," exclaimed Doña Isabel, "what is the matter with you? You look so happy, and yet I see tear-marks on your dust-stained face! Come—why you look like a white wall after the roof leaks for a day!"

"I have wonderful news for Rosendo," Consuelo answered. "He ought to be coming home soon. If you stay until he comes, you'll hear the good news also."

"I don't believe he'll be home till late tonight," said Doña Isabel. "He was here right after you went down to the village. The Mora priest was with him."

"Where did he go?"

"He and the Padre went up the valley to Las Colonias. It seems as though the small-pox is mowing everybody down up there. Word came to the Padre at Mora about a certain family at Las Colonias. The father died last week, and now the mother died this morning. Their two children are down with the disease. They have no relations, but even their neighbors cannot help them, as they have their hands full themselves. So the Padre asked for volunteers to help him bury the mother and see about the children. Rosendo offered himself, leaving his work to help the Padre. It's a sad case, all right."

Consuelo sat in silent pondering for a while. Her thoughts were centered on that letter. Oh, if Rosendo were home, so that she could break the glad tidings! Unable to contain herself any longer, Consuelo pulled out the letter and read it to a wide-eyed Doña Isabel.

The older woman was surprised at finding out that her young friends were not from Taos, but from Santa Fe. As for their being runaways, she had long nourished her suspicions.

"Many a time during the past three years," Doña Isabel spoke, "my husband and I talked about you when we were by ourselves. We wondered how long we would keep you near us, for we had learned to love you as our children, especially since little Genoveva came. We feared to lose you. We had our suspicions, for you and Rosendo acted at times as though you were here only for a time, waiting for an opportunity to return to some loved home. One day, when we were talking of these matters, my husband said he was willing to help you if you decided to go away. He'll take your little farm for a good price. Oh, my dear Consuelo, I feared to see the day when you and Rosendo moved away; I fear to say good-bye to you... and to my little Genoveva...."

"More people have died because they made their will than because they were sick," said the Señora Ortega to Pablito, sagely. Annoyed, Pablito merely listened, as he stared out the window over his mother's shoulder. Doña Genoveva had been talking and quoting maxims all afternoon. In the morning, the Padre Vicario had come to see her, as he had promised Don Vicente, and had found her in bed. He expressed his pleasure at the disappearance of the guitar. After many questions and repartees, he had persuaded the old lady to prepare herself for death.

"Señora," said the Padre, "you ought to know that you have many things to set right before you—"

"Oh, I know where the shoe pinches me," she remonstrated, just before giving in to the pastor's wish. "But, Padre, I do not feel death coming upon me."

"Suppose you don't," the Vicar retorted. "Death comes like a thief in the night!"

Gradually, the picture of a thief entering her room took form in Doña Genoveva's imagination. She glanced at the vacant spot in front of the fireplace. "Very well, Padre. Such a preparation will work no harm. As the old saying goes: The Doctor knows best as he does the killing!"

With the promise to hear her confession in the evening, the Padre Vicario went away. Doña Genoveva, however, did not feel sick enough to die. She crawled out of bed, dressed, and took a comfortable seat at her window. Afraid of being alone, she told Pablito to stay home with her, and Pablito stayed away from the Cathedral for once, sitting sullenly behind his mother's chair. All day she had been talking to herself, accusing herself, excusing herself, probing her soul in preparation for confession.

What had prostrated the old widow since Don Vicente's sudden death was the still unsolved mystery of the guitar. The sight of an unaccustomed empty fireplace had electrified her nerves and made her heart heavy. Now, however, since the Vicar had talked to her, she tried to make herself pleased that the guitar was gone. Yet, the Eve in her would ask now and then: "Where is the guitar?"

Whenever Pablito heard this question, he would begin to wonder if the guitar had already reached Consuelo. He had packed it securely in a green pasteboard box and was quite sure that the postmaster had written the address correctly for him. Meager though his faith was in the guitar, Pablito hoped that it might keep Consuelo away somehow.

"And my Consuelo?" asked Doña Genoveva of Pablito. "Did you mail that letter I gave you that morning after Don Vicente died?"

"I did," came the reply, as Pablito clamped his palm over his mouth when about to say, "—together with the guitar!" Then he grinned behind her back.

"Well, we must give them time to get ready, son. Rosendo will have to sell his farm, and they must pack their other belongings on the wagon...." The Señora could see, as if the Sangre de Cristo sierras were glass, the busy preparations that were going on in the Mora Valley beyond. "They'll be here this week, Pablito mine. Won't that be a blessed reunion?"

Pablito silently disagreed.

"I lost one of my treasures," she mused, "and now she's coming back to me, with other treasures, Rosendo and the baby. Oh, I'm ashamed of myself to think how I suspected poor Rosendo. Ay, suspicions are like spider-webs; they catch the little gnats and let the big hawks fly! But everything pointed to Rosendo, and by night all cats are grey!"

Secretly Pablito did not agree.

"And that other treasure, the guitar I lost! Yet, that was not a treasure," she corrected herself, signing herself. "Whereas that other treasure, my money and jewels which were nearly stolen—ah! I have them still. Do you know where I hid them, son, after I took them out of the fireplace?"

"You put them in that chest under your bed," Pablito replied.

"Ah, I thought you knew it! I remember that evening before the dance, when I pulled out the chest to give Consuelo my black Spanish mantilla. She gave the chest a suspicious look. That same night, after she ran away with Rosendo, I took my treasure out and hid it again. Ha, my Pablito! So you thought it was in the chest!"

The Señora arose and moved slowly toward her bed. Instead of lying down, as Pablito had expected her to do, she pulled off the covers, cast the pillows aside, and, producing a pair of scissors from the large pocket in her skirt, proceeded to rip the bare mattress open. To his astonishment, the youth saw her lift a small deep box out of the cavity whence the wool had been removed. She motioned to him and made him help her remove three other similar boxes. They were very heavy. When the boxes had been arranged in the middle of the floor, Doña Genoveva said, "Son, there it is; you never saw it before!" Rising, she locked the door.

Kneeling on the floor, she opened the first box. Pablito whistled. He had never seen so many coins at one glance. They were stacked in columns, and the columns were arranged in circles, like hollyhock seeds in a pod. Yellow money it was. It reminded Pablito of the Sunday collection at the Cathedral when he himself took it up. If the Padre Vicario took up the collection, as for Christmas or Easter, the box would be cluttered with nickels, dimes, and even large silver dollars; but when Pablito or the sacristan took it up, which they did every Sunday, the box overflowed with big copper pennies, just like these now, though not so bright and yellow. The Señora told Pablito they were gold, from her husband's saloon and gambling house of former days. She told him that Tules Barcelona likely handled these very coins once upon a time.

Pablito forebore to whistle as the other cases were laid bare. Some had silver coins mixed with the gold. Some coins had eagles, others had crowns. Some were new, and some were worn off at the edges, like a cast-off horseshoe. "Here are some," she said, "with a king's head on. See? See the castles and lions? It says *España* here, and on this side it's *Carlos Segundo....*" She explained to him the different engravings minutely, and Pablito agreed that they were nice and shiny and a lot of them.

The last box was filled with jewelry—rings, brooches, earrings, and chains, plain or strung with garnets, emeralds and sapphires. The Señora reached for them, and they clung in her hand in a radiant cluster.

"Wouldn't Consuelo be glad to see these?" she said. Pablito only smiled.

Having returned everything to the boxes, Doña Genoveva went to the fireplace and removed the loose slab where the guitar had stood. The hole was not much wider than one of the boxes, but Pablito's bewilderment knew no bounds when he saw each box vanish into it. The old lady then replaced

He had never seen so many coins at one glance.

the slab, which happened to be not a stone, but a rusty iron skillet without a handle. She made Pablito bring her some mud and with this she plastered the floor of the fireplace, so that only a minute part of the skillet remained exposed.

"There!" she said, with final pat. Now it's buried safely." Turning to Pablito, she began to speak in grave tones. "This, my son, is known to you alone. Now, if I should die, maybe next month or next year, do not dig out the treasure. Don Vicente Carillo left us his whole estate, and that will be enough for you to live on. But, in case you and your sister Consuelo are ever in need, then you may open it and use as much as is necessary. Otherwise not! Do you hear? Do you hear? Don't forget what I just told you!" She made him promise.

After supper, the Padre Vicario came to see the Señora. Pablito told him she had the chills again. After the priest had conversed with the woman for a while, she made her confession, and he gave her the last anointing. Without a warning, Doña Genoveva stopped breathing. The Vicar called Pablito in, but the boy didn't know what to make of it at first. After some thought, he went on a gallop to the Cathedral and tolled the big bell.

As the Señora Ortega, later on, lay in the Cathedral, facing the same vaulting ceiling that the old Archbishop had faced three years before, the old, black-shawled women huddled around to see her face for the last time. "That," said one of them, "that is the face of Genoveva when she was a happy and free señorita!" Another said, "How young and natural she looks!" Dona Genoveva, however, did not turn over in her coffin.

During the Mass of Requiem, Pablito tolled the bell according to custom. The people who filed into the edifice and saw his dry, expressionless stare wondered if Pablito realized that his mother was dead. He did; he also wondered why many of the people came in with moist eyes, as if that would raise the dead to life. He thought people were queer, indeed. From that time, Pablito Ortega stopped working in the Cathedral or in the Archbishop's garden. Locking himself up in the old adobe house that was his mother's like the species of crab which pulls himself into an abandoned shell on the sand, he waited for Consuelo and Rosendo, still hoping that the guitar might keep them away.

On the same day that the big Cathedral bell tolled for Doña Genoveva Ortega, all the bells of the Mora church rang out for fully fifteen minutes, like the joyous peals that answer the *Gloria in Excelsis Deo* of Holy Saturday. People paused on the streets, saying: "*Un angelito,* a little angel has returned to Heaven!" Mothers at work looked towards their cradles or at the playing tots around them, uttering a prayer of thanksgiving. For a baby had died, and it was the custom in New Mexico to ring all the bells whenever a little angel, as they called a child, returned to Paradise.

The news spread rapidly. It was the child of Rosendo Rael. Rosendo's baby had died, and the bereaved father had just notified the Padre.

"The small-pox?" one anxious woman asked.

"Yes, the small-pox."

Sad was the scene at the upper end of the valley. The little adobe house on the slope was quiet; nor was there any whistling sound from the pines on the mountain behind it. From the small corral nearby came the lowing of the cow for her calf, as no one had come to let her out on the field. A pair of mourning doves sat on the woodpile by the door, cooing in melancholy tones, as though an owl had destroyed their nest in the forest. All was sad.

Within the house, Consuelo and Doña Isabel sat alone by the little corpse. Rosendo had gone down to the village to tell the Padre and to see the town carpenter about the coffin. Long since, Doña Isabel had ceased to solace a sorrowful Consuelo, a Rachel who could not be consoled. Both sat silently together, the older woman's arm around the young mother.

Consuelo's sole thought was the motionless little one on the bed. Like many another sorrowing mother, she asked herself why her baby had been taken away. Why? She didn't know; yet, she thought she knew. For the last half hour her eyes had been roaming from the dead child to a green paste-board box on a high shelf, and from the green box to the child. Doña Isabel, noticing the glances, did not know what they meant. Nor did she know what was in the green box. She had never seen it before.

In Consuelo's mind whirled the sudden events of the last two days. The morning after Rosendo had returned from burying the woman at Las Colonias and had read Doña Genoveva's welcome message, Consuelo had sent him to see Doña Isabel's husband about buying the farm. The baby was still sleeping that morning, when Consuelo began sorting out the chat-tels which would be loaded on the wagon. After awhile, little Genoveva began to call for her mother. Consuelo found the child in a sweat; she was hot, the baby said.

Just then Rosendo returned, his face beaming. Under his arm he carried a large package. "My dear," he said, "the baby's godfather will buy from us any time! We'll be ready to leave for Santa Fe in two or three days. But, look, Consuelo! A package came for you!"

Pablito tolled the bell according to his custom.

Laughing, the two peeled off the wrapping, revealing a large green pasteboard box. Consuelo wondered if her mother had sent her some dresses, thinking that her returning daughter had no decent clothes left. Or was it a present for the baby? When the lid came off, both recognized the thing inside, the old Ortega guitar! What had made the Señora send it to Mora? Rosendo guessed that it was Doña Genoveva's manner of playing a joke. The Señora could be humorous in her brighter moments. Pulling it out of the box, Rosendo began to pluck the few strings, tightening them at the same time, so that the most bizarre groans emanated from the sound box.

On hearing the sounds, little Genoveva slid off her bed and noiselessly slipped from behind between her kneeling parents. One little arm was put forth, and a little hand began pulling at the strings, as though they were

One little hand began pulling the strings.
Simultaneously, Consuelo gave vent to her alarm.

rubber bands, letting them snap back raspingly against the letter-scarred front of the guitar.

"A violin!" the child screamed with delight. "A violin! Now I have a violin like my angel!"

Simultaneously, Consuelo gave vent to her alarm, for, like a flash, all the evil traditions connected with the guitar arose in her brain. Pulling the girl away, she turned her head in disgust and fear. Rosendo, taken back by Consuelo's gesture, knelt bewildered with the instrument in his hand. He had never imagined that his wife could believe such superstitions, for she had always talked lightly of the thing.

"Take it away, take it away!" Consuelo began to cry, pacing up and down the room with the child in her arms. "You and the baby have played the guitar! Take it away!"

Rosendo had never felt so angry in all his life. Dropping the hated thing on the floor, he was about to crush it to splinters with his heavy shoes, when Genoveva began to scream: "Papá, don't break my violin! Papá, don't break my violin!" Her little face was red, like a beet, almost purplish. Then it turned to a livid hue; Rosendo thought she would choke. He took her in his arms, shook her, slapped her back smartly, until she began to breathe again. "Papá," she said after many minutes, "you won't break my violin, will you?"

Genoveva's little forehead was steaming, her skin a sickly red. Consuelo thought that the excitement had caused it, and resolved to make her go back to sleep it off. But before she would allow herself to be put to bed, Genoveva wanted to see that her violin would not be broken. Rosendo replaced it in the green box, tied it with cord, and shoved it onto a high shelf. After that she fell into a long sleep.

Later, Consuelo found the child crying for pain. Her skin had broken out in blisters, which soon began to swell the more and to turn livid, like countless drops of cooled wax. Rosendo summoned Doña Isabel. She and her husband came, but could do nothing. Doña Isabel's verdict was *la viruela*—the terrible pestilence that had broken loose in the mountains. Consuelo suggested the wonderful *"ocha"* which her mother had commended so highly; but Doña Isabel said it was useless. The only course was to take good care of the child, as they might save her from death, but not from the *viruela*. The disease must take its course, since it could not be stopped. There was no doctor for miles around. There was one in Las Vegas, Doña Isabel's husband said, but he was one of those who would rather walk a hundred miles to attend an ailing horse, than ride thirty miles to see a dying Mexican.

"I'm an 'Americano' myself, he added, hot with indignation, "but this man belongs to a different breed, and there are too many of them in New Mexico right now!" The old gentleman was probably recalling the visit which a company of mounted Texans had made to the Mora Valley years before, when they trampled the ungathered crops and razed the houses.

Little Genoveva died in the presence of these few individuals who loved her better than themselves. Her little features were unrecognizable; they were white and yellow with the virulent matter and dead skin. Like a white and yellow daisy under an unbearable breath of hot wind, Genoveva turned her tiny head aside, never to bloom again till the coming of the eternal Spring.

Thinking of all these events, Consuelo had fallen asleep on Doña Isabel's breast. When Rosendo entered the room, she lifted her head. "Everything is ready," Rosendo said, referring to the priest and the carpenter. Walking up to him, Consuelo laid her brow on his shoulder. Rosendo, after glancing at the bed, bent his own head down to her shoulder, and both mingled their warm tears in silence.

"Consuelo!"

"Yes, madre."

"Consuelo!"

"Yes; I heard you, mother."

"Consuelo, Consuelo..."

Consuelo was fixing her white mantilla which Pablito had ruined in his botanical experiments. Doña Genoveva was sitting behind her at the window, her usual point of vantage, gazing at the verdant fields that spread like a carpet down to the *acequia madre.*

What would her mother want, the girl asked. With the mantilla in her hand, she arose, when a sudden dizziness stopped her. She shut her eyes tight for a spell and opened them again. The room was now dark, save for a pale gleam of dawn at the open window. Where was she? Consuelo rubbed her eyes and realized that she was sitting in bed, holding a corner of the blanket in her hand. This was Mora, not Santa Fe! What day was this? Ah, she remembered now. Yesterday, they had buried little Genoveva, her baby, her poor baby!

"Consuelo, Consuelo," again came the call, a plaintive call. Was she dreaming again? "Consuelo... Consuelo..."

Turning around, she noticed that the call came from Rosendo. She jumped out of bed and lit the oil lamp on the table. On raising the wick, she got a better view of Rosendo's shiny face, shiny with an oily sweat. "Consuelo," he said, smiling, "I thought you'd never hear me."

"What's the matter, Rosendo? Why didn't you shake me?"

"I can't move," came the weak reply. "My dear girl, it's got me, I think. I feel it all over."

A spirit of terror overshadowed Consuelo, as soon as she understood what he meant. "Oh, please, do not say that, Rosendo!" she cried. "Say it isn't that, please!" She fell down on the rug by his bed, her slender, arched back quaking with her violent sobbing.

"Consuelo—oh, don't—oh? Consuelo!"

She raised her wet face to his. "Rosendo, my Rosendo, are you going to leave me, too? Oh, do say it's not the small-pox!"

"It is; but that doesn't mean I'll die, dear."

"Oh, no; please don't! Please!"

"Don't touch me," he said softly. "This is contagious, you know. Come, get a chair and sit near me until the sun comes."

She sat by the bed in the pale beams of the lamp. After she had given him some water, to cool off his burning tongue, Rosendo begged Consuelo to talk of other matters, about their return to Santa Fe as soon as he got well. Invariably, their solitary conversation would turn to the light, the love of their young hearts—little Genoveva.

Consuelo sobbed out: "Oh, my baby, my baby—"

"Oh, don't cry like that, Please!"

"But she's gone from us—"

"Gone to Heaven, dear; she's happier—"

"Oh, Rosendo!" Consuelo thought her heart would break.

"Now, don't weep like that. Let's hope God sends us another little Genoveva soon. Let's talk about her, since we can't help it. Do you remember—Consuelo, do you remember what she said to me just before the end came? She said: 'Papá, you can break my violin now, because the angel will lend me his....'"

Consuelo didn't remember hearing that. But she had heard, or thought she heard, Genoveva saying to her: "Mama, you look so white, white, like a daisy. I bet your name isn't Consuelo. You're a *margarita*...Margarita is your name!" Margarita! Consuelo remembered that.

Until the sun crawled above the eastern ridges, Consuelo and Rosendo talked about the baby. Later on, after kindling a fire and getting a small breakfast ready, Consuelo began to attend to her sick husband. Shortly after, Doña Isabel and her husband made their appearance. They had come to see how the young parents had fared after the funeral and to make arrangements for their departure, for the prudent old man had said to his wife that, the sooner Rosendo and Consuelo left the scene of their sorrow and returned home, the better it would be all around. It would be tragic, he knew, to have another child born amid such heartrending surroundings and recollections.

Doña Isabel and her husband stepped back in astonishment on beholding Rosendo in bed. Blisters had already begun to form on his face, as they had broken out on the baby.

"Come in," Rosendo said brightly, in spite of his low condition. "I suppose our return to Santa Fe is postponed. Sit down."

The old gentleman came close. "That's the right spirit, my boy. You'll pull through as sure as God made a little apple. You're strong enough to stand the plague, lad. I had the dern same thing when I was a kid, and now look at me—going on strong at sixty!"

"You'll take the farm, won't you, dad?" Consuelo broke in.

"Sure will!" replied the old Yank. "That's one reason why my Isabel and myself came over this morning. Here's the five hundred you settled for, Rosendo. All in fine green paper. Where shall I put it for you?"

"Hold it yet," Rosendo answered.

"Hold it nothing, young man! I might spend it and have nothing ready by the time you want to pull out. Where shall I put it, Consuelo, my girl?"

Consuelo only pointed to a row of shelves on the wall. Examining them officiously, the old man selected the top shelf on which lay the green box. "Here's a nice place, eh? I'll slip the bills inside; this box looks like a little green iron safe, anyway."

Although Rosendo was strong, the *viruela* was stronger. That afternoon he reached the much-awaited crisis, which was to tell, like a dramatic climax, whether the end would be happy or tragic. To the dismay of all, however, Rosendo began to sink rapidly. A tragic finis seemed inevitable. One by one, his resources were being exhausted. The parish priest of Mora, sadly surprised on hearing of his condition, came in a hurry, heard his confession, and anointed him. All the while, Doña Isabel and her American husband assisted the dying man, the tears streaming down their cheeks. They took turns at leaving the room, to give vent to their emotions outside and to acquaint a few friends and neighbors outside of Rosendo's ebbing state. Consuelo, however, sat by the sick man's side, saying nothing, doing nothing, not even weeping—only staring disconsolately at nothing.

Weak though he was, Rosendo, with an uncanny penetration, took note of Consuelo's strange inaction. "Make her cry, make her cry," he pleaded. But she could not be moved. Rigidly keeping the same posture, she stared far, far away, as in a magic trance.

Consuelo did want to cry; she just could not. Her eyelids were dry, so dry that they would not shut to coax out the precious fluid beneath them. Her thoughts were always reverting to the contents of the green box, although she was really trying to meditate on the grim disease which, like a Horseman detached from that gruesome company of the Apocalypse, had come galloping down the mountains and had taken her baby away. Now the Rider had wheeled around on his tracks to seize Rosendo. Would he take her, too? It didn't matter. It would be much better that he did.

"Make her cry, please!" came the plaintive and weakening refrain from the bed. Doña Isabel noticed that Rosendo was sinking into a delirium. Consuelo heard the prayer, but could not answer it. She looked at Rosendo with wide, still eyes and thought he was beginning to lose his mind. Through swollen, glazed eyes, Rosendo saw the seemingly distorted face of his wife and thought she was going mad. "Make her weep, please," he whispered in pain. "Oh, this *viruela!*" After that, Rosendo remained quiet, as if asleep.

"La viruela!" Consuelo kept repeating in her mind. *"La viruela, la viruela,* la vi*r*uela, la vi*h*uela..." She caught herself pronouncing two words that were altogether different, but very much alike. Ghastly alike, she found out, as she interchanged *la viruela* (small-pox) with *la vihuela,* the old Spanish word for *guitar!* The guitar! There lay the solution! The guitar had done it all; Doña Genoveva Ortega was right about it! The guitar! With a piercing shriek, Consuelo stood up and fell unconscious into the ready arms of Doña Isabel.

On the advice of her husband, Doña Isabel had the unconscious young woman taken to her own house. She herself went with the compassionating mountain folk who had offered to help her, while others of the neighbors went in to assist at Rosendo's bed, excited as they were by Consuelo's scream.

Rosendo, however, had not heard the shriek. He lay quiet, mumbling something to himself which the old man could not grasp. At times, he thought Rosendo was calling his mother. He was almost convinced he heard a single word, like "conquistador" or "conquistadora." Then Rosendo said clearly and slowly: "I know you'll take care of Consuelo! Meanwhile, he had begun to rub down his ulcered arms with his hands.

"What is it, my boy?" the old Yank whispered close to his ear. "Sure, we'll take care of her, if that's what you mean."

But, in reality, Rosendo was not talking to him at all; he was kneeling before his little shrine of the Virgin in the dark Cathedral at Santa Fe, and he was telling La Conquistadora, his Lady of Victory, to make Consuelo listen to him in the bright dance-hall down on the Agua Fria. The image, however, nodded her head sideways, saying that he was not going to the Agua Fria dance, but must enter the hall of Paradise to join his little mother. That is why the old man heard Rosendo mutter, "I know you'll take care of Consuelo!" And that is why Rosendo was rubbing the dried ulcers from his arms; he was saying to the Virgin: "I enter Heaven like this? Look, Mother, I have been making adobes all day by the *acequia madre,* and the mud's dried all over me."

Part Five
Guitars and Adobes

8

Doña Isabel was holding a consultation with her husband some three weeks after Rosendo Rael's death. Since the day Rosendo was laid away in the old adobe-walled graveyard on the southern slope of the Mora valley, Consuelo had remained with them without health and without memory, as a result of the many sad events that had swooped in battalions upon the Rael household. Lately, Consuelo had been showing signs of restlessness, which worried Doña Isabel.

"She talks so outlandishly," Doña Isabel said, "and she stutters so much. You know she hardly spoke at all while she was in bed. It's plain now that she can't remember a thing."

"Can't you make her recall nothing?" the old Yank suggested. "Why don't we talk to her about Rosendo and the kid?"

"I do talk about him; but she doesn't know who Rosendo was. Remember when we first took her to her house yesterday? She pointed to the angel above little Genoveva's bed, saying: 'I had an angel like that, Señora; I used to have a little angel like that!'"

"That's bad, dear Isabel. It's better she would have gone, too, like the others."

"Don't—don't say that!" the woman stopped him. "And yet, it's strange that Consuelo didn't die also. First little Genoveva went, when they were merrily planning to return home. Then Rosendo. You know how she wouldn't cry, and how of a sudden she screamed and I caught her in time as she swooned. To make matters worse, the baby came, a dead child—and then the smallpox. It's a wonder that she lives."

"And I say again, Isabel, that she ought to have died. Look at her face now and what it used to be!"

Without answering, Doña Isabel went to renew the fire in Consuelo's room. The October days had steadily become colder, and tomorrow was the second of November, All Soul's Day. As a gesture of piety and with hopes for Consuelo's memory, the good lady had planned to take Consuelo down town to Mass for the first time. They would both pray for Rosendo's soul, while the sight of other familiar objects might help her to grasp a few threads from the past. Perhaps, the Sisters at the convent might do something.

Consuelo was sitting in a low rocker near the fireplace, peering at the smoldering logs through the lattice of her joined fingers.

"Are you cold, Consuelo?"

"No, Señora," came the reply, falteringly. Turning her pockmarked face to her kind guardian, Consuelo smiled graciously. Doña Isabel did not like to see that smile; to her it was the hideous grin of a mask, an unworthy substitute for what had been in happier days. It made the old lady's heart heavy to think that this could be the young wife of Rosendo Rael, a señorita so beautiful, so graceful, so neat. Now she did not care about her personal appearance, as if cognizant of the spoiled features—that face gouged by the poisoned fingernails of *la viruela,* which made Consuelo look much older and not like Consuelo at all.

"Your man was telling me," Consuelo spoke brokenly, "that the wolves are hungry and coming down from the sierra."

"I didn't know that," said Doña Isabel.

"I heard them last night."

"So?"

"Yes." Consuelo watched the woman nourish the coals and feed the flames. After a pause, she said: "Señora, I was thinking."

"Thinking what, Consuelo?"

"I don't think my name is Consuelo, as you call me."

"Why, sure it is, my dear girl!"

"No, Señora. I had a little angel once who loved me. She called me Margarita. My name is Margarita!"

"Oh," said Doña Isabel, turning to go out, when her husband appeared at the door. He carried a large green box in his arms.

"Look, Isabel, look! I had forgotten all about the money I put in here until today, when you and me started talking about Rosendo. The money's still in here, together with a crazy old fiddle!" He opened the box.

Doña Isabel had not known what the box contained; in fact, she had not thought of it during the past few weeks. The Rael house had been locked all this time, while she and her husband focused all their care on the unfortunate young woman whom they loved as a daughter. "It's strange," the lady said, "that we never gave that money a thought."

"How could we Isabel, with this poor girl on our hands, like she was. I was a-feared she might pass off any minute. It might have been better—"

"Not so loud," Doña Isabel interrupted him, "Don't say that—please."

"But the fiddle! It's a queer-shaped varmint, ain't it? Half guitar, a fourth mandolin, and the rest I don't know what!"

Consuelo had left her chair to look at the object of admiration. Picking it out of the case, she said with an air of recognition: "I know what this is. It's my little angel's violin." This said, she put it back.

"The jig there must have belonged to the baby, our godchild, eh? I never seen it, did you, Isabel?"

"I saw the box," Doña Isabel answered, "the day the baby died. But you're not leaving the money in there!" she exclaimed as he replaced the lid.

"Why not, honey?" replied the old man. "It's hers, and we'll just save it in here for her. Maybe something'll turn up soon and make her come to. She'll need it then."

After returning to her chair, Consuelo began to move her fingers across her lap, as though it were a keyboard. The two gaped at her wonderingly.

"What's the dear child up to?" the old man asked his wife.

Consuelo turned around. "I'm playing a song," she said with a grin, "See? It's about a little star..."

On All Soul's Day, the Mora valley lay draped in white, like a mammoth sugar-bowl. Doña Isabel arose early and went into Consuelo's room, as she intended to drive her down to Mass. To her amazement, Consuelo was not in the room. The bed lay untouched. The heavy coat and woolen mufflers were gone which Doña Isabel had set out for her morning trip to the church. So was the green box from the table! With a cry of alarm, the poor lady ran out to tell her husband.

They looked for Consuelo everywhere; the sheds, barns, the Rael house, all were searched to no avail. Presently, the whole village had joined in the search. After every structure in the valley had been examined in vain, all arrived at the conclusion that the young woman had gone away from the valley. Theories sprouted, as it were from the snow, as to the possible direction she might have taken. The snow, however, had obliterated all tracks and trails. "She must have left after we went to bed," Doña Isabel said, mournfully, "because I noticed it was snowing at midnight already."

That night, searching posses that had gone out in the morning in all directions, returned with empty hands. Those who had combed the mountains westward brought sickening reports of having sighted a mountain lion, as also several wolves and coyotes. A man who had logically searched eastwards to Las Vegas, the nearest railroad town, was told by a yardman of a lone woman who had boarded a westbound train. The station operator, however, did not remember having sold a ticket to the person described.

A few days later, Doña Isabel and her husband found themselves in Santa Fe, looking for their lost protege. Their hearts, which had been hanging to this last fiber of hope, almost broke when no sign of the fugitive appeared in her own city. The inhabitants, of course, still remembered Consuelo and Rosendo well, it was only about three years since they had gone away; but they had not seen Consuelo. Maybe she was dead, somewhere. *Quién sabe?*

As a last resort, the bereaved couple knocked at the old Ortega home. They had purposely left that place till the last, so as to feed the waning hopes. Pablito opened a window and looked out at them with a frozen frown.

"Are you Pablito, Consuelo's brother?" asked Doña Isabel.

"Yes."

"Have you seen your sister?"

"No," he said, slamming the window shut.

. . . .

In the morning of the feast of the Immaculate Conception, 1923, Doña Isabel, already a widow of more than twenty-five years, was walking home from Mass in the old Mora church when an automobile brushed her to the ground. Being an infirm and old woman, she died from the effects some time later, and with her died in Mora the dim memory of Rosendo Rael, his wife, and their baby.

In the latter part of September of the year 1929, a singular accident occurred in Santa Fe. It arrested the attention of the ancient city. As with all mishaps in modern times, the occurrence was gradually forgotten by all,

She came early to the Cathedral.

save by three individuals who knew a little more than the rest, but who were baffled by an unusual aspect of the accident that had for a moment disturbed the dreams of modern Santa Fe, the City Old and Different.

Santa Fe is not exactly the same as in the days of her first Archbishop, when overland stages and mercantile caravans drew up at the end of the famous Santa Fe Trail after traversing the plains from St. Louis, the mountains from Los Angeles, or the deserts from Chihuahua. True, the city stands on the same spot, with her historic landmarks intact, and the narrow streets follow their original meandering courses.

But these streets are now paved and they are thick with motor traffic. The plaza, too, has a new dress. The white wooden colonnades and the double porches with their spindled banisters which had sprung with the American occupation, like unsightly mushrooms in a flower bed, had given way to the upright, conventional scrolled-tin and brick fronts of Main Street. These also have gradually ceded their place to more fitting buildings of Spanish, Pueblo Indian or Colonial Santa Fe architecture, a scheme which would have delighted the eye of the old Archbishop in his time. Seligman's store is still there, also La Fonda, but no more the unsightly frame toadstools of the transition period.

Farther up the Calle de San Francisco stands the old Cathedral, as in the days when Doña Genoveva Ortega and Consuelo went to Mass or Vespers, when Rosendo visited his shrine, when Pablito rang the chime-toned bells. Further on, the purple and silver tips of tamarisks and spruces still sway above the original adobe walls of the Archbishop's garden. Across the street is the Sisters' Convent and Academy; the garden wall has been rebuilt of brick, but the wooden gate is there, recalling the hour when two lovers trysted there. Until a few years ago, a giant cottonwood stood in the middle of the street farther up on the Alameda. It had to give way to the merciless lava-like flow of the modern pavement.

The *old acequia madre* itself, however, still ripples along its serpentine, willow-walled bed, like the proverbial river—going down forever, but never gone. This hoary irrigation ditch, with its silver threads of cold mountain water, is Santa Fe's best-preserved relic. The road alongside is the same road, trampled and gored by wheels, modern and ancient, but rolling dustily along, unimpaired and unpaved. Yet the green fields are almost all gone; where Rosendo used to make his adobes and spread them under the sun to harden, one sees houses and houses of Spanish or pueblo pattern, but all of adobe, basking in the sun or hiding behind the very willows of the *acequia.*

The sunken road, really an arroyo bed, still shows the way as of old to the house with the ancient apricot trees by the kitchen door. Until a few years ago, an exotic and simpleminded old hermit lived in it, and there was talk about town that he had a treasure buried under an iron skillet in his fireplace. The old man either died or moved away. An artist who had purchased the house enlarged it considerably, added a second story to it in pueblo fashion, and artistically spared the old apricots. As for the skillet saga, no one knows

The Acequia Madre road cuts into the Camino del Monte Sol, a unique thoroughfare that winds up an incline in the direction of the Sun Mount.

whether the former occupant of the house took the treasure, or whether the new one found a skillet at all.

In the artists' settlement further up on the Monte Sol, it is customary in summer evenings to throw open the odd-shaped casement windows, not so much for the cool mountain breezes as for the sounds that are borne along by them. Sometimes there is a wake in one of the humble residences somewhere on the canyon road; soon the *alabados* float along to eager ears, loud dirges that bring to mind the Kol Nidri or the Lamentations of Holy Week. Ordinarily, it is the clean-cut chords of guitars which break the silence of cool summer evenings. Voices, young voices sound forth in old Spanish romances, old voices join in, voices of men and women, voices of girls and youths, children's voices around the guitar—happy voices!

A trio of young writers had learned to listen for a certain sound that came from the slope opposite the Atalaya. From afar off it sounded like an old piano, out of style, out of tune; the melody, or discord rather, was always the same. At times it could be recognized as the well-known "La Estrellita." What made these three persons listen, however, was the fact that, during the slow and labored playing, they heard the raucous chords, not of a piano out of tune, but of an untuned guitar. Another reason for listening was the person who dwelt in the little old house whence the sounds were broadcast across to the neighboring slope.

The inmate of this house was a pauper woman, of uncertain age, who was seen to walk down to the plaza every day. The face under her small black bonnet was withered, oily, and, if one looked closely, deeply pockmarked. To speak, she stuttered at every word. Her perennial dress consisted of a grey skirt and a red sweater, both sadly in need of repair and washing, if not substitution. She came early to the Cathedral, bringing her meager breakfast along. The first Mass over, she would come outside and eat, then reenter the Cathedral when the eight o'clock Mass was about to begin. Who the woman was, no one knew for sure. Nobody remembered when she had come to Santa Fe; she belonged there, they knew, in that little adobe house where she had lived for decades. The people regarded her with a familiar indifference, having a somewhat coarse nickname for her. She answered to the name of Margarita.

One quiet evening in late September, 1929, an evening made more quiet by an impending storm, these particular individuals were listening to the strange music. More than ever before, the melody bore a likeness to "La Estrellita," though the strains were much broken by uncanny guitar-like sounds. Suddenly, the storm broke loose. It was a cloudburst. Casement windows were pulled in, doors were closed, lights turned on. Still, when the noise of falling waters abated for a bare second, the listeners seemed to hear that playing, as if the musician had set herself to rival the clouds in noise. Then they heard a dull, weighty sound, as when a charge of dynamite goes off many

The lonely old house opposite the Atalaya had fallen in.

miles away. A tree, they guessed, a big pine had been felled by lightning in the Santa Fe Canyon.

The next morning, it was found that the lonely old house opposite the Atalaya had fallen in, killing the woman Margarita. The old structure, it was said, had never been repaired; the mid-summer rains and winter snows had eaten away the adobes under and around the heavy log beams, so that they had slipped away with the last night's rain, bringing down with them the foot-deep layer of earth which made up the flat roof. The men who dug away the debris found the woman in a crouched posture on the floor, hardly bruised, as the beams had missed her, but drowned beneath the thick cataract of sand and dirt.

Prompted by a curiosity which had been fed by the nightly recitals, the woman's audience of three went to the place later on in the day, to ascertain what musical instrument she had played. To their surprise, they found no instrument whatsoever among the ruins. The men who had dug Margarita out denied that they had found a guitar. Two of them said they had seen an old table-shaped piano, and they pointed to the spot where it had stood. The other diggers, however, denied it emphatically. There was a fist-fight, almost, but no definite answer to the mission of the three inquirers.

Next day the body of Margarita, enclosed in a fine casket, lay in the Cathedral during the Mass for the Dead. The St. Vincent de Paul Society, which for years had taken care of her in as far as a secret pride of hers would allow, were the cause of these ceremonies. Some of the most prominent men of the city, members of the Society, knelt beside the coffin as pallbearers. Old, old women in black shawls filed by and looked wistfully at the dead face, features which, in spite of the pock-marks, looked as though they might have been beautiful once upon a time. "I saw that face when I was a girl," one old lady said to herself. "Who? Margarita? Margarita what?" Others would turn to their neighbors and whisper: "How beautiful and natural she looks!"

The three authors, however, had to remain satisfied with an unsolved mystery, a mystery as intangible and uninterpretable as the one that holds the Old Santa Fe with the New in spite of the years, a tie of race, faith, and traditions, of love and romance, of guitars and adobes.

EARLY ILLUSTRATED STORIES
of the SOUTHWEST

Illustrations *by* Fray Angélico Chávez

Spanish and Irish

(October 1929)

Lupe Ortiz had her Spanish up; Rose Murray had her Irish up; and only a spark of an idea was needed to get them both in dutch.

Both young ladies rested their eighteen summers on either side of the *tapia,* or low adobe wall separating their respective back yards, as they faced each other in mild suspense.

"See here, Lupe," spoke the colleen, "we'll have to settle this some way or another. You want to be leading lady, don't you? Hm? So do I."

Now, the Academy was to stage a play in the near future. With the exception of the leading lady, the entire cast had already been selected; but Sister Antonia could not easily choose the girl for the lead. Lupe and Rose were the best talent in the school, and one was as talented as the other. To choose one was to disturb a nest of rattlesnakes, and the timid Sister would not do that for all the hollyhocks in Santa Fe. Only one alternative remained, and that was to ask these two girls to settle it between themselves. Thus, Sister Antonia shrewdly washed her hands of the matter, and this is why the colleen and the señorita were now in secret conference, neither nation willing to give in to the other, and both unwilling to sever feminal diplomatic relations.

"I have it!" Lupe at last exclaimed. "Let us gamble for the part; say—for example, a few sets of tennis."

Rose Murray thought for a moment. "You're smart, all right. And you very well know that I'm out of practice." A moment of silence, and she continued, "How about this idea? Let us both disguise ourselves and meet somewhere. Whoever recognizes the other one first is the winner!"

"That suits me," Lupe agreed. "Make-up and masquerade are quite appropriate for our contest. But when and where do we meet?"

"At three o'clock this afternoon. Lupe, you name the place."

"How about that corner of the Archbishop's Garden—by the bridge?"

"All right," Rose replied, and they shook hands on it and parted.

Lupe Ortiz had her mind set on being the leading female of the play, but she also knew that Rose Murray was no less ambitious. How should she disguise herself? "Ah, I have it," she breathed exultantly, and straightway began to make preparations for her incognito.

Shortly before three, she was making a stealthy detour toward the trysting place. But who could have made out the slim, graceful señorita in the person of a typical Santa Clara Indian woman, buxom and brown? Her face was dark and wrinkled beneath a shaggy mass of oily hair, bobbed at the temples and tied on the back of the head with strips of scarlet wool; the white buckskin booties, enveloping her legs up to the knees, and the tightly wrapped blanket, bringing out the contour of a multitude of concealed pillows, made her lateral girth quite that of the many squaws that roamed the streets.

At last she came in sight of the Garden;—but, horror of horrors—there on the assigned corner, holding a store of pottery in his arms, stood a real Indian. Quickly, Lupe darted behind a thick poplar near at hand, whence she could still see the man. She was not very desirous of being mistaken for a squaw—not by an Indian brave. Then and there, she resolved to wait until the Indian moved away, or until Rose would appear.

Quickly Lupe darted behind a tree.

But Big Chief Pot-Seller was a stubborn squatter. He sat down on the curb, laid his earthenware on the sidewalk, and began to roll a cigarette, while the girl behind the tree stamped her feet and gnashed her teeth with the impatience of her sex. Still, no Rose appeared, and still Mr. Redskin squatted. Fifteen minutes passed—a half hour. Disgusted, Lupe sneaked back home, laying innocent maledictions, as she went, on the Irish girl that "had played her dirty."

After washing up and returning to her former self, Lupe went to Rose's house. The first thing Rose said on opening the door was: "Well, you're a sport, you are; keeping me waiting almost an hour!"

"Waiting?" retorted the Spanish lass. "What about yourself! I waited that much for you—"

"Not by the garden corner," Rose interrupted her.

"No, not there," the other replied. "I was hiding behind a tree. You see—an Indian was standing at the corner, and I was dressed like an Indian woman."

"So that explains why I had to sit down on the street, eh? And smoke a couple o' dozen cigarettes while waiting for you to make your appearance!"

"Rose, you win," sobbed Lupe, embracing her. Thus was war averted between two countries.

Old Magdalena's Friend

(December 1929)

Clara Boyton had come to Santa Fe for no reason at all one week ago. She only wanted to forget— and also remember— George Duncan. For the last two years, she had traveled all over the world; had seen Paris, Rome, Shanghai, Sydney; had loitered awhile in Honolulu, Tangiers, Tokyo,—she had been almost everywhere save at the two Poles. And all these travels she had made by herself, and for what? To forget the man she loved and, perchance, to find him, the man she had lost through her father's fault, the only other friend she had in the world. And now she had found "a place different," a quiet spot in her own United States, but she could not tell how long her restlessness would allow her to remain in Santa Fe.

The friendly southwest sun was kissing the west walls of the "Santa Fe" house she had rented, and Clara could not resist its romantic charms. Bringing a light chair outside, she sat down and began to muse in careless contentment. The bells began to chime in the Cathedral towers a few squares away. Clara, struck by the musical interruption of a more musical stillness, listened with a quiet, breathless attention. Ah, it was Sunday, and that was a call for Vespers. Vespers? The word sounded very distant in her mind. Vespers! The young lady laughed to herself. Vespers meant nothing to a despairing woman who had not been to Mass, or even within a church, for ten, long, heartless years.

Old Magdalena, Clara's lovable housekeeper and landlady, came out in a hurry, her three-foot rosary swinging like a censer in her hand, as she wrapped her seven-league black shawl over her stooped shoulders.

"I go to the *Bendición,* Miss Clara," she said, very much out of breath. "Soon, pronto I come for to make the supper. What you want for supper, Miss?"

"Anything you like, Magdalena," came the reply from the chair. "Say a little prayer for me, will you?" she shouted at the vanishing form of the old woman; then she laughed at her little joke.

Again the chimes in the afternoon stillness, and again Clara's thoughts went back over a space of ten years. Vespers? Yes, the vesper bells were ringing at St. Patrick's, in New York, when they parted. She and George were returning to her home in George's shining, purring car, when she told him a little bit of her secret. Her father had to leave the country, and she was leaving with him. He had no other person in the world but herself. But where were they going? She knew not, she could not tell. Neither did she know when she would return. But George Duncan was a gentleman as well as a lover and he questioned her no further.

"But promise me, Clara, promise me," he said in tears, "promise to come back, if you do return, come back to me. I will always wait for you somewhere—"

"George dear," her tears drowned her words, "I'll come back to you someday—we'll wed at St. Pat's—someday—"

Thus they had parted ten years ago in old New York, a city that was beautiful then, when vesper bells were ringing for the beloved and her lover.

But the years of exile with her father, though made as comfortable for her as a wealthy parent could afford, were years of anguish, of longing, of despair. That little Spanish town near Buenos Aires was peaceful and beautiful, but to her bereaved heart, South America was as far as the moon from George Duncan, for nobody knew where she had gone. It was a "political" crime her father had committed, and he could not undergo the penalty imposed by his country by being imprisoned and impoverished. No, not while he had his daughter to care for. And, as Clara did not wish to disturb the peace he had found in exile, she told him nothing of her sorrow, and thus they lived in the little Argentine town until Mr. Boyton died, after eight years of longing on the part of the girl.

At her father's death, Clara found herself free and with an ample inheritance that would support her for life, even if she did not find her love awaiting back home. This last, indeed, was not her thought until she arrived at New York. To her sorrow, she learned that the Duncans had moved to England just the year before, and that George had probably gone with the family, George gone with the family! George, then, was not married, she thought. And the bells of St. Patrick's began to ring, but they meant nothing to Clara Boyton now. Religion was nothing to her, for God had not been kind to her; not now that she had returned and found George gone. Was there a kind God? No, she assured herself; but there was a beloved and true George waiting for her somewhere. "To England," she resolved to go, and to England she sailed.

But neither in England, nor in Scotland, nor in Ireland, could she find George Duncan. All over the world she traveled, seeking, longing, finding nothing. Where was he? Surely, he was either married or dead. But, no! Clara could not think that. She had lost confidence in God, and her confidence in man was also waning. And here she was remembering and recalling, when she had come to forget.

After a while, old Magdalena came up to the door puffing like a miniature locomotive, her rosary dangling at her side like a loose, heavy chain.

"Oh, Miss Clara," she whispered between puffs, "it is almost six, and you still sit you down outside. *Dios Santo,* Miss, I pray too much, the time goes like that!" and she snapped her tan, toil-worn fingers.

"And what were you praying for, Magdalena?"

"For you, Miss, for you. You see, I see you so sad and I pray for you to San Antonio—Saynt Ant'ny the Americans call him. Oh, you are so nice, I wish you was a *católica,* Miss Clara."

"I was a Catholic once," spoke the girl, rather sadly. "I have not been to church, though, for many, many years; and I'm beginning to think that I have not been fair to my God. You look so happy, even though you are poor, while I have all kinds of riches and am sad. Magdalena, do you think St. Anthony would help me find something or someone I want very badly, if I returned to God?"

"Why, sure, Miss Clara. Pray to the good Saint. Me and him is fine friends, and I will pray and introduce you to him, no? He sure makes answer, Miss."

Moved by the old woman's faith, the girl pondered a little, and a new confidence took hold of her soul. Telling her landlady to have supper ready for her return, she donned Magdalena's shawl and in the evening dusk made her way to the Cathedral. There she wept and prayed, prayed and wept, and asked forgiveness from her Sacramental Lord Whom she had for so long abandoned. The Angelus rang, and her heart simultaneously poured forth a fervent prayer for George Duncan. Finding her way to St. Anthony's chapel-altar, she knelt at the communion rail and gazed inquiringly at the beautiful statue of the Paduan. "Oh, Anthony," she prayed, "you have brought me back to God through an old lady's prayers. Hear my humble prayer, dear Saint, and bring my lover back to me."

As Clara Boyton prayed, and promised generous alms to the Saint, her attention was arrested by the peculiar gaze that was carved and painted on the eyes of the statue. It seemed at times as though the eyes met her own; but then she thought they rather rested on the railing before her. Clara smiled and, in her innocent humor, said: "And, besides all this money that I promise you, I'll ask the Fathers if I can wash your altar cloths and also make some new ones for you."

"Oh, Miss Clara, you look so different—so sweet—like our Lady Mary with my black *tápalo* on!" Thus Magdalena greeted her. "What did you promise San Antonio?"

"Why, I promised him money and money, but he didn't seem to be satisfied. So I promised to make new cloths for his altar and to wash the old ones besides."

"Oh, how nice," said the old woman, very devoutly. "Also," she said, "when you talk of washing, it reminds me I must wash and iron those shirts tomorrow."

"Shirts? I didn't know you took in washing!" Clara exclaimed, surprised.

"Oh, yes. I wash the shirts for an artist—a picture-painter, you see. He ain't married and he likes my washing. Oh, you should meet him, Miss Clara—a very nice man and a fine *católico* is Mr. George Duncan."

Sierra Moon

(February 1930)

We had just finished our supper on the mountain. Encouraged by a good mouthful of dry, fragrant, resinous piñon branches, the camp-fire lost all thoughts of death and began to lick the cool night air with voracious red tongues amid the hungry crackling of the wood. As the altitude of the sierras made the air cooler every moment, we four crowded around the flames, Fernando the cowboy, young city-bred Flicker, myself, and Buffalo Bill—Buffalo Bill was Flicker's dog.

Our little camp, if we could call it that, sat on a rocky promontory that faced a higher range of pine-clad bluffs just across a deep ravine or canyon. Together with the heights and the dark forests around us, this canyon seemed to make the night arrive before her time, for its hollow depths at the foot of our dizzy camp castle almost literally blew up puffs of mysterious darkness into the chilly atmosphere.

Just as the moon began to lift an opaque amber eyebrow over the ridges

The moon began to lift an opaque amber eyebrow over the ridges.

across the canyon, the tips of the taller pines in the ravine returned to our view, and Flicker, ever breathing forth his metropolitan book-ideas, whispered with a shiver:

"Gosh, don't it look ghoulish, though? This silent darkness, the ghostly trees—I sure wouldn't be surprised if there were some spooky stories about this place!"

"No, Flicker," I promptly replied, this is God's country. Besides, men are needed to make ghosts, and who ever lived here at the very source of the little Río del Pueblo?"

"Well, fishers and hunters, I suppose," Flicker retorted. "Fellows like you and me, like Fernando here—"

"Fishermen? Haw!" I laughed. "Why, men that can give up their work for fishing around here are found only in Taos or Mora, the nearest settlements that can be called towns—and they have their good trout-streams near by."

Flicker did not answer, as he was curiously watching Fernando. Fernando, in turn, was watching the moon, a large, bright thing that had floated like a balloon above the mountains and was outlining everything sharply, even the sly smile on the silent Westerner. Aware of our inquiring glances, the hardened and experienced Fernando turned that smile on us and pointed to the bottom of the canyon. We three, including the dog, followed the sights of his pistol-like finger, and the cowboy spoke:

"See that white something at the bottom of that gully?"

At first we could see nothing save the dark hollows interspersed with large boulders and towering evergreens. Then my city friend pointed with a gasp at a small white mass that at first resembled a snowflake as seen through a microscope. Slowly and with trembling excitement, I made out what seemed to be a collection of white, bleached bones, the legs and arms disorderly detached from a column of vertebrae to which clung a number of slender ribs pointing at the sky. In the moonlight, the sight was more than gruesome. I looked at Fernando, he looked at me, and we both turned our gaze on Flicker, while our canine comrade scanned us all with an expression that could have meant, translated from dog language, "These humans are funny. What are they scared about?"

"Skeleton," Flicker breathed, hoarsely and softly.

Fernando nodded in assent and began to examine us with a queer smile, saying, "And there's a story about that thing which I alone know. Are you boys too scared to hear it?"

We did not have to admit our terror; we showed it, even though we tried to dissemble. But our man did not have to be told that we were only too anxious to hear about the thing, and he began:

> Last year, about this time, I was out here rounding up some horses for my old boss, Old Man Bailey. Of course, I wasn't sure that the animals had strayed up this far, but I had come with the intention of asking old Isidro, who lives alone upon this sierra, if he

had not seen any of them pass by. That first day I came up, I was resting, down in this same canyon by that path which you can see from here—right around that cottonwood. That's the only cottonwood down there, and it means water—there's a spring right by it. It was about noon, and I was just about to take a nap after my dinner. Suddenly, I heard a harsh command and a noise of shuffling feet and loose stones from this same hill on which we're camping. I looked up and saw two figures coming down the path.

Immediately I recognized them both. The one uttering the commands was old Isidro himself, and the other, straining under the load of wood on her bent back, was Ramona. I knew them both—sure—I come up this way every year. Well, I stood up and waited for them to descend toward the spring.

Neither of the two had seen me. The ancient hermit and woodcutter was too busy with his cane, which he brought down at intervals upon the back of the poor thing before him. Ramona, as she drew nearer, seemed to be not at all right. Her legs were not so sure, it seemed, and, every time she halted for breath and the stick fell on her back, she would turn her head and look at her master with large, brown, pleading eyes. Then she would clench her teeth with the stubborn determination of her race and sex and weakly pick her way down the treacherous path. I knew something would happen. Once or twice she stumbled and swayed, but again that stick in old Isidro's hand. Can't the old fool see, I told myself, that there is something wrong with her?

Fernando stopped for a moment and eyed us as though about to ask a question, for we, especially Flicker, seemed quite troubled. At last Flicker said with disgust, "Why, Fernando, don't you think that was downright slavery?"

The storyteller only shrugged his shoulders and patted the dog's shaggy mane unconsciously. "Well, I suppose it was some sort of slavery," he said, "but I'm sure there's no law in the country against it. Everybody does it, and these mountain people have to live—but wait till I finish the story!" And he watched us with mild interest as we looked over our shoulders at the white thing in the gully below.

"As the two reached the bed of the canyon," Fernando continued, "I spied a pair of vultures hovering over us. They are smart birds, these. Now I was sure something would happen —and it did, too. A few paces away from me, Ramona stopped, her eyes rolling in agony. She sank to her knees without uttering a sound and rolled over on her side, dead. Isidro stood motionless, even after he discovered me advancing toward the scene. He was confounded, shocked, by the suddenness of it. There were tears in his wrinkled, red eyes as he looked at me, and he addressed me as though he had but seen me the day before.

"'I didn't know she was sick,' the old man sobbed. 'She was all right early in the morning when we came up for wood.' There was real grief in the old man's actions, and I pitied him much more than I did the dead. After a few moments, devoted to consolation and kind words on my part, I helped him remove the object of his sorrow from the path and into that gully down there. Isidro himself took the burden from her back and placed it on his own shoulders.

"We stood there for a long time. Boys, it was something sad to see a poor, lonely, old man sob as Isidro did. He was alone now, for Ramona had been his sole companion for many years, and I doubt whether he shed as many tears for his wife many years ago after whom he had named Ramona. At last I persuaded him to leave the place.

"As the vultures above our heads began to circle closer and closer to the gully, we turned from the sad place in silence, Isidro gave one last sad look at her, at those little hoofs and massive ears that would wag no more, and we moved away, Isidro continually swearing that there never was in the whole Southwest a burro so faithful and so lovable as his Ramona."

The Dude of Anchor Ranch

(August 1929)

Tim McKay stood before a large mirror in Father Donovan's study, his whole body at attention, as he examined his perfect form with an air of sadness and bewilderment.

"Well, Tim" Father Donovan spoke, "I suppose we must take the West Point surgeon at his word. Of course, you cannot tell by externals whether you have tuberculosis or not, but the doctor did find it out by his examination. This, however, should not discourage you."

"It is not that, Father," the young man turned around, "I am throwing no blame on the Academy doc. I guess he did his duty in having me dismissed for that. What gets me is that I don't know what to do or where to go."

"Well, as I told you a week ago, why not go West? A few months of roughing it will cure you, Tim. If you don't believe me, ask any doctor. You see, the disease is just starting in one of your lungs, and I know that the West will stop it. Besides, you'll enjoy the trip—the scenery is grand."

McKay laughed aloud and again stood straight before the mirror. Catching the priest's puzzled look in the mirror, he turned to him and said: "I was at a 'talkie' last night—a picture of 'Old Arizona,' or something like that. And you should have seen the legs on those cowboys! They certainly must be strange folks to be built that way. Why, when I think of my own straight pegs being like that, I have to laugh—"

"Oh, well, that comes from riding horses all their lives—"

"Horses? Pooh! It takes more than a horse to do that, Father." As the priest said nothing, Tim took him by the shoulders, and spoke in a deliberate tone. "Father Donovan, I'm taking your advice. I'll start packing and beat it to New Mexico. I'll ride the T. B.'s off on horseback. And, O boy—the scenery. By the way, what is the name of your friend's ranch?"

"It's Anchor Ranch, in Otowi Canyon—a beautiful place. And it's about forty miles from Old Santa Fe. Now, go with my blessing, Timmy boy. And be good."

"Thank you, Father, and good-bye. But, remember, no bow-legs for me."

It was three months now that Anchor Ranch had had the merry and pleasant dude in the person of Timothy McKay. The word "dude" among the ranchers does not necessarily mean a fop. It means exactly what "barbarian" meant to the Greeks and Romans. In short, a dude is a non-cowboy, and this is why Tim accepted the term with good grace. He did not care to be called a cowboy, anyway—not for their legs, at least.

By this time, Tim had practically and literally shaken off the tubercular germs by flinging them away in healthy breaths as he rode into the pure air, firmly set astride a broad Western saddle that was strapped on a broad Western mustang. Such was his zeal in regaining his precious health, that he always lived out of doors; and, if he had to travel far, he declined to use the kind ranch-owner's car, but always went to places on horseback, no matter whether the journey was twenty or even forty miles long. Day in and day out, the young ex-cadet rode up the mountains, through the pines, and down

As to bow-legs, Father, you were right.

the canyons; or he went down to the desert, picturing himself to be one of the "riders of the purple sage," where he galloped and trotted through the sage and the cedar, whooping and yelling in clouds of white and yellow dust under God's own turquoise sky, as he called it.

Frequent trips to the interesting cliff-dwellings, relics of time immemorial, and to the picturesque ancient City of St. Francis feasted his artistic nature; weekly trips down Otowi Canyon to the Valley of the Rio Grande, where rested a number of quaint and sacred Missions feasted his fervent Catholic soul; and, as all these trips were on horseback, they not only cured him of his malady, but also made him stronger and healthier than he had ever been before. Yet, they also did something else.

One evening, as Tim McKay rode up Otowi Canyon toward the ranch, he stopped and dismounted in order to witness the most beautiful sunset he had thus far seen. The western sky itself was indeed beautiful, but Tim turned around to see a more gorgeous sight that presented itself to him in the lowlands. Miles and miles of rugged and fantastically shaped cliffs danced in rich colors of deep purples, blue, red, orange and shining gold. The desert was a crimson carpet, dotted with purple spots; the sky an enchanting jade; the clouds a rolling surf of opalescence.

As he filled his sentimental soul with all this ravishing beauty, his gaze fell on the road immediately before him, and his eyes opened wide in good-humored astonishment. The setting sun behind him was throwing his shadow in sharp relief on the white gravel highway. There it was—was it his own shadow?—the shape of the sombrero that he wore, of his big shoulders, and of a pair of legs that formed a veritable elongated circle!

A few days later, Father Donovan opened a letter with "Otowi" inked on the stamp. The first thing he read was the postscript, printed in large, bold characters:

"P. S.—AS TO BOW-LEGS, FATHER, YOU WERE RIGHT."

Romance of *El Caminito*

(March 1930)

El Caminito is a popular thoroughfare in Santa Fe. It is not a boulevard, nor a street, nor a road; but neither can it be called an alley. To refer to it as a lane would be a gross exaggeration. The only term for it is "El Caminito," the Spanish diminutive for "road," and this also would be too big, were it not that in this case the thoroughfare makes the name, and not vice-versa. But, for the sake of means of expression, we may call it a mere path, a very narrow path, defined at one end by adobe walls and board fences, but lined most of the way by pesky willows and prickly wildrose bushes that make it necessary for the traveler to hold his hands high up in the air or deep in his pockets. Despite all these obstructions, lines of people use it day after day, as it affords a very handy "short-cut" between the ancient plaza and the many homes at one end of the city.

Hence, nobody would be surprised that Pancho and Mercedes met here every morning on their way to school. Pancho was a new boy in town and did not know Mercedes, nor did he care to know her, for that matter. Mercedes, on the other hand, winsome and coquettish, knew a handsome lad when she saw one. But Pancho, what with his natural timidity and reserve, was a hard trout to land, and he either followed her down the path or walked ahead, politely parting the brambles and bushes, but without a word or look after the usual matutinal "Hello."

To Mercedes, this conduct seemed rather foolish—ranch-like. In fact, her patience had been so taxed at times, that she often tried to snob him with the hope of curing him. But this ruse disconcerted the impenetrable young Gareth not at all. "You lead and I follow," seemed to be his knightly motto through the labyrinths of El Caminito, while the snobbish lynette made her weary way through the thorns, quite sure in her own mind that two persons could easily walk abreast, if only the other party were willing. And so, Mercedes planned and revolved things in her head with an ever-increasing zest, as the indomitable blood of the old *Conquistadores* in her veins spurred her on to glorious conquest.

It happened one day, after several weeks of this "lead and follow" routine, that Pancho really did look at her and smile in a very friendly, though somewhat distant, manner. This took her by storm, as she could not guess what had brought about such a change. "Perhaps," she thought, "perhaps—could it be this book?" The book she had with her was a large blue volume with red back and corners, and most of its leaves were filled with a motley variety of stamps. Maybe, it was the stamp book that caught his eye! Could he be a stamp-collector, too? This was possible, as there is surely more than one stamp-fiend in the Southwest. For, wherever there is mail, there are also stamps, and the "Amalgamated Stamp Corporations" of distant cities are sure to follow with their far-reaching tentacles. And Pancho a stamp-lover! Mercedes knew that her stamp book should complete and would close the romantic dream triangle of El Caminito.

On the following morning, the big blue book, suspended in mid-air, slowly meandered between the walls of rose and willow, clutched tightly in a

Something disturbed the bushes.

dainty white hand which peeped from a black velvet sleeve. Attached to the other end of the sleeve came a prim little jacket of the same material, fringed with a flutter of short, white skirts. And in them came Mercedes.

"Let me look at your book, will you?" spoke a voice, and the girl startled. She looked up and discovered a blushing, grinning Pancho blocking the path, his hand already on the book.

"Sure," she breathed with sudden ecstasy, "I'll show it to you." And the book was immediately opened on twenty eager fingers, all of which paged and pushed and turned its many stamp-laden leaves in nervous excitement.

"Austria, Spain, British Isles—" Pancho kept on muttering, "Japan, Denmark—why, this is rich! Oh, isn't that a peach of a stamp. That's a dandy—say, you have a wonderful collection—er—"

"Oh, yes," she answered, very musically, "but I wish I had another triangle stamp of Liberia, and then that set would be complete. Now, you didn't look at my Papal States yet," and she turned another page.

"Well, of all—why, this is great!" the boy exclaimed, unable to contain himself any longer. "Please, won't you give me this extra Papal State?"

"Here," she replied, promptly, and she handed him the tiny paper treasure.

"Thanks, dear," he burst forth in his exultation; then, he became a little disturbed at the deep blush on his companion's face and the expectant sparkle in her eye, and he wondered whether he had said something foolish. Anyway, he thought her very nice, and wished to repay her in some way or other.

"I—I want to tell you something," he stuttered, bashfully. A step and a noise as of disturbed bushes made him turn around, and he beheld one of the Padres coming down the path, probably on his way back from a sick-call. Immediately, Pancho hurried away and disappeared among the bushes in the opposite direction, while the girl stood motionless, not knowing whether to pity or to laugh at the youth's timidity and bashfulness.

Of course, they had to meet again; Mercedes knew that much. The next morning, as Pancho came sauntering along, she drew near to him and asked him very sweetly as to what he was going to say the day before.

"Oh, nothing, nothing," he answered, very much excited.

"Yes, you did want to say something," she prodded him, coyly. "Come, you'll tell me, won't you?"

"Well, you were so kind in giving me that Papal State—and you're so nice—why, I wanted to ask you if—"

"If what?" she prodded on, breathless with emotion.

"If you wanted," he muttered, "if you wanted a triangle stamp of mine to complete your Liberia set." This said, he turned and disappeared down the tangled ways of El Caminito.

The Blasphemer

(November 1929)

Buena Vista was a lively village before the Great War—and before new laws came to New Mexico. Set comfortably close to the pine-scattered foothills of the Rockies and overlooking the cattle-speckled plains, it was naturally the weekly rendezvous for the rough sons of this portion of the West. Two parallel rows of adobe huts and lumber shacks running up and down the slope defined what might have been Main Street. Isolated, at the uttermost extremity and close to the line of evergreens, rested a little church. At the opposite end, by the road that came in from the prairie, stood a saloon.

This was Sunday morning in Buena Vista. That is what any casual stranger might have concluded from his observations; for the missionary Padre had come, opened the church door, and rung the bell, while groups of black-shawled women were hurrying out of their dwellings, like broods of black hens running at the sound of grain shaken in a can. Also, if he had

sauntered into the imposing edifice on the other side of town, he would have known that the night before had been Saturday night.

On this particular morning, there was little life in Don Sabino's saloon. As usual, all the cowboys had come in the night before and had half wrecked the place in their revelry before they went away. Don Sabino himself, half-dazed and talkative, leaned his two hundred pounds of good nature among the broken bottles and glasses that lined the bar, while a handful of cow-punchers, who had awakened where they had unconsciously laid down, stared at him with bleary eyes. These children of the ranches were not really

bad *hombres*. The life they led had made them wild and prematurely old. Their pious Spanish mothers, it seemed, had not finished teaching them their prayers before they were already saddled to a horse and riding in the face of the western wind. Don Sabino, old in years and experience, was not only their bartender but also a father whom they all revered. Now that the husky old man felt particularly garrulous they listened with marked attention despite the sickly feeling in their heads.

"There goes the first bell for Mass," one of the cowboys spoke, as the mission bell pealed appealingly from the pines. "Just look at all the women going up the street!"

"Why, let the old women go to Mass if they want," drawled the bartender. "We men don't have to go to church." Setting his ample bosom firmly on the counter, Don Sabino leaned down and continued: "What is more, we don't belong there, anyway. What business have you blasted, drunken calves in the presence of the Sacrament? Answer me that."

"But," came in one of the men, "the poor Padre needs some extra dimes—"

"So?" Don Sabino interrupted him. "So? Are you sure that money of yours doesn't belong to me for all those glasses you broke and for all that liquor you spilled last night? Listen, that Padre does not need your money. He's rich enough without it. Besides, he does not work for every dollar he gets, while we have to break our necks on a steer to scratch a few cents. Let him keep away from this town if he doesn't like what I said—"

"You are right, Don Sabino!" The bartender stared with mouth agape at a new listener whom he had not noticed before. It was Zapata, that new cow-herder from Old Mexico, who spoke from the open door. "Yes, Señor, if there is anything these priests are after, it is the poor man's money." All the other men looked at him without breath or motion,—struck dumb, as it were. "Now, where I used to work, around Texas, we had a Protestant minister, and we never had to give him a penny. In fact, he and his good wife gave all sorts of clothes and food to our children. We didn't have to go to church either, just as long as we were Catholics no more. To speak the truth, there's where I found out that the Catholic Church is nothing but a creed of lies and a robber of the poor. Pooh! On the Sacrament!" And he made a blasphemous gesture at the church on the hill.

For a moment the cowboys remained confounded. But the richest part of their mothers' blood began to boil in their veins. Slowly and firmly, the big bartender moved away from the counter, not a word escaping his lips, his eyes fixed on the Mexican, but his feet slowly advancing toward the door. Suddenly, with a cataract of Spanish syllables, adapted from the English, Don Sabino launched himself upon the intruder, grasped him by the nape of the neck as though he were a mere pup, shook him, knocked him against the wall, dragged him outside, and, turning him around, used the heel of his boot in the exact manner with which he always hammered the stop on a whiskey cask. As the blasphemer raised himself from the ground, the bartender's fist shot out like a bronco's hoof, and Zapata lay motionless on the ground.

"Come on, sons of mine," shouted Don Sabino, hoarsely, "we're going to Mass. And, mind you, we're going to fill the basket for the Padre."

Notch Twenty-One

(September 1930)

Sheriff Miguel Armijo set his pistols, cocked and loaded, upon his office desk and leaned back on his swivel chair. His small eyes and big forehead registered intense excitement, while his big black mustachios went up and down with every twitch of his nervous lips. Close behind the broad-backed sheriff of San Miguel County, and in front of an open steel safe, sat young Jim Slocum, leisurely paging through the office books. He, too, had his six-shooters ready, but they were strapped to his sides, one on each hip.

"Jeam," Armijo spoke over his shoulder, "how does Pat Garrett and your men down in Lincoln County hold out with Beely de Keed? You seen de Keed, ain't you?"

"Sure I seen Billy the Kid," Slocum replied. "I kin tell 'im miles off, and 'at's why Pat Garrett sent me up here to Las Vegas, so's I could give yez a hand when the Kid shows up like he said he would!"

Las Vegas was in a state of nervous excitement. One who would look at the town today would never believe that it ever was excited. It wakes up once every year in July for the famous Cowboys' Reunion, and then dozes off again until the following summer. But this was in the late seventies, when cattle-raising was the chief industry of the southwest, when the railroad came with its cargoes of "bad men," when restless and hard characters had pushed in from western Texas into southeastern New Mexico. As stealing cattle and shipping them off on the railroad was easier and more profitable than going to the trouble of raising them, these men had taken the matter up as a profession. Then, after killing became the punishment for stealing, and thus the rustlers and bandits waxed more desperate and dangerous, no less than a bloody war had been raging for years among the plains' cattlemen. Especially was this true in the south County of Lincoln, where Pat F. Garrett was sheriff and the chief foe of all desperadoes.

The railroad town of Las Vegas in San Miguel County was the chief shipping center for stock from the south, and thus it became a hot-bed for raids, shooting scraps, and whatever goes with a frontier western town. The sheriff and his assistants kept their guns cocked, the committees of "vigilantes" slept with their boots on, and matters came to such a pass, that, united for the common good, the Spanish-American, Yankee, and Mexican citizens of "the city of Las Vegas" solemnly set up a high trestle and invited all bandits to a "neck-tie party" in the city square. (One of these invitations, by the way, may still be seen displayed in Santa Fe.)

The bandit whose name was expressly mentioned, and in large bold type, was Billy the Kid. Twenty-one-year-old William H. Bonney, hence called "the Kid," was the most notorious exponent of early frontier crime in these regions. His murders already numbered eight, although he himself claimed that they were twenty, and that he needed one more to match his age! Time and again he had evaded Pat Garrett and the Lincoln Co. cattlemen. Before their very noses he had at different times committed murder, and yet he always got away. And now he was about to make his latest threat good—to visit Las Vegas in person. Las Vegas had her local rustlers and desperadoes, true; but the Kid was something extra. Hence the excitement.

To make things take a more serious aspect, Sheriff Garrett promised to send up one of his men from Lincoln, in order to help Sheriff Armijo and his men get the Kid, dead or alive; for, since the Las Vegans had never seen the Kid, they needed such a man to identify the bandit, and Armijo was glad to get him. This is how Jim Slocum now found himself in Armijo's office. He had ridden under cover, so he told Armijo, all the way from Lincoln town and had overtaken and passed the Kid and his gang near Santa Rosa. They were driving several hundred heads of beef to the railroad, and it would take a few days before they reached Las Vegas. But the Kid was liable to leave the gang at any moment and reach the town before anybody expected it. And he was most sure to visit the sheriff's office first. But when?

"Going by my figgering, chief," Jim talked on, the while he kept on paging through the records, "I reckon the Kid'll be riding hot from Santa Rosa all day, aiming to hit this here town tonight. His gang and the horned critters is just a blind to fool yez, 'at's all. If I was you, sheriff, I'd get your old posse and the vigilantes ready in two or three hours. Else he'll have the draw on yez all for sure."

"I can get my posse ready in no time," Armijo spoke through his black mustachios. "But can you tell me what da Keed looks like?"

"He ain't no bigger and no smaller nor I am," replied Slocum. "And he totes two irons on his belt the same as I does. And, let me tell yez chief, he kin draw them shooters quicker nor greased lightning—and yez'll find hot lead pill in your innards with the Kid galloping out a range. I know young Bill, sez I. And this is how I firs seen 'im do his stuff.

"A couple years ago I had a pal cowpuncher from Fort Sumner. Me and Joe was real friends, just like Joe and Bill the Kid was real foes. And Joe was no coward neither. Pat Garrett hisself said that if anybody would get the Kid it was my pal Joe. But let me tell you what happened, Mr. Armijo.

"Me and Joe was filling up a bit in the old Lincoln town saloon one day.

We two was standing at the bar, and Joe he began to talk louder than he orter. Natcherly, he began shouting threats and cusses on the Kid and how he'd plug that young ornery gizzard o' his'n full o' lead balls. But, of course, nobody expected the Kid right in Lincoln town in broad daylight. Then Joe must have seen something on the bar-mirror, 'cause he reached for his six-shooter, and, by jingo! a shot rang out, and there was my pal Joe on the floor, with a neat black hole twixt his eyes!

"I seen who shot him. It was the Kid standing at the door with his two guns drawn at hip level. And, let me tell yez, chief, Pat Garrett hisself and brave old Murphy from the store was there, and so was other fearless and hones' cowmen there, but they couldn't do nothing. The Kid just backs out the door, jumps on his hoss, and gallops away, shooting hellfire at the shack all the while, so's nobody dare come out of the saloon until he's gone. That was Billy the Kid for you, all the time—"

The office door-knob clicked, and, before Sheriff Miguel Armijo could pull himself up from his leaning chair, a stranger had walked in and closed the door behind him. The sheriff was literally struck dumb, for here was a man that he had been picturing to himself all the while. About the size of Jim Slocum, and with a gun at either side of his belt, he stood there for a moment with arms akimbo, enjoying the sheriff's surprise. He made as though to speak to Armijo, when his eye caught the man behind the sheriff's broad back. Instinctively his hands dropped to his holsters, a shot rang out thunderingly through the small office room, and the newcomer lay sprawling on the floor, a neat black hole between his eyes.

Sheriff Miguel Armijo turned from the dead man and glanced cautiously over his shoulder. "Jim Slocum" was gone, and so were the contents from the open safe.

LESSONS *in* LOVE

Lithographs by Gerald Cassidy

Time and Tide

(September 1935)

Time and Tide were twin sisters; and they waited for no man. That is, although they did wait on the men who boarded in their Rocky Mountain plan hotel, they never entertained the thought of waiting for a man the way unmarried women folk are wont to do at a certain age. At least, Time and Tide were not supposed to, for they were now of such an age that, had some author tried to enter their girlhood memoirs in the Library of Congress, the memoirs would have been stamped "Ancient History" and shelved away beyond the "Middle Ages."

Time and Tide were not exactly their names, at least not their baptismal names. You see, Fructosa and Sinforosa Cana ran a hotel in Mora. Now Mora is a still little town, or rather a little "still" town, far up in the New Mexico Rockies. But it isn't too small to have a pretty good boarding school, and that is why the young folks there were smart enough to dub the Misses Cana "Time and Tide," thus saving their adolescent jaws from the wear and tear of Fructosa and Sinforosa.

Since, as the old proverb goes, time and tide wait for no man, these happy nicknames fitted the old maids to a pair of T's. But these young boarding school students had not reckoned with another quotation they had learned in school. Bill Shakespeare wasn't such a punk weatherman, after all.

There is a tide in the affairs of men, said Bill, which, taken at the flood, leads on to fortune. So far, life had been nothing but a desert to the Cana sisters, and, as far as romance is concerned, there had been no flood—as yet. Their hotel had brought them a fortune, however, and Time carried the said fortune in her stocking. But right now, fickle fate was about to reverse Bill's weather forecast, and Time's and Tide's fortune was to lead them on to a flood, to an inundation, to a deluge!

The Noah of this impending deluge was Spud Chisum. Spud was working on the highway, dynamiting, and his ark was the Cana Hotel. But he had never dreamed of turning the whole business into a Cana marriage feast until he laid eyes on Time's cash register. One day, snooping Spud, like nobody's business, happened to stroll into the Cana kitchen. Luckily for him, he was not seen seeing what he saw—Time had pulled her long skirt, modestly enough, up to her knee, and she pulled out a bank note from an unnaturally bulging calf and handed it to her sister, Tide. No wonder, thought Spud, that these dames stuck to their old-time petticoats.

And old-time fashions in general. Why, Time looked like Queen Victoria herself, while Tide resembled Queen Victoria's mirrored reflection perfectly. And right here is where Spud Chisum had to scratch his head. Both sisters stuck to each other, much like the real Queen Victoria and her reflection or shadow; and though Spud could have easily tackled Time and made away with her stocking bank, he was as yet afraid of their "United We Stand" attitude. They did not look like weak sisters, either. Besides, Time and Tide, pronounced rapidly, sounded too much like T-N-T in dynamiter Spud's ears, and he was prudent enough to keep his sparks of ambition at a safe distance for the time being.

Now, about the Cana wedding idea. As soon as Chisum saw that physical force was out of the question, he bethought himself of an old doctrine. If you want the canary to sing, don't cork the yellow bird; just feed him bird-seed. What this bird-seed is to a canary, flattery is to an elderly maid. Chisum's idea was to court Time away from Tide, or vice versa; just as long as they were separated, it mattered little. But as much as Spud knew himself to be a crook within, he was wary enough that his looks weren't a compliment to Frankenstein. Frankenstein's face makes a hit on the screen; Spud's mug would look better behind one.

His own participation as bridegroom, then, was out of the question. To make himself chief steward was easy enough, but he needed a pal to play the romantic Romeo. Whom could he trust? Ah, why not Dan Murphy? Slow, handsome, but sure Dan—why, he would be the cat's paw. Really, it began to look like the old story of the cat and the canary.

Of course, Dan was game. A thousand dollars, maybe two grand, walking around in a cotton stocking was nothing to turn up your nose at. Dan Murphy was a young road engineer, sure, mathematically exact, but rather slow. And though at first he could not catch on to Spud's proposition, he applied a formula with due figuring, and soon had the plan mapped out in his brain, to-wit:

"I flirt with this dame Time who has the dough," began Dan.

"Right," snapped Spud.

"Wait a minute. Let me finish. As I was saying, I flirt with this dame Time who has the dough without her sister, Tide, knowing it. Meanwhile, Spud, you leave for Santa Fe on a vacation. Anyway, that's what you tell them. Therefore, you become unknown quantity X. When you're gone, I elope with Time in the Highway Commission's car, and just out of town, down by the gravel pits, a masked robber holds us up. Masked robber is unknown—equals X. Therefore, X equals the robber and the robber equals Spud. Ain't I right, Spud?"

"Sure," Chisum replied, "and after I do some subtracting from the stocking, we both will divide."

"I gotcha down pat," Dan exclaimed. "Patter than a blueprint. What Roosevelt would say about this plan for flood relief!"

Well, Spud Chisum was no mean architect, if you asked Dan Murphy. Everything worked out true to specifications. Noah Spud went on a vacation, Romeo Dan made use of his good looks and the canary gorged herself with bird-seed. She fell hard. Still, hard is a soft word. Really, Miss Time just nestled into the Yankee's cat's paw.

Elopement night. O dear!

Queen Victoria left her reflection fast asleep in their Colonial four-poster, stole out of the hotel, and piled into the waiting car with a flurry of petticoats and bustles. Daniel Patrick Michael Murphy had never thought of sitting so close to Queen Alexandria or Dowager Queen Mary, or any other British royalty. But he made the most of his patriotic sentiments, and the Highway Commission's car rumbled down the freshly-graveled road, out of town, into the night.

Dan had already steadied his nerves with the moon. Ah, moon! It stirred up romance in the bride, but the groom only looked at the road before him. Perhaps Miss Cana thought that Dan's "moony" breath kept him from hugging and kissing her. Perhaps, too, if she had thought more on it, certain suspicions might have entered her love-mad mind. But she had no more time to think on it or on anything. By this time, the gravel pits appeared around a bend, and Murphy peeled his eye for unknown quantity X.

True to specifications again, a muffled figure stepped out into the glare of the car's headlights, and Dan put on the brakes. He also killed the engine, so that the lady beside him might better hear.

"Hands up, and keep 'em up," shouted unknown quantity X.

The groom did as ordered, rapping his knuckles against the cab roof, and he let out a soft curse. But the bride was not scandalized or shocked, nor did she put her hands up. She only sat there—in a dead, dead faint.

Dan felt her weight against his ribs, and he lowered his arms. "Swooned, by crackie," he whispered. "Easy work, now, Spud—with Time out!"

"Time out, me eye!" Chisum bellowed back, after running his hands up and down her stockings.

"What's the matter, man? Ain't she got the cash?"

"You dern fool! This ain't Time, it's Tide!"

Well, that terrible night passed, but not its memories. As the sisters were respectable ladies, no publicity of any sort or any kind of prosecution followed after the attempted Cananite abduction. The highway construction gang moved to worse roads, and Spud and Dan went with it.

Time and Tide wait for no man.

How Our Lady took a hand in bringing a Spanish and an Irish heart together.

Viola Comes of Age

(November 1936)

Señora Molinar had an explanation for everything, especially anything pertaining to her daughter. Blue-eyed and blonde, she looked all the more fair when among her Argentine companions. This her mother attributed to her Celtic ancestry, the Celts being the original people of Spain. In her many pensive moods, her eyes grew big and even dark. This, said her mother, betokened a strain of Moorish fiery blood. There was a reason for her name, too. Her grandmothers' names were Victoria and Olivia respectively, and each had wanted the child named after her. The Señora Molinar had compromised and called her Viola.

One thing she could not explain. Viola, known even to her olive-skinned friends to be a home-baby, had gotten into the habit of frequenting a certain shrine quite a distance away, over near the Alcalde's plantation. Why, why, wondered the mother, had Viola become so fond of Our Lady of Roybal?

"Daughter," she said to her one day. "Mamma's heart is heavy concerning you. Tell me, are you going to Our Lady of Roybal again?"

Viola's eyes dilated and darkened. "But, mother, there is nothing wrong in that, is there?"

"No, no, *vida*. No girl can be too devoted to the Blessed Mother, especially these days. But, *Violita mía*, there is a limit to everything. You are praying so much that you forget—well, Felipe Sánchez called yesterday when you were gone so long. Remember, you are our only child and heir, and I'm afraid that any day you will tell me that you—that you want to be a nun!" The old lady began to sob.

The girl's troubled expression gave way to one of her infrequent smiles. "Why, mamma, what put that into your head?"

"You pray so much," replied the Señora. "And you have neglected your dancing lessons of late, and you are to dance at the Fiesta next week—"

"I have already learned the Andalusian gypsy dance, the one with the castanets," Viola said, comfortingly.

"But you do not practice enough, going to that shrine so often. Why, several times your aunt at the convent, Mother Carlos Borromeo of the Sacred Wound, called for you; but I said nothing to you about it."

"You did very well, mother. I have no wish to lock myself up in the Carmel—as yet."

"As yet?" The lady put away her handkerchief. You have me worried, girl. Why are you so cold towards Felipe Sánchez? He is a gentleman, and very wealthy—don't tell me he is not handsomer than that Clark Gable we saw on the cinema at Buenos Aires!"

Again Viola's eyes became unfathomable ovals. Pursing her lips, she put on her hat and strolled down the path which led to Our Lady of Roybal, over by the Alcalde's plantation.

Still within sight of the Molinar homestead, Viola was thinking of the coming Fiesta, when she was to make her debut as "La Gitana," the Spanish gypsy. Yes, she could do the dance perfectly by now; that did not worry her a bit. Nor would there be a dearth of admirers. Felipe Sánchez would be there, of course, and all the rich young *caballeros* from the surrounding haciendas. But would *he* be back by then, he with the tall strong body and tanned handsome features?

Out of sight, the hacienda Molinar and all it contained were soon out of Viola's mind. Only *he* filled her thoughts. She began to picture him to herself just the way she first saw him. One day she and the Alcalde's daughter had gone out for a drive. She recalled how the Indian chauffeur had offered to take them to the new silver lode. A thick vein of silver, perhaps the richest in all Argentina, had been located in the Alcalde's vast estates, and the Alcalde had decided to work it by the most modern American methods. As they reached the spot where the imported machinery was being unpacked, he galloped up to the car and stopped—shining English boots, khaki breeches and shirt, a loose, leather vest over broad shoulders, and an Argentino hat perched jauntily over sleek black hair... and those smiling eyes and mouth....

The Alcalde's daughter had introduced him as the Señor Arnold Doran, the American engineer who was in charge of operations. Viola remembered having said nothing; she had blushed terribly and her eyes had become large deep pools into which he stared with unfeigned fascination. Even after they drove away, when she instinctively turned back, she saw him standing there like a bronze equestrian statue with grey eyes that spoke.

Since that day she had started her frequent visits to Our Lady of Roybal. The shrine stood close by the road that ran between the Alcalde's hacienda and the new mines, but that was not the sole reason for this sudden spurt of piety. Viola knew Mr. Doran would inquire after her and find her, whether she came to the sanctuary or not—she had read that in his eyes. She really came to pray. She prayed to the Queen of Heaven with all the fervor she could muster that he may be unmarried and a Catholic; she implored Mary to make him acceptable in her mother's sights.

And there he had found her praying, not long after. Often they sat together for long stretches at a time, right in front of Our Lady of Roybal, who had graciously granted the first two items, for Arnold was not married, and he was a good Catholic besides. He proudly added that he was Irish, the dark variety of Erin that inherited its brunette strain from shipwrecked survivors of the Spanish Armada.

Later he had gone back to the United States on business, and her pilgrimages had continued for his safe return. Would he come back? If so, would he be back in time for the Fiesta? So far he had not even written...

Viola's heart gave a jerk. Out of the leafy shadows of the shrine he came with that smile she had learned to reproduce in her dreams. Right away he noted her deep surprise.

"Sweetheart," he said, "what is the matter? I thought you expected to find me here! I told you in my last letter..."

Letter? More than one letter? But she had not received any, she told him.

"I wrote three times—no, not to you directly. I was afraid your mother would open them, so I wrote to your aunt, Mother Carlos with the long name."

"To my aunt?" she gasped. "Why to her?"

"I know her, dearest. I talked to her several times at the cloister grill. A wonderful woman, Viola. I told her in my first letter all about you and me. She only answered one, the last one. She said I must try to make it down here for the Fiesta, said you were making your big bow to society. And she gave me valuable hints as to how to win your mother over..."

Viola's eyes had become bigger and bigger; a crystal film covered each dark well for an instant, and then rolled like pearls down her flushed cheeks. She hid her face against his heart, and he led her to a stone bench in front of Our Lady of Roybal.

Señora Molinar was swept off her rheumatic feet by that dashing young *caballero* who looked so much like that Clark Gable she had seen once at the movies in Buenos Aires. The very first night of Fiesta, she noticed that he was one of the few young men who attended Vespers. And how sincerely

Never had Viola danced so ecstatically before.

devout he was. And such a gentleman at the street festival. No, not even Felipe Sánchez could hold up a taper to him. If only Viola knew him, she sighed, there would be fewer visits to the shrine and less danger from her Carmelite aunt's influence.

Viola came through victoriously, particularly in her gypsy dance. All the beautiful señoritas were eclipsed at that moment. Never was her hair more golden, or her lips more enticingly poutful, or her eyes more Moorishly big and enchanting. All the youthful *caballeros* applauded and whooped, but none more so than the manly object of the Señora Molinar's admiration.

And to him it was that Viola cast the crimson rose from her temple when the dance was over.

They still talk about it over there. The Señora Molinar explains the happy match by saying that a mother's choice is by nature the daughter's choice. But she wonders a little bit why Arnold and Viola still like to visit Our Lady of Roybal, and why they are so fond of the Reverend Mother Carlos Borromeo at the Carmel.

For years all the girls had called her Sister "Disappointed" and now at last they were to understand clearly why.

Eve of San Isidro

(June 1937)

Sister Consolata of St. Isidore's-on-the-Delaware was called "Disappointed," though nobody knew exactly for what reason. The name seemed to be as old as the Sister. Generations of graduates had used that appellation, but no one had figured out its origin or cause. The most plausible explanation was that dreamy, sad, and far-away look in Sister's dark eyes, a quality which was set off by the laughing eyes which belonged to the rest of St. Isidore's Irish community.

Ellen McIntyre, one of the graduates, was walking by herself on the Academy grounds. It was a warm May afternoon, the Eve of St. Isidore's feast. That is why the lawns were deserted, as both nuns and students were decorating house and chapel for tomorrow's festival. As Ellen approached the convent side of the gardens, she almost stepped on two little feet under a black skirt. There was "Disappointed" herself, sitting on a shaded bench, and devoutly telling her beads.

"Oh, I almost stepped on your toes, Sister!" Ellen stammered. "Were you saying your rosary for us graduates, Sister?"

"Not this time, dear," the wrinkled little mouth replied. "Sit down, Ellen. It's St. Isidore's Day tomorrow, you know—my patron's feast."

"Why, Sister, he's our patron, too—because this is his school and because we're all Irish."

"Was Saint Isidore Irish?"

"Of course," Ellen answered. "That's an Irish name all the way."

"But St. Isidore was a Spaniard, Ellen. In fact, there are two Saints by that name, the Archbishop of Seville and the Laborer of Madrid. The Laborer is the patron of the Academy, Ellen. But I have a great devotion to him because he was the patron of my home-church, and because I am also Spanish!"

The girl gasped. She had always been under the impression that only Irish nuns dwelt at St. Isidore's and that this old Sister had come from a place such as Killarney, or Cork, or Tipperary. Sister Consolata was enjoying the girl's surprise. Then, gazing away with her dreamy eyes, she began to move her shriveled lips. Her mouth began to tell of things that had often been thought of, but never spoken. So much did the old nun seem to be in a trance, that the girl beside her dared not move, lest she break the magic spell that was making her tell such interesting details.

"Five years ago, I celebrated my golden jubilee as a religious. That makes fifty-five years away from home. It seems like yesterday. I can still see the little town perched on the mountainside, with the New Mexico sierras looming behind, and the yellow plains spreading below for hundreds of miles. I can see my father's house so plainly, and the little white chapel of *San Isidro Labrador!* I can see the Padre teaching the children their prayers under that old acacia tree by the chapel door.

"My father was the wealthiest man of the settlement. In the mountain forests he had hundreds of fine horses grazing, and there were thousands of his sheep on the plains. His only child, I lived with him in our large hacienda, which was of adobe and which surrounded a spacious court, or patio. I remember all the servants we had, and my old *nana*, or nurse; for my own dear mother had died giving me birth... Isn't it queer? I remember all these things so plainly, but hardly anything that took place yesterday!

"When I was eighteen, my father said I should marry. He was getting old and wanted a man to run the hacienda if he died. They told me that I was beautiful, the people did. Also, from my grilled window upstairs, I used to overhear the servants and casual visitors in the patio below. So I suppose that I really was beautiful in those days. Yet, though all of the girls of my age had married, I had not given any man a thought. Why? I just hadn't, that's all. At this time my first suitor came.

"Antonio was the favorite among the youth of the settlement. But he was poor and an orphan. He was very handsome, clean, and an excellent rider. One day, while I was with my father and dear old nurse in the patio, Antonio came striding in. 'Don Gonzalo,' he said to my father, 'I come to ask for your daughter's hand.' I could not help but admire his boldness, for my father was hard to approach.

"'My daughter's hand?' almost shouted Don Gonzalo. 'What have you to offer her?'

"'Love!' replied Antonio.

"'Love?' Don Gonzalo laughed, coughed a little, and laughed again. Antonio then asked me directly if I would share the world's luck with him, and I said very humbly that I would act according to my father's wishes, as I knew well that it was the custom among our people for the parents to choose mates for their children. Besides, I was not so anxious to marry yet. Well, my father just told Antonio to get out or to sit on his boot. I had run up into my room and, as Antonio came out, his head hung low, I twisted off a big scarlet geranium from the window and dropped it on his big hat. He looked up, smiled joyfully, and kissed the flower. Why I did it, I don't know—silly me.

"Well, from that day Antonio pestered me with words, messages—why, I couldn't leave the house without being confronted by him. At first I put him off gently. But, when he insisted on begging me to run away with him, I told him in plain, even cruel, words that I did not like him, and that I would notify my father if he did not leave me alone.

"From that time on, Antonio became a different person. Once a gay lad, he turned bitterly melancholy. He became a shiftless idler. He began to drink heavily. I heard he even stole in order to buy liquor. One night however, the worst thing happened. Antonio was riding through the town, drunk, when a young lad playing on the road jokingly called him 'A Disappointed Lover.' Antonio pulled out a pistol, fired, and the boy fell. Sober enough to see the error of his deed and its consequences, he took the usual course of the murderer and fled. He was away into the night, no one knew in which direction, before any man could pursue him. The boy he shot, however, was not killed, or even seriously injured; he was playing on the same spot a week later. But we heard no more of Antonio, no more for seven years.

"But, oh, those seven years. A strange sadness came over me which neither I, much less my friends, could understand. I felt a longing and an emptiness in my heart which nothing could fill. After a time, I caught myself crying whenever Antonio's name happened to be mentioned. Others noticed this and said that I was in love. But it was not true. Perhaps, I was blaming myself for Antonio's misfortunes; but I was convinced that I had acted rightly. Still, I cried. My mother called the Padre of San Isidro, who began to do all he could to bring me to myself. He asked me if I missed, if I loved, Antonio. I said I didn't. Nor did I know why I cried. I guess he thought I was crazy.

"It was then, while he talked to me, that I began to look at the Padre and his lonesome work in a new light. The Padre was one of several French missionaries who had come to New Mexico. When he first came, he found the settlement of San Isidro in a sorry state. As our people hadn't had a priest, most of the families were not married by the Church, although they were good Christians. The Padre spent his first months in rectifying and blessing marriages. Next he had the old San Isidro mission church restored. Later on, he would gather all the children daily, not only for catechism instructions, but to teach them to read and write. Over and above all this, he taught the people how to do better building and planting; he encouraged, by word and example, the cultivation of flowers and vegetables. He himself brought the first twigs which were to become the beautiful orchards of San Isidro.

"Nevertheless, the Padre had his troubles, too. But he never told anyone of his days of loneliness and even discouragement. He carried on, because he knew his reward was in the hands of God, for Whom he was doing it all. From this viewpoint, I began to realize what the good priest had done for our people, and I wondered why these people took no cognizance of this wonderful benefactor. I now received whatever counsels fell from his lips with the utmost devotion. That is why I began to believe that I cried for Antonio, and that he would fill the void in my heart. For the Padre had concluded that I loved Antonio.

"One evening, about seven years after Antonio had gone away, the Padre came to our house with strange news. He had gone out to a distant mission on the plains and, on his way back, had stopped to visit friends at the Rancho Mariposa. What was his surprise to find Antonio there! Antonio told him that he had just returned from South America, where he had made a fortune, and had now purchased the Mariposa ranch. Of course, the Padre had to tell him that I steadily wept for him. Antonio smiled, the Padre said, for he thought that I was married. Before departing, the priest had made Antonio promise to visit us on the following day.

"Next morning my heart was aflutter, for soon its strange longing for possessing something big and noble was to be fulfilled. My father, now very old and feeble, was glad that I was about to marry, for I was twenty-five, quite an old age for beautiful maidens among our people. Besides, our hacienda had fallen off in late years, and my father was eager to annex it to the Rancho Mariposa.

"Antonio came. It was the eve of San Isidro, I remember well. My old nurse had decked me out in my mother's best finery—silken black bodice and skirts, solid gold earrings and necklaces that were ancient heirlooms, a large Spanish comb behind my ear, as also a big scarlet geranium at my temple, for the roses were not yet in bloom. Antonio came. My father received him gallantly and with apologies. I was all joy,—until we met; for when I saw him, I knew right away that I still did not love him, that it was not he who could fill the void in my heart. I had not cried because I loved him, but because I was sorry for him. Well, nothing took place.

"Shortly after, my father died. I opened my heart to the Padre entirely. Finally, I asked him why God had not made me a man, so that I could be an apostle like our pastor. That, I knew, was the only course which could satisfy my longings. Carefully, the Padre questioned me. Then he showed me what my heart needed to fill it up, and I became genuinely happy again.

"In a few weeks, I left for the East with enough money in hand for my expenses and my dowry. The rest of my property I left with the Padre with the provision that, if I made my perpetual vows, everything went to the church of San Isidro. So I became a religious fifty-five years ago. Fifty-five years! And I never was back home since then!"

Ellen McIntyre came to herself. "Sister," she said at last, "don't you get any letters from home?"

A little laugh came from the old nun. "Home? No, Ellen. The first ten years I did correspond with the Padre back home. But he died, and, sad to say, there was no priest to take his place. San Isidro went back to its former state. That was the plight of most of New Mexico. Oh, how I prayed that God would bless my poor people with spiritual shepherds. But for many years I was disappointed."

Ellen tittered: "Do you know, Sister Consolata, that *some* of the girls call you Dis-ah-"

"Disappointed? My Lord, Ellen, they've been calling me that ever since your own mother was a boarder here. As if I didn't know it!"

"They shouldn't do it, Sister. It's improper, and forbidden besides."

"As if you were entirely innocent, Ellen. I know, I know that it's a wrong practice. But you know that Mother Eve ate the forbidden fruit, even when God Himself, in person, told her not to!...Really, Ellen, I don't know why they gave me such a name. Perhaps, I looked disappointed long ago when I contemplated the sad condition of our Southwest Missions. But I placed my trust in God's Will, and my life-long prayers were finally answered. Do you know how? Just read the missionary magazines, and see what the good French priests have done to this day. Look at the Franciscans, how active and self-sacrificing they are. And don't forget the many Sisterhoods out there, and the Catechists. No, I'm satisfied now."

"I guess the girls thought you were disappointed in love, Sister—when you were a girl yourself, eh?" Ellen chose to explain.

"No, dear. You are the first to hear my story, and you can see that I was disappointed only in what the world had to offer. Besides, I was disappointed in my prayers, for a short time. But"—and Sister Consolata looked up at the big garden crucifix—"I was never disappointed in love."

What happens when the fate of a baseball championship hangs by a thread on a dressmaker's shoulder.

A Stitch in Time

(April 1936)

Lamech Andreas Levy, simply "L. A." to the community, emerged from his Saturday afternoon bath into a semi-formal attire. He was scheduled to give the boys a pep talk and was waiting for a call from Jake Swope, manager of the Newburg baseball nine.

Tomorrow they played the Brookland Bearcats in the final elimination game for the Inter-State pennant. L. A. expected them to win. They must. He had given them a financial boost from a scrub rural team to the crackest baseball nine in the State. It was his team, just as much as the Farmers' Bank was his bank and the Palace Theater his show place.

The phone tingled. L. A. picked up the receiver.

"Jake Swope? Ready? Yeah, this is Mr. Levy. What? Speak slower. I don't understand."

"There's been a break in the team, Mr. Levy," came Swope's excited voice. "The boys were rotten at practice this afternoon. No teamwork. A lot of growling and—"

"But, Jake, it can't be so, and just before tomorrow's game! You must lead them on the field and win. They must win!"

"I'd sooner go before the grandstand crowd with a hole in my pants than with a team all ripped up like they are."

"Listen, Jake. From where are you phoning from?" L. A. began eyeing for his hat and cane.

"From the dressmaker's."

"Cut the fooling out, Swope. You ain't making the team women's fitouts!"

"No, no, Mr. Levy. But this shop is the very seat of the trouble." Jake Swope was losing his temper, too.

"Och, leave your old pants out of it and—"

"But let me explain, Mr. Levy. And don't interrupt me, please. There's a cute little dame that works here. See? Until lately she was Ashby's girl, our star pitcher's girl. See? But she threw him off and started going around with our catcher, Bill Felder. See? Now Ashby and Felder aren't clicking. And the rest of the bunch knows it, Mr. Levy. There'll be a ragged split in the whole outfit by tomorrow afternoon, I'm afraid."

Old L. A. was gasping. "Jake! Can you maybe not fix it up with the young lady? Anyway at all?"

"Well, I could ask her to come over and see you right now. How's that?"

"Swell idea, Jake. You bring her right over. I wait."

Miss Gertrude Miller was a peach of a doll, the old financier said to himself as she settled down like a slim silver feather on his easy chair. While Swope stood by with his briar tight-lipped in his mouth, she sized up L. A. like a child looking up at a paunchy pachyderm at the zoo. L. A. put out his palms in the one ingratiating gesture that he knew.

"Miss Miller, you made that dress you wear all by yourself? It's a knockout. And you make the gowns for my wife, Reba—not? They are double knockouts. I wonder if you might sew up something for us."

The girl knew what he was driving at. "It's about Bill Felder and that Ashby, I suppose—"

"You hit the head on the nail, Miss Miller. Those two boys are mad with each other because of you. When our catcher and pitcher work together, we win. But when they don't—well, we lose. And we must win tomorrow. You explain to the young lady, Mr. Swope."

"It's this way, Gertie. Our boys are all pretty good. See? But our battery is our winning point. See?" And Swope went on explaining how Ashby was paying no attention to the catcher's signals. He wanted to make Felder look cheap and didn't give a whoop whether the team won or not.

"So you see, my dear," L. A. broke in, "how everything depends with you. We are willing to reward you for helping us, and I'll write you a fine check at once. I'll tell Reba to order more dresses, and I'll give you a permanent pass to the Palace matinee. All you have to do is—well, make up with Ashby."

Gertrude sat up straight. "Nothing of the kind, sir. Sorry. I hate that man, but I really love Bill Felder. Besides, Bill would then get sore, and you would be in the same fix."

"Exactly," said L. A. "I was thinking it would be better, maybe, that you make up with both, without each other knowing about the trick until the game is over."

"That's out, too," came her prompt reply. "I will have nothing to do with Ashby. He might be your best pitcher, but no gentleman. So your game can go hang before I have anything to do with that beast!"

Old Levy gasped and stared down at the insolent little face. Oh, these women! Always making trouble. All were alike, except maybe Reba. The wisest and strongest of men fell by their wiles. L. A. now recalled how old papa Levy, long since gathered to his fathers, had told him about Solomon and Samson. Those bad ladies had woven their spells about Solomon—yes, pulled the wool over his eyes. And Samson had lost his heavyweight title because he let Delilah a bit too close with a pair of scissors. And here was a little dressmaker cutting his baseball outfit to shreds! At last he erupted into a blaze of sound and fury.

"Yeah, you are another Delilah. She was like you, a—"

"A little snip," said Gertrude, curtly.

"Yeah, a little snipper with scissors! Oi, you modern womens. You ain't got no brains, no refinements, moralities, no—"

In a flash the girl was on her little toes. "No morals? What do you mean, Mr. Levy? I'm as good and straight as the best girl in this town. If I haven't high-hat refinement, it's because I've been too busy doing honest work. Dressmaking isn't any crime. I took it up to help mother, who couldn't afford to send me to the Academy where I should be now. Poor dad was robbed of his money and disgraced when I was a kid. It killed him, too. So, Mr. Levy—"

She suddenly stopped as Swope took hold of her flying arms.

"Calm yourself, Gertie," Jake whispered. "Mr. Levy just got excited. See? He hates to lose tomorrow's game. See?"

L. A. looked very humble now. "Please pardon me, Miss. Jake is right. I'd rather have the Palace burn down, or my bank robbed, than to lose the pennant to the Brookland Bearcats. Judge Peasely owns the Brookland club and he is mine biggest enemy. He is a crooked lawyer, a flirting bachelor, a skunk—phooey! He will laugh before my nose when he wins. Can you blame me then, I ask you?"

There was a queer twist to Gertrude's tiny mouth. "Well, I guess I did fly off the handle myself. Now, I won't promise anything definite, but I'll see that Newburg wins that game tomorrow."

And without further ado, Gertie winked at Swope and slid out of the house, leaving one Lamech Andreas Levy stroking his nose in wonder.

The game took off with a promise of excitement for both sides. The Newburg grandstand boards creaked and bulged with a full capacity of six hundred fans, while honking cars stood packed close together a few yards away from both sidelines. Out of a small coupe stepped Gertrude Miller, alone and with an anxious look. She squeezed into the crowded stand.

The Newburg boys had the outs. Ashby began lobbing the ball into the plate without any apparent effort. But Brookland began hitting, too. One, two, three well placed drives made the crowds hold their breath as each time an alert Newburg outfielder got under and made a really difficult catch. The battery of Ashby and Felder, that was sure, was not up to snuff, for the Brookland Bearcats had never hit Ashby like that before.

The game developed into a hitting spree for both sides. By the time the seventh-inning stretch rolled around, Newburg was barely ahead, 8 to 7. All the while Gertrude had tried to reach a spot behind a boxed off section directly in back of the chicken-wire nearest the home plate. In the seventh-inning scuffle and excitement she had managed to get closer to her goal. Felder, buckling on his chest protector at the beginning of the eighth inning, happened to see her and threw a kiss. She answered with the same gesture. But Ashby, on the mound, saw what was going on. His lips moved tightly and meaningly, his fingernails dug into the innocent ball. She'd soon see what a punk catcher that Felder guy was.

Felder knew the first man up could not hit them low. His glove went down. The ball was high and the batter caught it on the nose for a three-bagger. The next batter had two quick strikes on him when Felder signaled for another close low ball. Ashby released a wicked high twister which the batter missed by a foot. The ball glanced off Felder's mask and catapulted through the chicken-wire into the grandstand, while the man on third reached home. Tie score—8-all—and no outs. The crowd was razzing the catcher. But the rest of the Newburg nine knew what was really happening, and their blood boiled.

Ashby sent another pellet where Felder did not want it. The batter connected and sent a ripping grounder a few feet away from an angry shortstop who made no effort to grab it. Another run scored. The Newburg fans were mad. What if the next three batters hit flies that were caught? Brookland was leading, 9 to 8.

In the meantime something was happening in the grandstand. During the commotion caused by the ball breaking through the screen, Gertrude had slipped behind Judge Peaseley, owner of the Brookland Bearcats, and dropped her vanity case into his lap as if by accident. She reached for it, and he seized her small hand.

"Hello, girlie. Some game, isn't it?" He continued to squeeze her hand.

"I'll say. And it's a cinch for Brookland," she said, making no effort to remove her chin which, by this time, had dropped to his shoulder.

"You bet your pretty eyes, kid. The game's ours. That Newburg battery is shot to pieces. Our boys are knocking Ashby right and left, and what they miss, Felder also misses. It's ripped up the support also. Did you see how that man on short let that easy one go by? Boy, won't old Andy Levy feel sore! And look at Swope trying to pump air into his flat tires!"

Gertrude saw Jake looking at her, and he called Ashby's and Felder's attention as the boys were lining up to bat in the last of the eighth. That the boys saw her snuggling close to Judge Peasely she knew. But she didn't know that Ashby and Felder shook hands in the dugout. A new spirit suddenly took hold of the entire team.

The first two Newburgers struck out to begin the last half of the eighth. They were too anxious. The next got on first by a walk, and Ashby rushed over to Rohan, who was picking up his bat. "Rohan, you bring this man in, and I promise you they won't get another run."

Well, the fans around Newburg are still talking about that drive of Rohan. It shot straight over the pitcher's head and kept going up, up at a depressed angle, like a rocket, pushing itself past the center-fielder, and into a cornfield. A homerun. Newburg was ahead, 10 to 9. What if the next batter popped out? Nobody cared.

What followed went fast. Felder didn't feel so happy behind the plate since he had seen Gertrude's face next to Peaseley's jowl. But he would be a good sport, anyway. None of Ashby's former tactics for him. He gave the signals and Ashby answered perfectly and with unusual zest. One, two, three strikes—three times! The Bearcats couldn't see them. The game was over.

In a deafening bedlam the crowds arose. Gertrude slipped away towards the home dugout. She must explain to Bill. There was no need to cause him a lot of mental pain. But Levy and Swope crossed her path.

"Great work, Miss Miller," said Jake. "Mr. Levy, she won the game at the last minute."

"You telling me!" L. A. screamed. "My dear, it was a knockout! You sewed up the breeches—I mean, the breach in the team at the right time."

Swope laughed. "A stitch in time saves nine! See?"

"You might call it a double-stitch," Gertrude replied, with a catch in her voice. "You see, it was Judge Peaseley who robbed and ruined dad."

"Oi-yoi!" L. A. shouted. "For why you didn't tell me sooner?"

Swope chimed in. "She's a dressmaker, Mr. Levy. And she knows how to punch an eye when she has to. See?"

Why must death plunder the strong and the beautiful? And all for an apple! Nurse Ellis wanted to know.

Daily Apple

(September 1936)

Nurse Ellis stole into the nurses' lounging room and opening a book which lay on the table next to a large red apple, took a seat by the open window. Four stories below, the service trucks on the side street were roaring and screeching as she listened expectantly for some other sound.

Then it came. A voice that reminded one of silver and velvet, yet a manly voice, rose clearly above the mechanical pandemonium. It was singing, "Come back to Sorrento." She waited excitedly for the song composed especially for her. He had told her that morning as she left the nurses' home that he would sing it around this time. "A song about you," he had said, handing her a large crimson apple from his cart.

Every morning Tony Valentino gave Nurse Ellis an apple, a particularly large and particularly polished pippin. Several months previously she had begun buying fruit from him. He sang beautifully, and she loved music so much that in no time they had become fast friends. Tony's voice was more than a good Italian tenor; it had that silver clarity and strength which she delighted to listen to at the Metropolitan, and at the same time the velvety smoothness of a Spanish or Irish voice, McCormick's, for instance. She could never understand how he had not landed in opera or the radio. She was in heaven when he sang, and he worshipped her very shadow—she could see that.

And every morning Tony gave her a bright red apple, which she, in turn, handed over to any of her patients, or even to young, handsome Doctor Nelson. The Doctor, however, accepted the gift rather coldly, she observed. "Nellie" was always so serious; one would never think that she was engaged to him. If only he were half as romantic as Tony Valentino, she mused.

Suddenly Nurse Ellis leaned over in taut attention. A charming new melody floated up to her ears, half-hymn and half-serenade, it seemed, as if the singer had the Madonna reverently in mind whilst he told of his human affection. She could not make out the words of the verses, they went so fast. But the oft-repeated refrain, slow and solemn, stuck to her memory. *"Angelo bianco e puro senz' ale, Tu fai un cielo di questo spedale..."*

Paging feverishly through her book—an Italian grammar and dictionary—she made out the meaning with delight. Something about a white angel and a hospital. Yes; that was it. She was no poet, but the English rendering took some sort of form in her mind, something like this: "O wingless angel, pure and white, You make this hospital a Heaven bright!"

The door opened softly and young Doctor Nelson paced in towards the window. "Well, Mary, have you decided to read *Anthony Adverse* between sessions?"

She closed the book and smiled, blushing a trifle. "Why, not exactly. It's more than a novel. It's a dictionary—an Italian dictionary and grammar combined."

Doctor Nelson arched his brows and made big grey eyes, wrinkling his high forehead in the attempt. "You don't expect us, if and when we're married, to join Mussolini's medical staff in Ethiopia, do you?" Then he spied the shining apple on the table. He was figuring out something to say about it, maybe something sarcastic, when the call-bell began tingling madly for Doctor Nelson.

"An accident," he said, curtly, and turned to rush out. "You better come along, Mary. Get the business end ready in Operating Room 31."

Mary Ellis almost fainted in her tracks when she heard an orderly in the corridor say to another, "It's that Eye-talian peddler what sings now and then on the side-street—got slammed bad by a van!"

There was no need to operate on Tony Valentino. A projecting hook on the side of a moving van had caught his belt as he was gazing up at the building, and had hurled him beneath the double wheels of a heavily loaded trailer. Doctor Nelson gave him a bare half-hour to live and tried with anxious solicitude to lessen his sufferings as much as possible.

But Tony seemed to have no pain. After the chaplain had administered the last Sacraments, he lay quietly on the bed, his wrinkled face and his hair almost as white as the pillow, his large sharp eyes showing the only signs of life. For a while he had been watching Miss Ellis, his "white angel of the hospital," who with tear-filled eyes stood by, afraid to see death come. Countless times she had witnessed such scenes with a cold professional concern; but now trembling and with eyes moist, it seemed that she might faint any moment.

The young doctor, too, looked unusually upset, ashamed maybe. Tony saw him move close to the nurse and clasp her hand sympathetically; consolingly he placed his other arm around her shoulder. Their eyes met and then both turned to the dying old man.

Tony Valentino smiled wanly. "Miss Ellis, you make dis place a heaven for all. Tony, he go up to da big heaven. He pray for you two. He sing plenty with many white angel." Then came the ghost of a twinkle to his eyes. "Maybe better dis way. What do American people say—an apple a day keepa da doc away?"

Folks say there's gold in "them thar hills." Mosses, too—and a bit of romance, if you know where to look for it. Here's a girl who did.

Rolling Stones

(July 1936)

It was an old mill, the kind you often see on calendars, its lichen-faced walls shining in the Tennessee sun against a rolling shoulder of the Crab Orchard Mountains. There was the great wooden wheel on one side, motionless, with a stray streamlet bouncing off its front in a shimmering bridal veil.

That was the closest Flora Leech had ever got to a bridal veil—until two weeks ago when Algey Ludlow pitched his white tent near old Paw Leech's mill. Algey had fascinated her from the first. True, Jim Huskin had been asking for Flora's hand for more than a year, but Paw Leech was reluctant. He wanted his only daughter to get a good start in married life. And all that Jim possessed was the little unproductive Huskin farm down the creek. Even Father Duffy, who came to the mission chapel uptown, twice a month, said that was hardly enough.

"Oh, Flora!" came a high-pitched call from a window near the mill wheel. Algey Ludlow, his ordinarily sallow city features flushed with a vivacity she never thought him capable of, was beckoning her with the magnifying lens in his bony hand. "Flora, dear," he whispered ecstatically, as she approached him among the big millstones, "you and I and the mill are now famous. Eureka! I have found it!"

"Found what?"

"A treasure. A new contribution to science! Your father has been complaining about these millstones standing idle, and meanwhile they have been busily gathering this!"

Algey Ludlow held out some greenish thing in his open palm as though it were a precious emerald. On seeing it, however, Flora's elation gave way to puzzled disappointment. "Why, there's oodles of that stuff all over," she said, frowning. "The idea—moss!"

Yes, the very wall cried out with the green growth; the water trough and the big wheel were starting to rot with it; and the woods behind the mill were carpeted with it.

"But Flora dear," Algey remonstrated, "this is a new species. It is unique. It baffles me." Algey brought the lens into play. "Even without my compound microscope I can discern its peculiarities. See? It obviously belongs to the *Pleurocarpae*, but, while it shares the characteristics of two related families, it is neither *Fabroniaceae* nor *Neckeriaceae*. In short, my dear, it is a new moss! New! See, the leaves of ovate-lanceolate, the calyptra quite hairy, but the perichaetium..."

Outside, where the second floor met the ground level in front, Paw Leech was talking to Jim Huskin and laughing at the young fellow's witty remarks. "I Reckon, Jim," said he, stroking his long Whittier whiskers, "this here old mill is shot for good. Ever since them Yankee Marmons put up that there new-fangled rolling mills at Gatesville, I ain't ground nothin' 'cept maybe them sacks of your'n last year. I cain't see how you—"

"Listen, Paw Leech. My scheme's doggone good. You take me in as pardner and I'll get all the farmers in Bledsoe and Cumberland counties on our side. They don't fancy these pert Yankee millers nohow, 'cause they buy the grain off'n 'em darn cheap and then sell back their flour and stock feed at darn high prices."

Paw laughed, but not very fully. "You ain't jokin' me now, be you, Jim? Come, son, what price you askin' these here farmers for us grindin' their wheat and corn?"

"Nothin', Paw. No kiddin'. It's this way. My cousin, Caleb Jarvis, who is the Justice of Peace at Gatesville, he's been nominated Proc'rater of that there new government experimental farm. He promised me jest last night he'd buy all the cow and hoss feed off'n me alone—in case I can produce it. Now, Paw, say we grind all the folks' grain for nothin' so's only they allow us to keep the bran, then all them people are sure to come to us. Besides, they'll be glad to spite them Yankee Marmons."

"Got you, I reckon, Jim. But we only got two old-time grinders, son, and they's got modern machinery and steam and—"

"That's it, Paw Leech. We don't have to pay for no power. We got nature to push the old wheel and Cradle Creek's always runnin'. Besides, these old-fashioned millstones don't grind so good and fine like modern machines do and so we can't take all the flour off'n the bran. Get me? We get a richer and heavier stock feed and at any price we want for it from the good old U.S. government. It's a cinch."

Old Paw Leech was convinced, and his whiskers trembled. "Jim, you're a heap smart boy, a genus, a darn-right genus. You deserve more'n half the pardnership."

"I'll take Flora to wife, Paw."

The patriarch laughed. "Still harpin' on my daughter, eh?"

"'Course, she don't look at me like she used to since that overgrown boy scout, Algey Ludlow, come trotting along. He sure hits her fancy with them words longer'n a wagon-tongue. You don't take to *him* for a son-in-law!"

"Well, Jim, I reckon I ain't so awful keen on him. But if Flora wants him, it's her feud, I says. I had enough trouble t'home when I picked her mother from the McMinn clan. I'd much ruther have you, Jim."

Jim smiled and showed a row of white teeth, evidently greatly pleased. "I was talkin' to the postmistress yesterday down Gatesville. Told me this here Ludlow is an authority on Flora—"

Old Leech gasped. "He ain't got her, by gum, not till he's wed her proper."

Jim Huskin chuckled. "One on you, Paw. I also got all het up when I heard it. But the lady explained as how Algey Ludlow knows everything 'bout flowers and mosses and pond-scum."

"Well, even 'twere 'totherwise, says I, if that pond-scum should harm my maiden daughter, I'd tie a millstone 'round his neck, like the Good Book says, and chuck him into the depths of—of the mill-pond!"

Jim roared heartily. "Paw, there's one big difference twixt you and Algey Ludlow. You read the Book of Moses and he writes the book of Mosses."

Paw Leech doubled up with merriment and was still extricating his beard from his shoe laces when Flora and Algey came out of the mill.

"...and I disagree with Brotherus in *Die Natuerlichen Pflanzenfamilien* where he puts this family in the Neckeraceae. All the characters are truly hypaceous except, possibly, the areolation...Ah, good day, Mr. Leech, and you too, Mr. Huskin. I have ravishing news for you."

"Pappy," Flora shouted, buttonholing her father. "Pappy, Algey's found a brand new moss, and he's christened it after me—*Flora Leech's!*"

"More correctly," said the botanist, "it will be called *Floralacea.* Mr. Leech, your mill will be to Tennessee in history what Sutter's Mill was to California. One stone wheel of your mill, sir, standing idle for many months, was most fortunate in nurturing and developing the stray spore of a most rare moss. Your mill is forever famous!"

In a few days the old Leech mill became a Mecca, not for tourists with kodaks and botanists with microscopes, but for wagon-loads of grain from all the surrounding counties. In the meantime everybody was busy. Flora was occupied helping Ludlow dry out his specimens as soon as her kitchen chores were done, while Paw and Jim went about setting the machinery in order and repairing the troughs that led to the water wheel.

A week later everything was ready to start. Paw had driven down to Gatesville for a license to operate, one of these—to him—new fangled ideas of politics. Flora and Algey were sitting close together on the supporting wall by the mill-wheel. They did not see the grim scowl on Jim Huskin's usually merry features as he passed by them, for every day his antipathy regarding the botanist was growing stronger. He had cussed Ludlow and his mosses under his breath while scraping moss from the old millstones, or while replacing planks on the sluices eaten away by their loads of moss.

"Oh, Flora, look!" Algey exclaimed, pointing into the big wheel. "There's another rare specimen. I must get a ladder—"

Flora stopped him. "I can get down there without a ladder." Before Algey could stop her, she had tiptoed across the thick axle and was letting herself down into the wheel through the big spokes. No sooner had she dropped lightly to the bottom when there came a deafening splash overhead. The mammoth wheel grunted and began to turn. Running counterwise, like a squirrel in a revolving cage, she was shouting something to Algey, while tongues of water lashed her face. Witless with agony, Algey picked up the cedar post nearby and stuck it between the moving spokes, but it snapped in two and barely missed the girl's head. It was like trying to stop a wagon wheel with a pencil. His specimen book fell into the churning chasm below.

Luckily, Jim Huskin had heard the first terrified scream. Running down, he saw Algey standing there alone, paralyzed. Promptly he hurried back to shut off the sluice gates. A few minutes later, he was climbing out of the dripping, but motionless, mill-wheel, with Flora in one arm. She was conscious though exhausted. When Algey began to beg Jim to drop Flora and retrieve his book also, she put her hand across Jim's mouth, for she saw a torrent of words coming, much longer than any botanical terms Algey had ever used. Her eyes spoke what was dearest to his heart, and he held his peace.

And when old Paw Leech returned to his house, the first thing his eyes beheld was his daughter nestled in the arms of one Jim Huskin.

"I ask you for the hundredth time," pleaded Jim, "if you prefer me and the millstones to that cracked moss-gatherer."

"And I answer for the hundredth time," said she, smiling, "that a rolling stone gathers no moss."

Winds of trouble were brewing. In fact, it looked like a cyclone of destruction to Jim Archer. But then, it's an ill wind that blows no one good.

It's an Ill Wind

(January 1936)

The swag from the Simpson burglary was divided, like gall, into three parts: the bag, the juice and the stones. Tony Corell and Joe Starkas took the juice, twenty grand in cash, and also the stones, diamonds valued at the same amount. Jim Archer was left holding the bag.

That bag, to Jim, was like those the Greek gods used to keep the winds in. And it's an ill wind that blows no one good. The way the wind of ill luck was blowing toward Jim Archer was enough to fan his bitter dejection into utter despair. "Why did I fall for those two yeggs?" he kept on saying to himself. "Why did I consent to such a crime, in the first place? Why did I quit my job in the orchestra at the time the burglary was pulled off?" But the blackest question was: "What will Millie say when it's found out?"

True, his conscience as such was now clean. He had gone to confession and made the sincere promise to pay everything back, even if it took a lifetime. But would the matter remain hidden always...?

That Simpson burglary was really one of the slickest jobs ever pulled off in town. Years ago, rich old Miss Simpson had had a secret vault built under the basement of her 19th century mansion. There she stored her rare collections of art, antiques, and gems. It also served as her bank. Very few people knew the exact position of the strong room. Jim was one. When he was a mere kid he had gone down with his dad, who had been Miss Simpson's attorney. Poor old dad! If he were alive, this disgrace would surely kill him!

Well, Jim had remembered the layout of the vault. How Tony Corell and Joe Starkas, two minor characters in New York's underworld, came to find out about the vault and Jim's knowledge was pure accident. While stopping in town, they had somehow gotten several bits of information by chance, and these they pieced into a valuable whole. They made Jim's acquaintance in the hotel where young Archer played the bass tuba in Jan Ross's orchestra. It took only a week for Jim to fall.

"You'll be on easy street the rest of your life," said Joe Starkas, who had a very glib tongue. "You'll never get anywhere playing second fiddle—I mean, blowing that oompah-oompah in that hick band. Think of it, Jim! You'll be able to marry your girl, Millie, who is used to big dough, anyway. It will never leak out. Starkas and Corell leave no tracks for the cops to follow."

The job came off as smoothly as Joe's line. The trio quietly broke into the manse one night, and Jim led them down the steps and secret passageways he recalled so well. In half an hour Corell had made the safe-bolts slide. They hid the loot in an old barn, and Starkas decided they'd meet when the storm blew over and divvy up.

But that following noon Jim got a letter, posted in town. It read:

Dear Sap: We two have beat it with the swag. Don't you open your trap except to blow into your horn. If you squeal, Millie will learn naughty things about her boy friend. And before you can testify they'll find you dead with all signs pointing to suicide. Good-bye and lots of kisses.

Millicent Davis was giving an afternoon party, and it was the first time that Jim had seen her since the burglary three days before. Inclined a little to plumpness, she looked luscious in her black satin gown, which made Jim feel and appear all the more haggard.

"You look so worried, Jim," she said, as they slipped to a deserted veranda. "I never saw you looking so sickly, Jim. What is it?"

"I'm all right, Millie—except—well, I can't get a good job; and you can't marry a beggar."

"Jim, you know that won't come between us. Dad likes you. Your father was his best friend, and he is willing to give you a position at the office. But you're too proud to ask. Besides, why did you quit the orchestra? Jan Ross called up and said you had quit, disgusted or something."

Jim explained with flickering eyelids. There was little money and no future in blowing a sousaphone. If his father had not lost all his money before he died, he would have taken up law and stepped into his shoes.

This last thought brought up the Simpson burglary to Millie's mind. "Who do you think broke into the vault?" she asked. "Do you think it was anybody in town?"

Jim's heart skipped a beat. But he saw not the faintest gleam of suspicion in her eyes. Moreover, didn't the papers say the safe was opened by an expert? Nevertheless, he felt as though his guilt was plastered all over his features.

An hour later, the ill wind he feared began to blow against his face. As he steered his car out of the Davis driveway, a voice hailed him by name. It was Sheriff Silbermyer, who came up and squeezed his two hundred pounds of good nature beside Jim's slight frame. The latter's momentary relief, when the sheriff asked him for a lift into town, flopped into a feeling of fear as he was ordered to park in the shade of a deserted side street.

"How ya feeling, Jimmy boy?" Silbermyer spoke, still good-naturedly.

Jim noticed the searching points of the big man's pupils and turned his head away.

"I think you're in a tough spot, Jim. I can see it on your face. Tell me, do you know anything about this Simpson business?"

The youth jerked about with a shocked expression. "I know anything? Why surely you don't suspect me, Mr. Silbermyer! You know me too well, and you knew dad."

"That's it, Jim. That's why I want to help you. Here's how I came to think about you, Jim. I just recalled this morning that I drove past the Simpson home about twelve on the night of the burglary. And I remembered seeing you walking down the street. Now, neither your rooms nor the Davis home are near that place. Besides, you should have been at the hotel."

"I quit the job, Sheriff, the day before. Nothing wrong about walking—"

"Yes, Jan Ross told me you didn't want to waste any more wind on an old horn. And on the eve of the burglary, Jim. Then, I have never seen you so far away from your rooms without your car. Since then I have watched you closely. You're not yourself, boy. Who did it? Where's the loot?"

"Mr. Silbermyer, I know absolutely nothing. That's final."

"Very well, Jim. Then it is my duty to arrest you and lock you up. If you're guilty, they'll make you tell everything. Sorry."

Jim broke down and told everything then and there, pleading with his father's friend to save his reputation. Yes, to save his life, for Corell and Starkas had promised to kill him. The sheriff listened patiently.

"Corell? Corell?" Silbermyer repeated, then jerked a newspaper from his pocket. "I guess you hadn't seen this, Jim." The item read:

> New York, May 10—A body, identified as that of Tony, alias Toby, Corell, was found in the East river yesterday afternoon. It was apparently a suicide. Corell had served ten years at Sing Sing for safe burglary...

"Starkas did that, Sheriff! That's what I was promised—apparent suicide!"

"Nobody is going to hurt you, Jim, if you do as I say. You're free, so as to help us catch the thief. Jim, I trust you."

"Many thanks, Mr. Silbermyer. I'm willing to risk my life to help catch Starkas and have the stolen goods returned."

"Listen. You go back to work. Ross said he'd take you back anytime. I'll have a man watch you, so that no stranger gets close to you. Then I'll send a wire to the New York papers, saying that the authorities here suspect a certain Joe Starkas as the Simpson burglar. Your life will be safe, Jimmy."

"But what about my reputation? And—Millie?"

"You'll have to risk that. There's no other way. Besides, there's a fat chance of keeping you out of it. I'll try to find a way, though."

Two days dragged on for Jim Archer. From the bandstand in the hotel he could see the detective who had followed him in another car to and from his boarding place. The same man parked his car a short distance away when he visited the Davis home. As for Starkas, according to Silbermyer, he could not be located in New York. As if there anybody could be accounted for! Anyway, Jim felt a storm brewing.

On the third night after his secret confession to the sheriff, the cyclone came. Ross had hung up the baton early, and Jim drove home, followed a block away by his guardian. He caught a glimpse of his headlights as he turned in towards his garage, which stood a hundred paces away from the unpretentious boarding house where he roomed. After throwing the doors open, he drove in and, of course, could not see them close again, or hear the bar on the inside fall into place.

The first intimation of someone else's presence came from an automatic stuck into his chest as he reached to shut off the engine.

"Keep the cylinders hopping, mug! And step out. No funny stuff either, or—"

It was Joe Starkas.

"Ya, it's me, sap! So you decided to squeal, eh? Well, nobody can double-cross Joe Starkas. Tony Corell tried to grab my share—oh, so you read about the suicide! Turn around, and put your mits behind you!"

Jim did so and felt a pair of cold bracelets clap about his wrists. What was the thug's idea? To take him for a ride in his own car?

"Another case of suicide, lily. Afraid to face the D.A., and so choked himself with car-smoke. Lay down, sister, and let me tie your feet. I'll take them off after you've croaked."

Asphyxiated! Jim could see it all now. With him gone, Starkas would slip out of the law's clutches with the aid of a smart lawyer, while everybody would pin the guilt on Jim Archer, a cowardly suicide. The small garage was filling up with smoke, which began to gag him. The murderer was very impatient.

"Lay down," he ordered.

Close to him in the dark, Jim saw Millie's face, clouded with carbon monoxide—with disgrace, rather. A more real face came close, that of Starkas, and his eyes were smarting.

"Lay down, I say!" he repeated, unwittingly lowering the ugly muzzle of his gun.

Jim had read about a certain wrestler's scissors-grip. Without considering whether it was wise to try it, he made a desperate leap. Gasping with surprise, the yegg found himself on the floor with a pair of thin, long legs locked around his arms and waist. The gun had gone off into the floor as he fell, but the report sounded no different from the coughing, poison-spewing engine.

Starkas was a much stronger man, and Jim lacked the use of his arms. But this, and the fact that all depended on it, made Jim squeeze all the more tightly with his legs. The thug turned over with a mighty jerk and tried to pry his arms free, which made Jim feel as though he was being ripped in halves. He held on, however, noticing that the other's efforts were weakening fast.

"So this is your game, sissy—think I'll go under first. Not on your life—"

Jim kept his lips and jaws shut. The more Starkas growled the more gas he inhaled. Feeling his adversary go limp altogether, Jim extricated himself, rushed to the doors and wrenched off the bar, and pushed out into the fresh night air, falling unconscious on the gravel driveway. He did not see half a dozen men leap from a car as it drew up in front of him.

The first impression he got on opening his eyes was that of whiteness. White ceiling, white walls, a man and woman in white, the white face of Millicent Davis. When he muttered her name, she quickly bent down and kissed him, saying something about his being a hero. He could not understand. The doctor explained that the crisis was now over, but that the patient's recovery depended on complete rest. And so Millie retreated through the door.

Just then a big gray blur of a man came in and whispered to the doctor and nurse, who left him alone with the patient. It was Mr. Silbermyer.

"Jimmy, you shouldn't be disturbed, but I explained to the doc that my message is worth a thousand rests. Jimmy, everything's OK! Starkas never came to and passed out completely an hour ago. We also found the loot in his car—must have been heading West. And say, old Miss Simpson has deposited five thousand in the bank in your name for being a hero!"

A look of protest came upon Jim's face. "I can't take it—she doesn't know that I helped Starkas and Corell..."

"Quiet, Jim. Doc's orders. You can take the reward. You see, I figured you would look at it this way, and that you would let me tell her the whole case. The old lady was sure glad to know that the honest Archer blood triumphed in you, for she admired your father very much for his honesty. All this means a lot to you and Millie!"

Ah, Millie! A gorgeous peace overwhelmed Jim Archer, and he closed his eyes.

"Before I leave," said the sheriff, "I want to know how a kid like you could handle brute twice your size, and with your hands literally tied behind your back."

"It was a lung-capacity contest, Sheriff. Starkas was a dope-fiend, and I've been blowing a bass horn for a couple of years."

Chuckling to himself, Silbermyer left the room. "It's an ill wind that blows no one good," he said to the puzzled nurse outside.

You might say that Carrie didn't have much of an idea—but look what Elmer did to it!

Carrie's Notion

(June 1937)

Elmer Vogelmeister went cautiously along the storefronts of Third Street one Saturday noon. He had the lean and hungry look of those who depend pretty much for a living on their manuscripts, and who gorge themselves with nothing more substantial than dreams of literary recognition.

"Komnenos Billiard Parlor" read a sign above his head, and Elmer stuck close to the wall until he came near a shiny large window with the pretentious legend: "Ye Olde Sugar Bowl—Basil Panaiotes, Prop." Letting one eye slip past the brick corner, he caught sight of Carrie standing behind the candy cases, and talking to the omnibus that paraded as Basil Panaiotes. The girl saw Elmer, and Basil swiveled about, but Elmer had slipped back to the vicinity of the pool hall.

"Just my luck," muttered the spy. Elmer was not merely love-sick for that slim, small, round-eyed person called Carrie Hopewell. He was dead in love from heel to hair. Carrie thought a lot of Elmer, too; to her he was a genius who hadn't got a break yet. His bad fortune extended even to the simple (or complex) matter of courting, for big old Basil also had his beady eye on the girl who handled the sweets in his candy shop. Of late the Greek had begun to manifest his dislike for the young fellow, and he kept a strict watch over Carrie. She, however, had to stand passively by in order to keep her fifteen-dollar a week job.

"If only my rejection slips were dollar-bills," said Elmer to himself, feeling at the solitary dollar in his pocket.

Suddenly Basil came out and brushed past the figure pressed against the wall. He had not seen Elmer. With a bound the youth reached the door and slipped in. There were no customers, and Carrie was arranging the trays in the glass cases. She looked up.

"Oh, it's you, Elmer. You better not stay too long."

"Say, how about a date to-night, Carrie. Or is that fat bozo taking you out?"

She nodded. Basil was taking her to a show. Elmer groaned all the way up from his toes and began to complain about more rejected manuscripts, and then this amorphous Adonis stepping in besides.

"I've got a notion, Elmer," Carrie replied. "Listen—"

"Can we sarve you, my frand," croaked a voice close to Elmer's ear and a hand big as a first-baseman's mitt parked on his shoulder. Turning his head a bit, Elmer caught the sharp stare of Basil Panaiotes upon him. He felt like punching the brute, but thought better. Although a shapeless and graying Hercules, Basil yet reminded him forcibly of Jim Londos ready for a bone-crushing grip.

"I was just buying some candy, mister," he managed to whisper.

"What kaynd, baddy?"

"This pink fudge here," Elmer answered. "I'll take a pound."

"This fadge is fifty sants a pound when dry," said the big voice. "And saventy-five sants when it is frash. This was jast made this marning. Wrap it up, Carrie. Thank you ver' mach and don't come again."

With a pound of priceless fudge in his coat pocket and his twenty-five cents in his hand, Elmer walked away with the feeling that he was carrying a gold brick. But even this was light compared with his heart, which swung like a tolling bell of two tons. What to do with the fudge? It bore down on his spirits like an "old man of the sea." He himself hated fudge, and Carrie smelled so much of the stuff from morning till night that she despised anything under the name of candy.

A little girl waiting for a street-car at the corner gave him an idea. The child looked up and around with wondering eyes when he offered her the fudge.

"Hop along there! Keep moving, smart guy!" came a sharp command, and Elmer felt the end of a policeman's stick under his ribs. Too many kidnappings these days.

As Elmer walked down a deserted side street, another figure lumbered toward the corner. Basil's suspicions had been set aflame, and he wanted to make sure that the young fellow was not waiting for Carrie when she came out for lunch. Basil saw Elmer toss something in front of him, and then kick it as if it were a football—or maybe the back of Basil's pants, the Greek surmised correctly. A lump of fudge lay splattered on the pavement. Smiling with satisfaction, the old fellow was about to return to the Sugar Bowl, when he noticed that his youthful rival had walked across the street and up to the Catholic Rectory. The door closed behind him. "Ah-ha," Basil grunted. "Fixing up for a wadding, eh?"

Father Bergan was hilariously glad to see his one-time server boy. "It's a long time since I saw you, Elmer my boy. How's the quill trade coming along? Sit down, sit down. Say, you don't look overly cheerful."

"Everything's gone haywire, Father. I just dropped in for a little bit of advice. Got the time?"

"Oh, certainly. What is it, old pal?"

"Father, you wouldn't ask a girl to marry you when you're broke, would you?"

The priest chuckled. "No, I wouldn't, broke or brimming with gold. But you're talking about yourself. Well, who is the lucky lady?"

Starting from their very first meeting, Elmer recounted the great Romance of Sir Elmer and Lady Caroline, lady-in-waiting in the Palace of the Sugar Bowl, or rather the captive damsel in the Fudge Den under the power of a big ogre. Her he painted as an incarnate fairy in dainty slippers, whatcha-may-call skirts, and a brick-red leather jacket. Father Bergan was patient. Gradually the storyteller passed over to his own failures. His short stories were not so poor, he said; yet they always returned, except for a few, with pink slips attached. Pink slips and pink fudge were his Nemesis.

"I know you have ability, Elmer," the priest said at last. "Don't give up. It's there. Your chance will come. By the way, here's something you ought to try. It's a new magazine for men—*The American Scion*. They have started a short novel contest, and the prize is 2,000 dollars."

"Two thousand bucks for a story!"

"If the story is worth it. How about trying it? You stand a good chance, I believe. If you win, you'll start a reputation; besides, you can rescue this Miss Hopewell from the big bad wolf."

Elmer's elation went so far as to make him swing the priest's arms up and sidewise in a most irreverential manner. He was confident that he could have a novelette in three weeks when the contest closed. He must tell Carrie.

Hardly was the boy gone when Father Bergan had to answer the doorbell again. He immediately recognized one of Elmer's descriptions in the hulk before him. The wolf was at his door.

"How do," Basil growled, and squeezed in. "Naw, I gat no time to sit down. I jast come to ask if that kid speak to you about a wadding."

"No, he arranged no wedding, so far as I can recall. Elmer Vogelmeister is a good friend of mine; I knew him since he was a baby. Are you from this, parish, Mr.—"

"Panaiotes, my name. Basil Panaiotes. I go to Greek Church sometime when I go warship. What I want to tell you, Mr. Priest, is that you keep out of my affires; or maybe I blow up your ractory to bitses!"

Father Bergan smiled, but with a firm mien. "You will oblige me very much if you do blow up this old place. There's heavy insurance on it, and I could build a new rectory. But please warn me to get out before you light the fuse. So good afternoon, sir; and call again."

All that afternoon Elmer racked his brains for a suitable plot. None of the ideas filed away among his projects seemed to fit in with the requirements of a prize-winner. Towards supper-time he locked up his working desk and took a bath. He put on his best clothes, snatched a bite or two for a meal, and was off at a trot toward the carline. He knew which car Carrie took to return from the city to her rooms across the river. He wanted to talk with her about the contest. Not that she would give him plot and characters just offhand, but that she would fill him with hope and confidence in himself. That, surely, was most important.

Not until he had boarded the outbound car did he remember that Basil was taking Carrie out tonight. But he'd talk to her before Basil drove over. The aisle was crowded with workers and Saturday shoppers returning home, but, by pulling himself up on the strap, Elmer momentarily surveyed the length of the car and made sure that she was on it. It was already dark when the trolley crossed the bridge and made its first stop. Elmer jumped off and met Carrie as she was stepping out at the other end.

"Why, Elmer," she gasped. "I told you he was coming for me tonight."

"Oh, sure, don't I know it? I just wanted to see you about something before he comes."

Instead of following the sidewalk, Elmer led the girl a few feet into a grove that touched the water's edge near the bridge. They easily made themselves at home on a fallen sycamore—they had been there often before; that is, before Basil grew too fond of Carrie. To form a romantic background, such as the young author had given to many of his unaccepted stories, a generous moon was rising above the light-dotted skyline on the opposite bank. All this made a shimmering display on the black deep current. Elmer, however, noted that the moon wrought a sharp silhouette of the Greek Cathedral of the Theotokos. An ill omen. Imagine Carrie walking up its great aisle with that pudgy palooka.

"I wanted to ask you a question," he whispered close to her ear. "Remember this afternoon, when that rhinoceros horned in on me? You said you had a notion—about what?"

"Oh, yes; about your writing, Elmer. Don't you think your name has something to do with it? Well, it—it isn't literary, don't you see?"

"I get you, Carrie. I ought to have a pen-name. Say, I never thought seriously of that! Elmer Vogelmeister. Not so romantic, eh? How about 'Elmer Hopewell'? That's a dandy."

"Don't have me taking credit for your work. Couldn't you translate your family name? What does it mean, anyway?"

"Gosh, I learned more Greek (darn it!) than I did German when I went through high school. But I'm pretty sure Vogelmeister means 'Master of Birds,' or something close to it."

"Fine!" Carrie exclaimed. "How about this: E. Byrd Masters?" She spelled it out. "See? The two names are very bookish, and many of such folks like to carry their initials first!"

Elmer thought it a colossal idea, especially since it fell from those small, rounded, cherry lips in the moonlight. Moments of ecstatic visions into the future followed, and an hour had slipped by before Carrie gave a thought to Basil Panaiotes. What if he had come and found her not at home? She was not afraid of him, however, for she said that every inch of the big Greek was a bluff. Any prompt affront was enough to unarm him. No sooner did they reach the street level, when a car grinded to a stop by the curb. A husky voice in the dark called Carrie by name.

It was Basil.

"Say, Carrie," he growled. "Why I not find you at home?"

"I had some important business, Mr. Panaiotes," she replied, indifferently.

"Let's drive over to the house, and I'll change my dress and fix up a bit."

"Impartant business, you say? Ah, with that squart, eh? Say, rant, I gotta mind to stap out and panch you on the noss. Keep off this garl. Hear me?"

"All right, come out of that car," Elmer retorted. "I'll knock you cold and then roll your walrus' carcass into the river." He was now hoping that Carrie's appraisal of her employer proved to be correct. To his relief, the machine purred around and away, and he stepped forward for a town-bound trolley that came clanking around the corner towards the bridge.

Carrie Hopewell saw little of Elmer during the next two weeks in which he was working at his masterpiece. Shortly before the contest closed, he sent her a card, announcing that the MS had been mailed. The following weeks dragged along miserably for both. Elmer vainly tried to sell some minor stuff in the meantime; Carrie trafficked all day in crisp peanut brittles, chaste marble taffies, buttery caramels, and frozen-faced fudge. Every time she wrapped up a purchase of the pink variety, she breathed a prayer for good luck in behalf of the purchaser, just as she prayed for the success of Elmer's venture.

One hot day, nearly a month later, Carrie was slipping on her jacket, as it was her lunch-hour, when a bunch of Basil's pals came over from the Komnenos Billiard Parlor. They asked for Basil.

Suddenly the front screen-door flew open with a screech and slapped back angrily against the fuming bulk of Basil Panaiotes. He was holding an open magazine in one paw and beckoning his friends with the other.

"Look here, fallows," he roared. "I have been insalted in the prass! It jast come out." The men came forward, while Carrie stood by like Lot's wife to watch the conflagration. "Look! Some wise guy, he write something fanny about me and my place!"

"What is it, Basil?" asked a fellow they called Eli, who at the same time hid his copy of the magazine behind his back.

"Tack a look," Basil replied. "Some san-of-a-gan he write a story about a candy shap, and he call my Sugar Bowl 'The Fadge Dan'!"

"Oh, The Fudge Den," another repeated, with a grimace.

"If I know who writes this, I kill the booger! I sue him for label!"

"You can't sue him for libel," interposed a little fellow. "He don't mean you. How can you prove it in court?"

"I know he means me, Cyril. See? He say Plato and Dick the hero after same garl Susie. Plato he sells pink fadge to hero and puts a drop of strychnine in it. The hero he don't like fadge and so he gives it to strange little garl. The kiddie she die on the trolley-car. Then the police start an invastigation and find nathing. But the hero saspects the candy man. There!"

"See now?" said a certain Georgy. "You never poisoned no kid, Basil. It can't mean you at all."

"Yas, but the writer he descrabs my parson and my Sugar Bowl. He say I am cuckoo in the upstars! He say I have one parsecution camplex; he say I am crazy—nats!"

Carrie, coming to herself, involuntarily cleared her throat. Basil faced about and came to the counter, almost pushing the open magazine into her face.

"Carrie, you know something about this abamination!"

But Carrie could hardly conceal her surprise, which, happily, the rest took for sheer fright. The title of the story glared and blared at her in large black and red types: "THE FUDGE DEN" by E. Byrd Masters. The $2,000 Prize Short Novel—Beginning this Month."

Basil brought his boar's head closer. "Garl, I think I brack your little nack!"

"You do nothing of the kind, you bully!" Carrie gave full rein to her long-suppressed disgust. "I have nothing to do with this thing, and you know it. You have publicly insulted a lady, and I ought to call the police. I will call them, Basil, if you ever bother me again. I'm through with you and your fifteen-dollar a week charity!"

With this she deliberately paced out the door, being careful to slam it vigorously, while Basil sank into a chair, looking more forlorn than Job amid his circle of silent cronies.

Elmer Vogelmeister waited at the door of the Cafe where Carrie usually lunched. He wanted to be the first to break the happy news. But her pale features and heaving breast told him that something was amiss. She took away his fears after explaining briefly what had taken place at the Sugar Bowl, and both laughed heartily as they left the Cafe far behind.

"Isn't it grand!" he said. "They were so crazy over the story that they sent the first installment to press before mailing me my check. Besides, they have offered me a contract to write periodically for them."

"Two thousand dollars to start with," she breathed. "And a name for yourself and—say, where are you leading me to?"

"This is a priest's house, Carrie. I want you to meet that Father I've often told you about."

Father Bergan was very cordial, but somewhat funereal when he looked straight at Elmer. "I just received my *American Scion,*" he said, picking up the magazine. "I see that someone else was the lucky man."

"Someone who?" Elmer shouted gaily, and Carrie smiled. "Why, I'm the man, and you ought to be glad about it!"

Nonplussed, the priest looked at the open pages and then whistled softly. "Oh, so you are this bird, this 'E. Byrd Masters.' Congratulations, boy. And you, Miss Hopewell. Elmer, where did you get the classy nom-de-plume?"

"That was a notion of Carrie's, that is, Miss Hopewell. Say, Father, should a guy marry a certain party if he's got the money?"

COURAGE *and* FAITH

Lithographs by Gerald Cassidy

Honest Art

(February 1938)

"Lucky young fellow, that Arturo Vásquez," said old Pedro Luna to me the other day. "Most exact and earnest. Scrupulously honest. And he's well-to-do; that's why I call him lucky. You would imagine him chiseling his statues in some squalid adobe hut (there are no Parisian attics in Santa Fe) like those art beginners I've read about."

Yet it isn't luck so much, Arturo himself would tell you.

One afternoon I stopped in to see that San José he is carving for the old chapel back home in Chimayó. He owns a neat little home and studio pueblo style, right off the Alameda under the cottonwoods. I squatted down by his fireplace and engaged him in a friendly chat while he hacked away at a big pine trunk that stood upright on a stool. He told me he had plenty of commissions, but liked to work on this San José. As for the other jobs, he was certain of having them finished by the time stipulated.

"Fortune has surely favored you," I said, admiringly. "Of course, you tell me it's honesty, as you're always hinting to me, friend Vásquez. *Pero quién sabe?"*

"I know it's hard for a county politician of New Mexico to grasp such a lofty idea," he retorted, winking at me with good nature. "But you'll understand when I tell you—"

"That being honest sent you to a school and then showed you how to chip silver dollars off a piñon plank."

"Exactly!" Arturo lay down his tools. "However, Señor Luna, you must presuppose that the good God gave me the knack, or call it talent, for shaping things. The rest came in great measure from that which makes art, Art—honesty. Where falsehood is, there Art cannot be."

I smiled condescendingly, thinking what a valuable campaign orator this young Vásquez would make. "It sounds very beautiful—"

He hesitated; then sat next to me. "Listen, Luna," he said at length. "You will be surprised at this. Nor am I ashamed to tell it. Here it is, you know how I came to town from the *rancho*—a green boy, greener than Chimayó green chile, but not so hot. I came to Santa Fe because some artist people had liked my carving and the Government was starting to aid promising talent at the time. They said I had the makings of a genius. Maybe I did. Only the gift had to be brought out, they said. I carved a figure of Padre Padilla with an Indian which he displayed in the Museum. Remember? Everybody came to see it.

"Well, all these compliments made me yearn for a good knowledge of sculpture. I wondered how I could scrape enough money to send me away and start me off in school. There were plenty of wealthy folks who patted me on the back; but their hands never went down into their pockets.

"One morning I met Miss Donahey under the Old Palace porch, and she invited me to a small gathering of notables at her house that evening. Some New York artists and writers had stopped over on their way to Los Angeles, and it seems they had been very much fascinated by my Padilla piece. Some even said they'd love to meet me. Miss Donahey herself told me this, so I went up to her rambling adobe on Canyon Road.

"I met a famous French painter there; also, a rich theater manager, a couple of New York novelists, a woman scenario-writer, and a poetess from New Hampshire. When I came in they fell all over me; but soon they left me severely alone. I was not hurt by it; that's the way these people act. They hung around that lanky, wax-skinned, red-topped poetess, like moths around a lit candle. She had personality, all right.

"Shortly before dinner, while I was studying a Taos landscape on the wall, I overheard an interesting remark the French artist was earnestly making to Mr. Palmer, the theater mogul. 'The trouble with modern art,' said he, 'is that there is too much dishonesty....' His voice lowered as he vigorously tapped his fingers on his other palm, as if recounting specific instances. As I was glancing at them over my shoulder, Palmer drew a beautiful morocco wallet and handed some card or envelope to the Frenchman. Just then Miss Donahey called us in to dinner, and the poetess' admirers formed a chattering wave which carried Mr. Palmer and the painter into the dining room. I tagged along after them, but not until I had picked up something Mr. Palmer had dropped—the morocco wallet.

"*Amigo,* I don't understand to this day how I stole that wallet without any deliberation. So naturally, although I had not pilfered a thing in my life. It was only until I sat down, that qualms of conscience began to stir and then to writhe in my chest. And fear also came. When Palmer happened to look my way, I felt as though he knew, as though he recognized that bulge on my breast pocket. All the while, my conscience was poking me inside, pinching, biting. But then I thought of the Art Institute.... I would first see how much the wallet contained.

"After dinner I excused myself. I examined the wallet behind a locked door. Five one hundred dollar bills, and many smaller ones—847 dollars! A neat sum. Just what I needed. My flushed face looked at me from the washstand mirror, and I turned away from it; I sank the wallet into my hip-pocket.

"Yet all through the evening I suffered from fear. If I left early, as I wanted to, they would suspect me afterwards when the loss was discovered. The climax came when Miss Donahey announced that Mr. Palmer had dropped or misplaced his pocketbook. Nobody knew, of course. Nor was anyone searched."

"For a few minutes I felt coolly relieved, until Mr. Palmer walked over to where I was disinterestedly peering at some Baumann wood-prints. You see, I preferred to keep my face to the wall.

"'Young man,' he said to me, quietly turning me around by the shoulder. 'I admire your work very much, very much.' My answer was a nervous blush and grin which I hoped he would take for modesty. It began to look that way, his eyes were so kind behind his thick glasses.

"He brought his face closer and whispered forcefully: 'You have unusual talent, boy. Surprising, indeed. And no training at all, my hostess tells me. Wonderful. Would you care to take up studies in sculpture?'

"That was my main desire,' I told him."

"'That's fine, very fine! Perhaps, matters could be arranged. But you must do your part; you must not spoil your talent, your chances. Young artists are often spoiled, you know—taking the easier path. As Mr. Boutain was telling me right before dinner, Art today suffers from dishonesty. Many artists of the present, afraid of work and privation, follow the line of least—'

"*Amigo* Luna, I, Arturo Vásquez, felt very funny, felt like screaming like a woman in hysterics. The old gent looked at me somewhat queerly too. I pulled out the wallet and slipped it into his hands, explaining how I came to have it. Right away, something told me I made what Mr. Boutain would have called a *faux pas*.

"You see, Mr. Palmer did not know. He had no suspicions. What he was giving me for advice referred to something else. Modern Art suffers, the French painter had told him, from members of the profession who are not sincere, who cheat in their work, like painting over photographs, putting wax or plaster on imperfect statues, using the arts for pure propaganda, and all that sort of quackery. You understand, don't you?

"Take it or leave it, friend Luna, that gentleman complimented me on my honesty, although you can see I did not deserve it. We had a private conversation the rest of the evening. Mr. Palmer is the one who put me through school. He is the best of my patrons.

"*Sí, mi amigo político,* where falsehood is, there Art cannot be."

Beads

(August 1937)

The other day, upon swapping my berth in an A.T. & S.F. Pullman for a mess of footage on a crowded street-car platform in Denver, I received a heavy tap on my skull. I looked up.

"Well, well," says Joe Sterkes, "if it isn't Chappy himself, and in the skin!" We managed to shake hands and began to explain our respective presences in this western metropolis.

"I'm drumming," said I. "But where have you been keeping yourself these last ten years? Didn't I see you reporting for the Louisville *Courier-Journal?*"

"I've been all over," answered Joe, in a hurry. "I must get off now. Are you busy today? No? Good. Wait for me in front of the *Denver Post* at 5 P.M. Then we'll have supper together. By the way, old Chappy, our office force is having an intelligence test today!" With this he jumped off, and I was left with an intelligence bug humming like a dynamo in my ear.

It was still buzzing at 5 o'clock when I spied Joe leaving the printing house of the *Post.* I picked him out of the crowd by the neck—I mean, his neck and head showed about six inches above other heads. He literally stood out in a crowd, this Joe. He was not yet forty, of very tan complexion, and afflicted with perpetual motion about the lower jaw.

We shook hands again, but with more leisure, as we walked off.

"Sterkes," I said, "you haven't changed. How's work? Did you pass the intelligence test? Are you settled down? Do you still smoke as much as ever? Are you still a Christian?"

"Here's a taxi, Chappy," he answered. "Jump in and we'll be home in time for a good old feed. Meanwhile, I'll answer your simple question in a few words." Joe was a man of few words; that is, he had the gift of making a few words do for one. That's why he never had any trouble in landing a newspaper job in any town.

"Have a cigar," he continued, settling down beside me. As he pulled out two cigars, I caught sight of a little rosary tangled about the cellophane wrappers. He saw me look. "Oh, yes, I'm still a Christian. I've said my beads for twenty years, ever since my mother died. I would have dropped it long since, were it not for a promise I made to her. There's many a fellow, outside of Catholic magazine stories, who keeps that kind of a deathbed promise. However, many of them don't say their rosary with much prayer in mind. I do." He looked at me doubtfully.

"But that's another story, Chappy. I've got a fine job, a nice home, and a swell missus. We live on the other side of town. Everything has been running smoothly like the presses, until a brood of research psychologists made up with the *Post*'s boss to have the office crew examined as to brain fruit. Mere experiment, so they say. So we went into their roller mills this afternoon."

"Cheat your way through?"

"Cheat? Never. Flunked, says I. Flunked. What do you expect? A couple of wax-cheeked robots first take individual measurements of the bunch. They ran miles of tape around my ears, up and down my cranium, and down my nose to my gold uppers, marking it all down with curving lines on a chart.

They examined my teeth, like the big horse that I am, and set that down also, until the chart looked like a sketch of Pike's Peak yonder, or the tracks of the Big Four leading into Cincinnati. 'Regular cephalic' says one of the wax-cheeks, and marks it down. When everybody was converted into charts and figures, they give us ninety-one questions to answer. Easy? Say, what do I know about the formula for bicarbonate of soda? Who wrote 'Hark, hark, the lark?' Or, what would you do on a burning aeroplane if you had no parachute? And such questions.

"Well, after the inquisition I asked my boss if I'm fired. 'Joe' says he, handing me these quarter cigars, 'as long as you have brains, that's all we want.' And then I remember you are waiting for me outside. Is your very simple question answered?"

"Generously, Joe, generously. A very intelligent reply." Too late did I discover my blunder. It was like shoving chewing gum in a monkey's mouth. For Joe's jaw began to chew and churn at that word "intelligent." The taxi kept on going, nevertheless.

"It isn't the height nor the girth nor the shape of his chin," says Joe, "that makes a man intelligent. Nor the hue of his hide either. Take my experience for example. Some years ago I was reporting for the *Texas Free Star*, an independent daily of El Paso. That's where I had gone when I left old Louisville, where you last saw me. Well, old Gordon Murphy, editor of the *Free Star*, calls me to his sanctum and makes me an offer. As you know, at that time Calles was playing the double role of Nero and Stalin down in Mexico. The paper needed some sensational stuff to survive, for competition by the chain papers was strong. So Murphy tells me to cover Calles, expenses paid and pay in advance. I shake hands and am ready to start across the Rio Grande next day.

"Of course, I had to go incognito. That is, turn Mexican. Do you see this school-grid complexion of mine? Smoky, isn't it? Well, my folks come originally from Bohemia, where dusky gypsies must have tampered with the Sterkes family blood. Besides, I happened to be born in Pittsburgh. And another thing, I had lived long enough with Mexicans on the border to speak their lingo to a T. So in a couple of days you could have seen me riding a train through Chihuahua and all points south. I was Pablo Rocha now, a common peon, though somewhat taller than the ordinary citizen of the white flannels and half-barrel hats.

"When I finally dropped off at Mexico City, I found me a room near the great plaza, dirt floor and mice, for five cents a day in our money. I had to play the poor peon, you see. Here I slept and wrote my reports by candlelight, for a typewriter would have meant a machine-gun for me, with me at the dangerous end of it. During the day I trailed Calles and the other big shots, whether at their hangouts or at a bullfight in the *Corrida*. At night I would return to my little pad and pencil, and in the morning I would stealthily mail a letter to a certain Mexican gent in Juárez, who knew how to forward it to Editor Murphy across the Rio Grande, as prearranged.

"But there was danger of suspicion. I found this out when an army officer caught me loitering near the President's palace. 'What's your name?' he asked.

"'Pablo Rocha, at your service,' says I, grinning rather foolishly to hide my alarm.

"'A big man like you,' he continued, stepping under my big sombrero, 'ought to be working or in the army!'

"I laughed aloud. I in the army? I explained to him that I couldn't march a mile with a gun, that I was no man. Loose living and *pulque* had sent me to the dogs, Mexican hairless at that, adding that I might take a job if I found one. I blew into his oily mustache, as I had bought a glass of *tequila* shortly before, and then I walked off like a collegian after a New Year's party.

"However, I got tired of reeling about; it was getting too mechanical. Later in the day, as I made for my dingy headquarters, I came upon a tossing sea of sombreros with little brown peons under them. On a box stood a military officer whom I recognized. He saw me. *'Oye,* long stick,' he hollered, 'I have a job for you—digging foundations for the new arsenal— twenty cents per day!' I bowed and raised the street dust with my hat, while a mob of less lucky job-seekers looked up at me with envy.

"The new magazine of artillery was to be erected right across from my hotel suite. I was one of a gang of twenty men set to dig the foundation trenches. We picked and spaded all day in the blistering sun while our foreman, an armed guard, walked up and down nearby. Being a stranger, I was not talked to by the rest of the crew. They seemed to sense that I was more than they in other things than stature, maybe one of Calles' stool-pigeons, just because the recruiting officer had singled me out, and because now and then I managed to swap a joke with our guard.

"After the first day, I began to look around me more closely. I noticed that my companions were particularly fond of one of their number, a puny brown peon, gray-haired, somewhat nervous, and very queer. His wrinkled mouth was always going like a rabbit's, although he didn't speak much. I also noted that, when the guard visited the saloon down the street, and if I was not looking toward him, he would squat down on the embankment, all played out. What struck me was the funny twitching of his fingers, slowly, one after the other, until he would jerk up his thumb and look at it, like little Jack Horner and the plum. When the soldier returned, he was back on the job.

"Then a queer thing happened late one afternoon. In fact, it was our last day, for the trenches were ready for the masons. I was resting on my shovel, talking to the guard about the price of drinks, when I felt a heavy weight thrown against my thighs, as if a sack of wheat had rolled down the embankment. I turned around. There at my feet was the still form of little Jack Horner himself, in a dead swoon. As I lifted the old fellow in my arms, the way you pick up a run-over kid, the rest of the gang saw what had happened and hurried toward us. They stopped, however, and turned back to their tools, for the sentinel was pointing his rifle at them. I understood their prudence, for a Calles soldier is liable to shoot you without excuse.

"Lowering his gun, the soldier stood looking at me. I said: 'I'll take the poor hombre to my home across the street, if you don't mind. I got a nice bottle of *tequila* that'll bring him to.'

"The guard rubbed his sweaty chin, '*Bueno;* but you must not use too much of the spirits, and bring what's left to me.' So I promised.

"Back in my room, I laid the limp old man on my rickety cot. Then I forced some liquor between his teeth and began to massage his arms. Slowly his mouth began going rabbit-motion. I listened. He was praying. Suddenly, he opened his eyes and blinked at me, bewildered.

'You're all right, *amigo,*' I says. He looks at me rather nervously and tries to get up, but he groans and falls back. When he fainted, he must have struck his back against my shovel, I guessed. So I prepared to investigate.

"'No, no, señor!' he protested. 'I am all right. A few minutes and I shall be up.' But I wasn't finicky and so, before he knew what I was about, I pulled off his cotton blouse and left him there naked to the waist. I saw his fist close around a little crucifix that hung around his neck by a string, and he stared up at me somewhat defiantly. Laughing, I said, '*Viva Cristo Rey!* I am no Calles man, if that's what you are thinking. See? I pray on this every day!' And I pulled out this little rosary of mine. He stared. After a while, I had won him over to trust me.

"The old man said at last, 'It is dangerous to carry a rosary around. They might see it. I pray my rosary, too, but on my fingers—so!' And his fingers began to jerk slowly, the way I had seen them do many a time before. After the tenth jerk, up came his thumb. 'That is an Our Father,' he explained. I felt somewhat shrunk, I tell you.

"Then I remembered the old fellow's injured back. Pouring some liquor in the cup of my hand, I began to rub it all over his back. As I did so, I was puzzled by a little white rope that he wore, doubled, around his brown waist. I pulled out the ends from under his trousers. One of the ends carried a couple or more knots which I'll bet no Boy Scout ever tried. 'Say,' I asked my patient, 'if I ain't too personal, may I ask the meaning of this thing?'

"'Don't you know, señor? That's to show the world that I am a religious, if it is necessary to do so. I am a Franciscan priest!'

"I tell you—I lay my hands off that man as though he were a hot potato. But he smiles kindly and bids me keep on rubbing, as it does him good. By and by, he is able to sit up, but I make him lie down and rest a bit, while I tell him what I really am. Then he begins telling me more about himself. At the time of the Calles outbreak, he was stationed at the Franciscan convent of Tapopan, State of Jalisco, where he taught science and literature to young men. Boy! the way he described what the soldiers did to their convent! They burned their big ancient library and smashed their laboratories to pieces. That was besides stabling their horses in the chapel. The friars, of course, had to flee the country. But Padre Juan de Dios (that was his name) got permission to remain in hiding and minister to their scattered flocks. As he was too well known all over Jalisco, he fled to Mexico, the very heart of all the trouble, and there he was the camouflaged pastor of half the city. To avoid capture, for the hunt for priests was hot and thorough, Padre Juan, besides dressing like a beggar, had to work like a slave, despite his age and dignity.

"Did you ever hear Shakespeare quoted in Spanish? Padre Juan did that. He also quoted Cervantes and Lope de Vega, talked chemistry and bugs and stars, as though I understood everything. Now and then he would let out some bright remark that made Bob Burns' postscripts sound like post mortem reports. What a man! When I told him I was sneaking back to the States and asked him to come along, he thanked me. No, he wouldn't trade places with the Pope. As I shook hands with him, apologizing for thinking him a half-wit old Indian, I said under my breath: 'All power to you, Padre. Stay where you are. Anyway, if they saw you in civilized places out my way, you wouldn't graduate to kindergarten in an intelligence test—not by your looks. Yes, sir, they'd put you with St. Francis and the Curé of Ars in a county institution. They would.'

"Just then, the priest closed his eyes as if asleep or in a faint. It was a *feint,* for the guard, our foreman, stood at the door. He had waited too long for the bottle and now asked me for it.

"Well, I left Mexico with one memory. The *Texas Free Star* had gone under, and so I hiked up here to Denver, landed a job in the *Post,* as also a wonderful little wife. But nothing has erased that memory of the Padre. And, let me add, there's push behind my prayers now when I pray my rosary."

Joe Sterkes leaned over to the cab driver and told him to let us off. We stepped out in front of a church. Looking at his wristwatch, Joe said to me: "I live just around the block. Do you mind waiting a few minutes while I go in here to say my beads? There's an excellent book-store across the street where you can entertain yourself in the meantime."

I looked at Joe and kinda smiled— feebly.

"Joe," I replied, "I've contracted an inferiority complex somehow. Do you care if I go in with you?"

Sometimes it pays not to talk too much—as old Mateo learned with pleasure.

Mateo Makes Money

(November 1937)

The sun was beating unusually hard upon the stretch of prairie highway between the Indian Pueblo of Santo Domingo and Santa Fe. Puny, wrinkled Mateo seemed bothered not at all by it as his short but steady moccasined steps lightly touched the ground, although the old man was burdened with two heavy blankets and a generous consignment of silver trinkets and earthen pottery.

Mateo, despite his sixty southwest winters, did not mind this trek of thirty miles from his own village by the Rio Grande to old Santa Fe, nestled far up against the mountains. He had done it since he was a boy, and had liked it; but now he more than loved it, for later years had brought on flourishing trade conditions for Indians like himself. As you shall soon see.

What the aged redskin did not relish, though, was the uncertainty of his losses and profits. He had no set prices and it all depended on the character of his customers. If the tourists were green and gullible, he made a hundred percent profit, or even more. If on a bad day they happened to be tightfisted and suspicious, he would often give in to concessions that a careful inventory later on proved alarmingly disastrous.

Especially was this true with regard to customers who were young and good to look at. If a girl wanted a bracelet or a ring and thought the price too high, Mateo would give it to her for practically his own picture, and a buffalo's, stamped on either side of a coin. This was a weakness, and Mateo regretted it after finding himself in the hole; but, no matter what resolves he made, he would fall when the next temptation flapped around.

Now, there was one beautiful lady whom old Mateo loved and venerated passing well. Her picture hung in his room back at Santo Domingo, the only decoration on the bare white walls, save for a Navajo rug or two. It was the dear Virgin of Guadalupe, dark-complexioned and very modestly posed, robed in a gold-embroidered tunic of Indian red, and with a large mantle of Aztec deep blue, spangled with myriad stars of Mexican gold, that covered her head and fell over her shoulders as far as the crescent moon at her feet.

Mateo had prayed to her daily for years. She was the Mother of *tata Dios,* true; nevertheless, Mateo loved her the more because she was of his people, an Indian, and she was dressed in the Indian colors of earthen red and heavenly blue.

No friendly tourist had so far given Mateo a lift. He had already come to the foot of La Bajada, a thousand-foot cliff of volcanic lava, which the highway has to climb in scores of hair-pin turns before it reaches the plateau that stretches away to the base of the *Sangre de Cristo* range where Santa Fe is situated.

Slower still did the old Indian begin to ascend on foot. But, to lessen the tediousness of the climb, Mateo began to revolve the Guadalupe legend in his withered brain, which was as follows:

> Once upon a time, far away towards the wind where the ducks fly in autumn, in the far land *Mexitli,* whence the first white man came up the Rio Grande to Santo Domingo, there lived a giddy old

Indian, called Juan Diego. One day, when Juan Diego had followed a path over a certain hill, a beautiful lady in red and blue and gold, wearing a golden crown, and surrounded with bright rays, appeared to him, saying: "Juan Diego! Juan Diego! Go you and tell the bishop that he must build me a church on this spot."

But Juan Diego was humble enough, and sensible enough, to realize that his Lordship would not believe an ignorant old Indian. Wherefore, Juan did not obey the lady and he afterwards avoided that path. But, wherever he went, the lady stood before him and demanded her strange request. At last Juan explained to her how matters stood, and that he needed a proof to make the bishop believe him. And hence she told him to gather some roses on the hill.

The giddy Indian did as he was told, and he found many beautiful roses on the barren hill, even though it was mid-December. And, the beautiful lady having arranged the flowers on his *tilma*, or fiber blanket, he folded it up and went to the Franciscan bishop of Mexico City, before whom he spread the blanket. And lo! The venerable prelate knelt down in veneration before it, for, when the roses rolled out on the floor, he beheld the picture of Her, whom Juan Diego had seen!

A faithful copy of this miraculous picture was the one which hung in Mateo's home, and now, though the old Indian's wrinkled form was laboring up La Bajada, his spirit was in the presence of his Lady. Mateo was very imaginative, for an Indian. He now began to picture the Blessed Virgin appearing to him on the crest of La Bajada; he already imagined himself plucking all sorts of roses from the thorny cactus on the mesa; he began to see himself kneeling before the Franciscan archbishop of Santa Fe, ready to unfold the wondrous treasure of his own blanket: then, of a sudden, he found himself rising to the clouds. At first they were red, like the sunset, and traced with golden pictographs: and then, lost in a sky of deep blue, he found himself surrounded by countless golden stars.

And close (oh, so close to his face!) came the sweet strong fragrance of many roses, and he heard a mild voice speak in a tongue unintelligible to him. Mateo was seized with joy and without opening his eyes, said in delightful ecstasy: "Guadalupe!"

"Guadaloop must be the chief's name," said a man's voice behind Mateo, and the old Indian awoke to the fact that he was surrounded by a small group of wealthy-looking persons. Not far stood a large, shining automobile.

"Thank God, he isn't hurt a bit," cried a lovely young woman. When she continued to wipe the dust from Mateo's face with a dainty kerchief, he caught the smell of roses again.

"He's all right, sis," a young fellow came in. "I didn't touch him at all. Just as I made the sharp turn, the front fender caught his blankets and knocked him against that wall of tufa rocks. Let him be, sis, and let's go!"

The young lady pressed a handful of crumpled green papers into Mateo's fist in payment, so she said, for the pottery that lay scattered in shards over the road. "How about us chipping in for the benefit of Pocahontas' grandpa?" said the man that was holding Mateo up, and he thrust something into his shirt pocket.

The other tourists followed humorously enough, while Mateo sat on a stone with mouth wide open, like one of those little clay rain-gods that he often sold. It was not until the car was but a speck of dust on the plain below that Mateo began to count his newly acquired wealth, an amount that proved of more value than all his wares put together. It was a miracle that the Lady of Guadalupe had worked for him, Mateo concluded. Should he not tell the archbishop of Santa Fe about it? Or should he sing her praises before the whole pueblo of Santo Domingo?

Mateo, however, like Juan Diego, had enough sense to realize that the kind archbishop would hardly believe his story, no matter how well his Grace received him. Were he to tell it to his people at the pueblo, they would be sure that he had gone through somebody's pockets. He decided at last to keep it a secret between himself and his Lady, content with the thought that he ought to love her more than ever.

From shell-torn Spain comes this tale of a modern Joan of Arc who died that others might live.

Spanish Joan

(December 1936)

It was the night the Red Terror broke loose in Málaga. The *Calle del Toro* was but one of the streets that ran red with fire and blood, but to young María Jaén, in her dark little room upstairs, it was the worst in the city, the most horrible in all Spain.

It was a picture of hell. The Communist mobs surged about like incarnate demons, shrieking blasphemies and applying the knife and torch to everything that was God's. That is why María was so scared as she peered down from her latticed window. She was God's, and so were her aged father and her brother Manuel. Mercifully, her mother was already *with* God, and so was spared the present anguish.

"Lord Jesus, O Sacred Heart!" she whimpered in terror. "O Mary most pure! Do not let them take Papá and Manuel. They are all I have!"

But the Reds could not pass the Jaén house by. Old Señor Jaén had presided at an anti-communist meeting the week before, the very day that some rowdies attacked one of the Canons on this same street and Manuel ran out to defend the helpless old priest. No, they could not spare these two. As she prayed, too weak with fright to rise from her knees, María saw some of the government military approach the door and begin to pound on it.

Manuel rushed up to her dark room, her father behind him. "My sister, my sister," he said in a low voice. "The sons of the devil are come for us. Quiet, now. Papá and I come to say *Adiós*. We could fight back, but then they'll burn us all together with the house. You stay here. *Adiós, hermanita mía!"*

"Adiós, hija!" said the Señor Jaén. María hugged his stooped frame as he kissed her softly and turned away. Manuel caught her against his breast and kissed her mouth *"Adiós*, María. Pray for us. We go to God." Whispering this into her left ear, he kissed it and disappeared after his father. And in María's ear her brother's last word tingled like a little bell: "To God—*Adiós!"*

"Adiós—go with God!" she managed to say at last, but by this time the soldiers had led the two men to a guarded group of captives in the middle of the Calle del Toro.

What followed sent a more than sickening shudder through the girl. Before she realized what the Soviet fiends were about, they had herded all the prisoners into a large van, which they promptly padlocked, splashed with gasoline, and ignited. With a deep boom the truck became a mammoth blowtorch. For a minute the hoarse cries of agonizing pain within the furnace drowned the rumble of the flames—then only the fire could be heard as the Reds began to shout blasphemously amid the revolting smell of burnt human flesh.

María Jaén began to faint. She fought against the nauseating feeling. Why had not God made her a man, so that she might defy and fight these foes of her home, her country, and her Faith? But women had fought, too! There was St. Joan of Arc. And also María's own compatriot, the Maid of Saragossa. Why not she? She was seventeen, not weak by any means, and she was a Spaniard like the heroine of Saragossa.

On the point of hysteria, she stood up, a strange strength vibrating through her plump body. She was resolved to snatch up a butcher-knife, anything, and run berserk among the sacrilegious crowds. A sudden cry from below stung her heart.

"El convento de los Franciscos!" the cry was taken up. The Franciscan convent! They were going to burn that and the friars with it! María could already see the small building in flames, a funeral pyre for kind old Padre Víctor, for Brother Carlos and the rest of the community. She must help them escape. She must get there before the mob.

In the hallway she stumbled against Manuel's hunting-rifle. Loaded or not, she grasped it in one small fist and stole through a rear window onto a neighbor's terrace. Over irregular roofs of loose tiles, along the dizzy top of crumbling garden walls, around yawning patios, the long-skirted figure flitted in the dark, guided by some sixth sense—some guardian spirit, maybe. As she reached the street in front of the convent, a masculine voice called her by name. It was one of Manuel's friends. "María Jaén! It is you! *Por Dios*, hurry! There's an Italian battleship in the bay, and our people are being taken aboard."

"But the Padres?" she asked.

"It is too late to warn them—look! The mob is coming toward the convent. Follow me!"

María did not follow. Gun in hand, she reached the friary door ahead of the Reds. The Porter, who was watching the frenzied crowd approach, quickly unbarred the door for her and barred it again.

"Padres," she said, out of breath. "Hurry out through the rear door, climb over the wall, and run down the alley through the gardens of Doña Clara. From there you can make the waterfront easily. I will hold the Communists here."

While the Reds rammed the door, the Father Superior tried to remonstrate with her. He thought her act was mad. Impatient at the loss of precious time, she pointed her rifle at the community. "Padres, I *am* mad! Away as I tell you, or I shoot you all down!"

The friars disappeared a few seconds before the front door was battered

She wore a defiant little smile that matched the glint in her black eyes.

down. Rifle in hand, she stepped over the splintered boards and faced the rabble in the orange glare of their torches.

"You will not harm these poor helpless men of God!" she screamed at them. "I shoot the first one who dares to make a move this way."

The unexpected sight stunned the blood-thirsty throng for the moment. Suddenly a leering youth in officer's uniform started toward the door with a show of bravado. María herself was startled by the report a she pressed the trigger. With a screeched curse the corporal grasped his shattered knee and struck the cobblestones with his shoulder. The crowd's grumbling arose above their seething fire-brands, but, like any mob, they were hesitant, waiting for some external force to break the spell.

María did indeed hold them spellbound for a space. She was not afraid any more. Her round pretty face was flushed and begrimed, her raven hair was disheveled, and the rose near her temple hung awry. But she wore a defiant little smile that matched the glint in her black eyes.A rifle spoke from an adjoining building behind the rabble.

María's weapon cluttered to the ground as she clutched her breast with both hands and leaned against the door-post. She felt her breath stifled as everything went dark, and Manuel's last words began to ring again in the ear he had kissed—"To God, to God, *Adiós!*"

Her expression, however, remained the same. Scores of savage eyes were fixed on María Jaén's face as she sank slowly to her knees and remained kneeling upright against the door-post, her eyes still open, her mouth still set in that little firm smile. The only difference was that her teeth were no longer white, but tinted with a dark rich flow, like the precious muscatel which for centuries has made Málaga world-renowned.

Once again hell broke loose. And as the human devils tramped over her body to get into the convent, the spirit of Joan of Arc, the Maid of Orleans, rode down from the starry sky for the soul of María Jaén, the Maid of Málaga.

Winnie the Breadwinner and Saint Anthony

(June 1938)

"Mother, the leaves are flying south!"

A strong wind from Lake Saint Clair was working havoc with the maples and elms along Detroit's residential streets. Autumn had tinted the leaves red, orange, and yellow, and now, like flocks of goldfinches and orioles, they were chasing one another around corners.

"Mom, the leaves are flying south for the winter," repeated the same voice. The voice belonged to a boy of five, whose little nose was pressed against a cold window. The window belonged to an old red-brick flat facing a street, and the flat belonged to a landlord.

Laying aside a copy of the *Free Press,* Winifred Pugh looked at her tiny son by the window, then, turning to an elderly woman who sat knitting by the gas-stove, she whispered: "Did you hear, Mary?"

Mary, Winifred's elder sister, smiled sadly. "Bless his wee heart, Winnie; if he knew that we might be flying south, too."

"Not to a warm south, like the birds," Winifred corrected. Then she added sadly: "But from street corner to alley corner, like the leaves." Again she picked up the newspaper and began to tear out a small slip. "Mary, I'm going to try this ad right now. And you pray that I get the job. It's either this or—join the leaves!"

Although everything was turning dark before her, Winifred was trying hard to put on a brave front. She had done it before. Two years ago, Llewelyn Pugh had died. No insurance, of course, and three mouths to feed—her own, little Llewelyn's and Mary's. But she had found work in an office and succeeded, until lately, when she had been discharged, just as many other employees of longer service were losing their jobs. Daily she scoured the want ad columns, and many a time she applied, to no avail. Today she had found a call for "a middle-aged, respectable lady to do clerical work." Perhaps, there was something in it. She'd try.

"Mother," it looks like Mr. Jewell is also blowing south—oh, no! He's coming this way!" Winifred grew pale, and Mary waxed paler still. What the boy had spied was a tall, prosperous-looking man, in a gray overcoat, whose steps the wind had been accelerating. As he turned about and walked toward the house, clamping his cigar between two perfect rows of teeth, he looked like a shark as viewed from below. The doorbell rang just as Winifred opened the door, and there stood the man, grinning, like a snake—you know, like one of those sleek bluff, puff-adders, the cigar playing out of his puckered mouth like a red-tipped black tongue.

Mr. Jewell slid in at Winifred's gesture and coiled himself into the big chair which she had occupied, as though this were his own house. Of course, old Mary said to herself, it was his house, but not his home.

"So!" the visitor said. "How's business? Work?"

"None to be found," Winifred replied.

"Depression, all right," he commented. "So. Most of the renters can't pay their bills."

"And we're some," she retorted.

"Thanks, Mrs. Pugh, for coming to the point right away. And now that we're there, we'll stick to it. So. Your month's dues didn't come in last week so I guess you've come to the end of the stocking, eh?"

Winifred faced Jewell squarely. "Not quite to the bottom, sir—there is some change left, about enough to meet last month's bill. But that is all we have and we need it to live on."

"So—" Jewell drawled out amused. "So you would rather have something to live on than to *live in*! So."

The woman said nothing. The boy, having left the window, was examining the man with the wonder of a schoolchild before the boa's cage at the zoo.

Old Mary, who had held back with fear, now broke the silence. "Mr. Jewell, think of us two helpless women and that innocent child before you. What would happen if you turned us out —oh—"

Flipping some ashes into Mary's knitting basket, Jewell asked: "Ain't you people got any relations?"

"Not here in Detroit, nor in all America," Winifred replied. "We have them a-plenty in Wales, though—in Carnarvon and Llanrwst."

"So. Well, why in the world don't you go home then?"

"Go home?" Mary stood up, trembling. We would go home if we had the means, Mr. Jewell. The British government offers to pay half the fare for its subjects who wish to return to the Isles. But where can we get our half? Our brother David wrote and said he would help us, but that is not enough—oh, please, can't you see?"

"I guess I'm supposed to buy you steamer accommodations, first class, and a carton of cookies for the kid here to munch on the way, eh? So. What's that you got there, Mrs. Pugh?"

Winifred showed him the newspaper clipping. "I'm going to try it."

"Hm. You might land the job with your brains and looks, Mrs. Pugh. And I'll show you that I ain't so scroogey as you think. So, if you get the position, I'll wait until you can pay."

After the details of the contract had been concluded, and Jewell had left, Winifred put on her hat and coat, while Mary sat down to drop tears into her knitting. "Oh, if we were home in Llanrwst, Winnie! Or could we journey to Holywell and pray to St. Winifred—there would be nothing to fear, Winnie dear. Oh, St. Anthony, help us!"

Tearless and firm, Winifred put her arms around her sister. "You can pray here, too, dear Mae. Pray to good St. Anthony again. Do. Do. You and Llewelyn start praying real hard, while I apply for that job—and I'll get it!"

Five minutes later, a determined and trusting Winifred was being blown briskly along with the leaves down the street, while an old lady and a child knelt before a statue of St. Anthony, praying for miracles that seemed impossible in these dark hours.

Winifred got the job. From among several anxious-faced applicants she was picked out and given a cashier's desk at the entrance of a restaurant. But what a job! Only two hours daily, in the evening, at a dollar a day, weekdays and Sundays. However, it was better than nothing, but its uncertain duration! What if the job wouldn't last through the winter. "St. Anthony would take care of that," said Winifred with determination.

A whole month passed, the snows came, and Mr. Jewell got his pay. St. Anthony, said Mary and Llewelyn, was keeping Winnie's dollar-a-day job from drifting away; for the three had begun a novena from the very day Winifred started to work, and their only petition was that the job would last a least through the winter. Every Tuesday morning, the devoted trio could be seen going to the novena services, Mary resting comfortably on Winifred's right arm, and Llewelyn hanging on to his mother's left hand. It was at the end of the first month that Winifred suggested to her companions to ask St. Anthony for the means of returning to Wales. At the present rate, though able to pay the rent, she had to stint herself considerably for her child's sake, and Mary's, too. If they could only go back to Llanrwst!

No sooner had this new attack on heaven begun on the fifth Tuesday, when the restaurant dollar-a-day job collapsed, fell flat like a toy balloon. New fears arose. Desperately, Winifred began to realize that they would sure be turned out at the end of the month, unless something turned up. The novena continued with renewed fervor.

"St. Anthony will take care of us," they said, even at the end of the second month, the eighth Tuesday, although there was no money to send to Mr. Jewell, and very little left for food.

On the following Monday, Jewell served notice that they must send in their dues, or else leave the house to accommodate new boarders. Winifred's face was sunken yet firmly-set, while Mary sat the whole day by the stove, rocking, knitting, praying, weeping, telling Llewelyn of St. Winifred's Well at Holywell where she and his mother used to pray and gather stones and moss to take home, and about Uncle David who was waiting for them with open arms in Llanrwst.

The next morning, the three stood for a while on the church steps after novena services, as had become their custom. There was snow on the ground, but the sky was clear—an unusual sight. Everything was so still, now that the worshippers had all departed for their homes. It was a little chilly, thought Winifred, but it seemed far more chilly to go to those rooms which they must give up in a day or two. And where would they go? "O Saint Anthony, pray for us!"

The heavy church door swung open behind them, and Winifred, turning around suddenly, met the gaze of a well-dressed lady older than herself maybe, but not so old as Mary. Winifred had not seen such happy smiling eyes for ages. She was charmed by them, and soon she found herself smiling back, her eyes riveted on the stranger. Even Mary had turned and was smiling feebly.

"Good morning," smiled the stranger, "Are you making the novena, too? I just ended mine."

"So did we," Winifred replied.

But the stranger saw a distress in those smiling eyes, which touched her to the quick. "You weren't answered," she said.

"Not yet," said the two sisters, almost in a breath.

"Not yet?" the lady gasped. Not yet? What kind of people were these with such hope, such faith. She wanted to know more. Winifred promptly told her all in a few words, and, as she stopped with a final sigh, the lady opened her purse, produced a checkbook, and began to write on it. Then she tore off the slip, waved it two or three times in the cool air, folded it, and closed Winifred's thin hands around it.

"Don't," she said quickly, "don't refuse—it's really for you, for your trip to Wales. It's St. Anthony answering your prayers; answering your prayers as he answered mine. I have plenty of money, my dear woman, but I had to go begging for health and peace of soul to St. Anthony, and I got it this very day. And it's because I'm well and happy again that I turn out to be so generous. This is how St. Anthony works his miracles. Good-bye! And don't forget to pray for me occasionally."

The strange benefactor slipped away, entering a large automobile which soon whirred away out of sight. Winifred thought she was dreaming, but Mary, sobbing close against her arm, proved to her the reality of things. Her sister was saying tenderly: "Now, Winnie and Llewelyn boy, we need not fear the cold...now we can go back to Llanrwst, back to Uncle David's and someday we can also go to St. Winifred's Well...your patron Saint, Winnie...a Saint of the *Cymry*...."

But Win'red thanked St. Anthony.

GLOSSARY

acequia madre: "mother ditch," the main irrigation ditch

adiós, hermanita mía: good-bye, my little sister

adoberos: makers of adobe bricks

alabados: Penitente hymns

Ave María purísima: Hail Mary most pure

ay de mí!: poor me!

bailes: dances

Bendición: a Catholic Benediction liturgy, or a blessing

buenos días le de Dios: good morning, or may God give you a good day

Buena Vista: good view, also the name of the street where Witter Bynner lived in Santa Fe

caballeros: gentlemen; horsemen

carretela: a carriage or wagon

censer: incense burner carried in religious ceremonies

chiquita: little girl

converso: convert, a Jew forced to convert to Christianity in order to remain in Spain

curas: priests

Cymry: the Welsh

Dios de los cielos!: God in heaven!

estrellita: little star

feminal: female

fortuna: luck

gallo: rooster

gaucho: Argentine cowboy

hombres: men

Malaya: from Malaysia

manitos: little brothers

ma vie: my life

La Noche Triste: "the night of sorrows," a historical reference to the Aztecs driving the Spaniards from Tenochitlán in 1520

O mi Dios!: Oh, my God!

O María, madre mía: Oh Mary, my mother

oye: hey, or listen

padrinos: godparents, sponsors, or witnesses

peineta: hair comb

piñon: pine tree

por Dios: on God's honor

pulque: alcoholic drink made from agave cactus

quién sabe?: who knows?

sabe?: you know?

sala: parlor, living room

tápalo: long shawl

tapia: mud wall

vida mía: my life

viga: wood ceiling beam

Viva Cristo Rey!: Long Live Christ the King!

March 26, 20

Aloha Shalom Marta & Denito:

May y'all live long and know joy and warm embraces as you journey together with each other, and with your children, family & friends...

Hugs,

J  y